DISCARD

RANGER'S APPRENTICE

THE ROYAL RANGER BOOK 3

DUEL AT ARALUEN

RANGER'S APPRENTICE

THE ROYAL RANGER BOOK 3

DUEL AT ARALUEN

JOHN FLANAGAN

PHILOMEL BOOKS

PHILOMEL BOOKS
An imprint of Penguin Random House LLC
New York

Copyright © 2018 by John Flanagan.
Published in Australia by Penguin Random House Australia in 2018.
Published in the United States of America by Philomel Books in 2019.

Philomel Books is a registered trademark of Penguin Random House LLC.

Visit us online at penguinrandomhouse.com

Library of Congress Cataloging-in-Publication Data is available upon request.

Printed in the United States of America.

ISBN 9781524741419

1 3 5 7 9 10 8 6 4 2

U.S. Edition edited by Cheryl Eissing.
U.S. Edition designed by Jennifer Chung.
Text set in Adobe Jenson Pro.

Dedicated to the memory of Bill Paget,
1942–2018

PROLOGUE

DIMON, FORMER COMMANDER OF THE PALACE GUARD AND now the leader of the rebellious Red Fox Clan, leaned on a windowsill, looked upward, and scowled. He was in a room on the top floor of the Castle Araluen keep. The south tower loomed above him, several floors higher.

He came here regularly, to stare up at the ninth floor of the south tower, where Princess Cassandra, King Duncan and their men had taken refuge. Occasionally, Dimon would see movement on the balcony that surrounded the ninth floor and once he had recognized Cassandra herself peering over into the courtyard below.

He cursed bitterly when he saw her, but she was unaware of his presence. The people on the balcony rarely seemed to look in his direction. They were more interested in the courtyard, and Cassandra's archers had already taken a savage toll on anyone who moved incautiously down there, straying too far from the shelter of the keep walls.

Under Dimon's leadership, the castle had been taken by soldiers of the Red Fox Clan. He had chanced upon the Red Fox Clan some years before. They were a disorganized, poorly motivated group of malcontents who protested against the law that allowed a woman to succeed to the throne. The law had been put in place by Cassandra's grandfather, and it meant that Cassandra would eventually become Queen of Araluen in her own right. The Red Fox Clan clung stubbornly to the old tradition that only a male heir could succeed to the throne—a position Dimon heartily endorsed, as he was distantly related to Cassandra and, so far as he knew, the only possible male heir.

Under a false name, he had joined the Clan and quietly worked his way to the top echelons of power within it. The Clan was big on angry talk and short on action. Dimon, on the other hand, was an expert orator, capable of rousing the passions of an audience and swaying them to his point of view. He had a powerful and charismatic personality and an inborn ability to make people like and respect him. He rose rapidly in the Clan, until he was appointed as their overall leader. He organized them and motivated them until they had become a potent and efficient secret army. He pandered to their beliefs and, most important, he gave them an agenda and a goal—rebellion against the Crown. His cause was aided by the fact that King Duncan had been an invalid for some time and Cassandra, his daughter, was acting as Regent in his place, providing an obvious example of the result of the law change.

Dimon used the Red Fox Clan as a tool to further his own ends. He planned to usurp the throne and have himself crowned king. He saw the Red Fox Clan as the vehicle by which he would achieve this ambition.

His chief obstacle, he believed, was Cassandra's husband, Sir Horace—the paramount knight of Araluen and the commander of the army. Horace was a highly skilled warrior and an expert

strategist and tactician. He was assisted in his leadership role by
the Ranger Gilan, Commandant of the redoubtable Ranger
Corps and Horace's longtime friend. For Dimon to succeed,
these two had to be lured away from Castle Araluen and, prefer-
ably, killed. Accordingly, he had devised a plan whereby Horace
and Gilan set out to the north to quell a rebellion raised by a
small force of the Red Fox Clan, taking most of the castle's garrison with them. They were intercepted along the way by a much
larger force of Sonderland mercenaries and Red Fox Clan members. Outnumbered three or four to one, Horace's men had
staged a fighting retreat to an ancient hill fort. Although they
were currently besieged there by their ambushers, Dimon knew
that a leader of Horace's ability wouldn't stay contained for long.
It was vital that Dimon should act quickly to seize the throne.

Initially, all had gone well. Dimon had tricked his way past
Castle Araluen's impregnable walls and massive drawbridge
with a force of Red Fox Clan troops and came within an inch of
capturing Cassandra and her father.

But then Maikeru, Cassandra's Nihon-Jan master swordsman, had interfered, holding Dimon and his men at bay long
enough for Cassandra and Duncan to retreat to the upper levels
of the south tower with a small force of loyal palace guards and
archers.

The eighth and ninth floors of the south tower had been
built as a last refuge in the event that the castle was captured. A
section of the spiral stairway, just below the eighth floor, could
be removed, leaving attackers with no access to the upper two
floors—while the defenders could move between the eighth and
ninth floors via an internal flight of timber stairs. The refuge
was stocked with food and weapons, and large rainwater cisterns

in the roof above the ninth floor provided water for the defenders.

So far, Cassandra had resisted his attempts to force his way into the eighth floor of the tower. But now, he had an idea that might just prove to be her undoing.

He turned as he heard a tentative knock at the door.

"Lord Dimon? Are you there?"

He recognized the voice. It was Ronald, the leader of his small force of engineers and siege specialists. "Come in," Dimon called.

The door opened to admit the engineer. Like many of his kind, he was an older man, his gray hair denoting years of experience in his craft. He hesitated, deferentially. All of Dimon's men knew that their leader was in a foul mood since the Nihon-Jan swordsman had foiled his plan for a quick result.

"What is it?" Dimon said testily, unreasonably annoyed by the man's nervousness.

"The materials have arrived for your device, my lord," the engineer told him. "We can begin building it immediately."

For the first time in several days, a smile crossed Dimon's face. He rubbed his hands together in anticipation.

"Excellent," he said. "Now we can make things extremely unpleasant for my cousin Cassandra. Extremely unpleasant."

1

"Dad's outnumbered and the enemy can see everything he does," Maddie said. "He can't surprise them. I thought if I could get some men and stage a surprise attack on the enemy from the rear, that would give him a chance to break out."

While the traitor Dimon assumed that Maddie was confined in the south tower with her mother, the apprentice Ranger had discovered a series of secret tunnels and stairways that allowed her to move freely in and out of the castle. Maddie had infiltrated a Red Fox Clan assembly and overheard Dimon's plan to attack Castle Araluen and trap her father and his men in the north.

Now she had returned to the castle and made her way to the ninth floor, where she and Cassandra were formulating a plan to aid her father.

Cassandra considered the idea. "It would work," she said. "But where would you find the men?"

Maddie shrugged. "I thought maybe I could mobilize the army," she said. The castle maintained only a small regular garrison. The army was made up of men-at-arms, knights and foot soldiers from the surrounding farms and villages who could be called up in the event of war or other danger.

Cassandra shook her head. "It'd take too long to gather them," she said. "And Dimon would quickly get wind of what you were doing." She stood up and began pacing the room, her brow furrowed in concentration.

"We can hold out here indefinitely," she said. "But what we need to do is find a way to break your father and Gilan out of that hill fort. Then, if they march south and hit Dimon from behind, we can break out here at the same time and attack him from both sides. You say there's a tunnel into the gatehouse?" she asked and Maddie nodded. "Then you could lower the drawbridge and let Horace and Gilan's men in."

She turned, pacing again, her mind working overtime.

"But if you're going to have to launch a surprise attack on the force holding Horace and Gilan, you'll need men. Good fighting men. The kind who will put the fear of the devil into those Red Fox scum . . ."

Her voice trailed off as she racked her brains for an idea. Then, her brow cleared, and she looked at her daughter with a wide smile on her face.

"And I think I know just the men you need," she said.

Cassandra moved to the window, looking out over the green parkland below. There was a positive note in her voice that hadn't been there previously, and Maddie looked up curiously.

"So tell me," Maddie said.

"The Skandians," her mother replied.

For a moment, Maddie was confused. "What Skandians?"

"Hal and his men—the Heron brotherband." Cassandra's manner was becoming more positive by the minute. "They're due back from the coast any day now."

"But why should they help us?" Maddie asked.

"Because they're old friends and allies. We helped them when the Temujai tried to invade their country years ago. And we organized the ransom when the Arridans captured their Oberjarl. They owe us. And they're not the kind of people to forget a debt."

"If you say so." Maddie didn't share her mother's confidence that the Skandians would immediately come to their aid, but Cassandra knew the sea wolves better than she did. There was another point, however. "Aren't there only twelve of them?"

Cassandra smiled. "Twelve Skandians. Your father says they're the best troops in the world. If a dozen of them hit the Sonderlanders from the rear in a surprise attack, they'll cause the sort of panic and confusion you'll be looking for. Take my word for it."

"I suppose you're right," Maddie conceded. "But how will I get in touch with them?"

Cassandra walked over to a large-scale map of Araluen Fief on the wall. Maddie followed her and waited as her mother studied the map, running a finger along the River Semath as she talked to herself.

"Let's see. They headed down the Semath to the sea. The wrecked wolfship was here . . ." She stabbed her finger on the coast at a point south of the mouth of the Semath. "Hal said they'd be back in around ten days, so you've got a few days left."

She traced the path of the winding river back inland, stopping at a point where it took a sharp bend to the south. She tapped the southern headland formed by the apex of the curve.

"Here, I'd say. This would be the best point for you to intercept them. You should see them coming for some time. That'll give you time to attract their attention."

Maddie studied the point on the map for a few seconds. The promontory did seem like the best choice—close enough for her to reach in good time to intercept the *Heron* and with a good clear view downriver. And it was sufficiently distant that Dimon would have no inkling about what she was doing.

"I'd better get going then," she said.

Her mother raised her eyebrows. "What? Right away?"

"Yes. I'll go while it's still dark. That way there's less chance that Dimon's sentries will see me. I'll pack some provisions for the trip and be on my way," she said.

Cassandra nodded. "And assuming Horace and Gilan manage to break out of the fort, what's your plan then?"

"We come back here and I bring a small party through the tunnel under the moat. Once we're inside the walls of the castle, there's a hidden stairway to the gatehouse. We'll lower the drawbridge. After that, it'll be up to Dad and his men."

"And once they're inside the castle walls," Cassandra said, "I'll bring my men down the stairway and hit the Red Foxes from behind." She touched the hilt of the *katana* that was thrust through her belt in its scabbard. "I rather fancy the idea of having Dimon at the end of my sword."

Half an hour later, with a sack of food slung over her shoulder, Maddie stood by the door into the secret stairway. Cassandra stood beside her. She was loath to let her daughter go, having only just discovered that she was safe. She gestured toward the door.

"Maybe I could come down to the tunnel entrance with you," she said.

"Mum, it's eighteen vertical ladders. Do you really want to

climb down all those steps, then climb back up again?" Maddie asked her.

Cassandra shook her head ruefully. "Not really. Just . . . oh, I don't know . . . just take care of yourself."

Maddie nodded several times, not trusting herself to speak. Then she quickly embraced her mother, opened the door and disappeared into the dark stairwell.

2

THE MEN IN THE HILLTOP STOCKADE WERE STIRRING WITH
the first light of dawn.

The sentries on the walls, who had been on duty since midnight, were red-eyed and yawning. They greeted the men who
relieved them with a mixture of reactions—some grateful that
the long vigil through the dark hours was over, others irritable if
their relief was a few minutes late. Then they all headed down
the stairs for the compound, where the fireplaces by the lines of
tents were being stirred into new life. The smell of woodsmoke
filtered through the fort, along with the welcome aroma of coffee
brewing and bacon being set to sizzle in pans.

Horace and Gilan paced the timber walkway inside the wall,
offering words of encouragement to the men who had taken over
the watch.

"Keep a good eye out," Horace said from time to time. "We
don't want those Sonderland beggars to surprise us."

The sentries answered cheerfully enough. After all, Horace
thought, they hadn't been on the midnight-to-dawn watch,
which was the most fatiguing one of all. Along with the body's
craving for rest at that time, a sentry felt alone and vulnerable

while his comrades slept. He would be peering through the uncertain darkness for five hours, straining his eyes, imagining he saw movement where there was none, dealing with the sudden surge of panic: *Should I sound the alarm? Was that someone crawling through the long grass?* That constant tension sapped a person's energy—mental and physical.

Horace saw the cavalry lieutenant who assigned the sentries each day. The man was patrolling the wall in the opposite direction to Horace and Gilan, making sure the men were alert. Horace beckoned to him, and the officer approached and came to attention, straightening his shoulders a little and raising his forefinger to the brim of his helmet.

"The men on the midnight-to-dawn watch," Horace began. "How are you selecting them?"

The lieutenant thought about the question for a second or two. "Usually it's a punishment for the odd minor offense, sir," he said. "Dirty equipment or an untidy sleeping space."

Horace nodded several times. "I thought it might be something like that. In future, just assign it on a routine schedule. Don't have the same man pulling that duty two or three days in a row."

The lieutenant hesitated. He looked doubtful. "Yes, sir," he said, but his tone indicated that he didn't understand.

"Those hours before dawn are where we are most vulnerable," Horace explained. "If a man is put on watch as a punishment, he'll be resentful and he'll tend to think about how hard done by he's been. That'll make him less attentive to his job."

The lieutenant's face cleared. He hadn't considered that. In the three years he'd been in the army, being assigned to the dawn watch had been a traditional punishment for minor infringements. And since men who were lazy or untidy often infringed more than once, they were often put on the dawn watch repeatedly.

"Yes, sir. Sorry, sir," he said, straightening a little more.

Horace smiled at him. "No harm done. Just change things up in the future."

He dismissed the officer with a casual gesture, and he and Gilan continued their pacing along the walkway. He sniffed the air experimentally. "Nothing like the smell of frying bacon in the morning," he said.

Gilan shrugged. "Enjoy the smell. There'll be precious little of it to eat." Several days previously, Horace had cut their rations, trying to eke out their limited supplies of food.

The tall warrior nodded, a worried look on his face as he thought about the inevitable day when they would run out of provisions. He moved to the wall and rested his elbows on top of the logs, peering down at the enemy camp below them. Gilan joined him.

The Red Fox camp was coming awake, just as the men in the hill fort were. Smoke from their rekindled fires could be seen at half a dozen points. There was no wind yet, and the smoke streamed up vertically until it dissipated. Men were moving around the camp with the lack of urgency and energy of early risers who still wanted to be in their blankets.

"No shortage of bacon there," Gilan commented.

Horace grunted in reply.

"What do you think their next move will be?" the Ranger continued.

Horace pursed his lips. "They don't really need to do anything," he said. "They know they've got us trapped here and they must realize we're short of food. They can afford to wait us out. Of course," he continued, "they'll probably try the odd night attack, trying to catch us napping. If nothing else, it'll spoil our sleep and keep us awake at night."

"That's no good," Gilan replied. "When I'm asleep is the only time I don't feel hungry."

"You're lucky," Horace told him. "I dream of food when I'm hungry."

"You dream of food when you're not hungry," his friend said.

As if prompted by their discussion, Horace's stomach rumbled mightily.

Gilan feigned shock, stepping away from the big knight. "My god! I thought we were having an earthquake there," he said in mock alarm.

"If we don't get some food soon, we may well have one," Horace replied.

"There's always the spare horses," Gilan pointed out.

Horace snapped around to look at him. "Are you suggesting we slaughter some of them for food?" he asked, the anger evident in his tone.

Gilan shrugged apologetically. "Well, it has been done before," he said, then, seeing the stubborn set of Horace's jaw, he continued. "But I don't think things are as bad as all that yet. What I was thinking was that we might let the spare horses go, drive them out through the gate. That way, the grain and fodder we have for the rest of them will last twice as long."

Horace's angry expression faded. "It's a good thought," he said. Then he frowned. "Mind you, telling a cavalryman to abandon his horse is a hard thing to do."

"Better than eating it," Gilan pointed out.

"That's true. We'll see how things go. One thing's for sure, we don't need remounts while we're stuck here."

They studied the enemy camp for some minutes in silence.

"They've gone to a lot of trouble to lure us here," Gilan said thoughtfully.

"I'd say they planned to kill us," Horace said.

"Precisely. But why go to all that trouble? What else did they have in mind? Surely they didn't just say, *Let's trick Horace and Gilan into coming north and then we'll kill them.* There must have been some further part to the plan."

"Like taking Castle Araluen?" Horace said.

This was the conclusion they always came to when they discussed the situation, and Gilan sighed in frustration. "I can't think of anything else they might have in mind. Can you?"

Horace looked troubled by the question. "No. I can't. But the castle is no easy mark. It's virtually impregnable. Even Morgarath knew that, and he had thousands of troops with him." He paused. "And Dimon is a good man. Even with a small force, he'd manage to keep them out."

"Unless they trick their way in," Gilan suggested, but now Horace was more definite in his rebuttal.

"They wouldn't fool Cassandra," he said, then added a little ruefully, "I've never managed to do it in nineteen years of marriage."

"Still, they must have something in mind. I can't help wondering what it might be."

"I guess we'll find out when we send that lot packing." Horace jabbed a thumb at the camp below them.

Gilan looked at him in feigned surprise. "Are we going to send them packing?" he said. "How are we going to manage that?"

Horace patted him on the shoulder. "You're going to come up with a masterful plan to do it."

Gilan nodded several times. "I suppose I should have realized that."

"That's what you Rangers do. You're plotters and schemers—and you're very clever with it. I have every confidence you'll come up with an idea. Just don't leave it too long."

"I'll see what I can figure out. Maybe I'll have a nap. I plot and scheme much better when I'm napping. In the meantime, let's go and get some of that rapidly shrinking store of bacon."

Horace pushed off from the parapet with both hands and turned toward the stairs leading to the compound below.

"Now, *that's* a good plan. I knew I could rely on you."

3

THE SKANDIANS HAD STRIPPED THE DAMAGED WOLFSHIP until she was no more than an empty shell lying on the coarse sand of the beach, where her crew had beached her some days prior.

Weapons, shields, bedding and stores were all stacked well above the high-water mark. For the past hour, the crew had been busy removing the deck planking and setting it to one side. The mast, yardarm, sails and rigging formed another well-ordered pile. By now, the ship should weigh no more than half her original weight.

Hal Mikkelson stood with his hands on his hips, looking at the stripped hull. "All right," he said. "Let's haul her up to a more level spot."

Wolfbiter currently lay at the water's edge. Her crew took hold of ropes attached to the bowpost and to purchase points along the hull. Hal's crew moved to the stern to add their weight to the effort of moving the ship.

"Ready?" Hal called, and receiving no sign that they weren't, added, "One, two, three, heave!"

The ropes came taut as the men threw their weight on them,

their heels digging into the sand. For a moment, the ship resisted their efforts, then she slowly began to slide up the beach.

"Put your back into it, Ingvar!" Hal ordered.

The huge warrior gritted his teeth and bent almost parallel to the ground as he shoved with all his might. The ship began to slide more readily with his additional effort, moving with increasing freedom up the slight slope that led from the water's edge until she was on level ground.

Hal held up a hand. "All right! That'll do," he called.

The two crews relaxed, letting the ropes fall to the ground at their feet and the ship heel over to one side. Jern Icerunner, the ship's skirl, dusted off his hands and walked to stand beside Hal.

"You picked a good spot to beach her," Hal told him, glancing round the narrow cove, whose tall headlands protected the beach and the bay from the worst of the wind.

Jern shrugged. "Luck more than judgment," he said. "I could feel the hull flexing after we hit that rock and I just wanted to get her ashore as quickly as I could."

Hal grinned. "Sometimes luck's better than judgment anyway," he said. Then he moved toward the ship. "Let's get those props under her and get her level."

Earlier in the day, he had supervised the men in cutting and trimming stout props from the trees that grew around the narrow inlet. Now he directed them as they pushed on the port gunwale to bring the ship upright, then placed four of the props under her to keep her there. Some of the crew took four more props and placed them on the opposite side, to prevent the ship tipping the other way. Hal studied the props closely, making sure they were well seated and the sand under them was compacted and firm. He shoved hard against the hull, trying to tilt it one way or the other but it remained solid.

Stig, Hal's best friend and first mate, stood watching, a concerned look on his face. He knew what was coming next. He gestured to Ingvar, the largest man in the two crews, to come closer.

"Just stand by in case we're needed," he said.

Ingvar nodded, understanding.

Hal dropped to his hands and knees, peering under the propped-up hull. He raised one hand and ran it along the smooth planks, testing, pushing. The planks felt solid under his exploring hand. Then he crouched lower and scrambled in until he was well under the ship, feeling the weed and barnacle-encrusted timbers a few centimeters above him. He took a small timber maul from his belt and hammered it against the hull at different points.

Stig and Ingvar took an involuntary pace forward as he did so, watching for any sign that the ship might move, or that the props might be dislodged with the impact of his blows. Jern was watching anxiously as well, although his concern was more for his ship and what Hal might discover than for Hal's well-being or safety. He knew Hal was an experienced shipwright and he'd done this sort of thing before.

Hal scuttled farther aft, duck-walking on his heels. He stopped at a point about a third of the way down the ship's length. "Jern? Is this where you struck the rock?" he called. He prodded experimentally at the hull.

Jern screwed up his face as he considered the question. "Pretty much, Hal—as far as I could tell."

"Hmmm," Hal said thoughtfully. He hammered again on the hull. This time the sound was slightly different. It sounded duller, somehow. Hal hit the planks twice more, swinging the maul awkwardly in the cramped space.

Ingvar had his hand resting lightly on the side of the hull, and he felt the vibration of the blows. "Wish he wouldn't do that," he muttered, glancing at the nearest prop.

"He knows what he's doing," Stig replied, although it sounded more like a statement of hope than reassurance. "Good. Here he comes," he added.

Hal scuttled out from under the beached ship. Stig stretched out a hand to help his friend stand. Hal grinned at him, dusting sand off the knees of his leggings.

"Mother hens," he said, including Ingvar in the statement. "I know what I'm doing."

He reached up and took hold of the ship's rail, hauling himself up and over it and lowering himself into the hull.

There was more hammering and banging from inside the wolfship, the noise echoing in the empty hull. Stig and Ingvar relaxed. There was no chance now that a dislodged prop could send the ship crashing down on their skirl.

Jern, however, was still concerned as he waited for the verdict. *Wolfbiter* was the assigned duty ship for the year—the ship provided to King Duncan of Araluen by the Skandian Oberjarl to patrol the coast, pursue pirates, smugglers and slavers, and carry urgent messages. Some two weeks prior, she had come to grief in a fierce storm, being driven close inshore and hurled onto an uncharted rock. Jern had heard the sickening crunch as she made contact and felt the hull flexing badly. Fearing that the keel was broken, he had hurried to beach the ship before she broke in two.

The accident happened to coincide with the arrival of Hal's

ship, the *Heron*, at Castle Araluen. Hal was on an unrelated mission, but when word came that *Wolfbiter* was seriously damaged, he had hurried back to the east coast to provide assistance. Jern counted himself extremely lucky—Hal was possibly the finest shipbuilder in Skandia.

But that luck might not hold. If the ship's keel was in fact broken, Jern knew that there would be no repair. They would have to abandon her, burn her and find their own way back to Skandia. It would also leave Araluen without a duty ship until another crew could make their way to Araluen across the Stormwhite Sea. That would take months, and word would get around among the smugglers and slavers who infested these waters that the coast was unpatrolled. They would quickly begin their predations once more. Bad news traveled swiftly.

The hammering stopped, and Hal's face appeared at the railing. With the decking removed, he had to heave himself up so he could roll over the gunwale.

Jern took half a pace forward, not wanting to hear the worst.

But Hal smiled at him reassuringly. "Pretty sure the keel is sound," he said.

Jern let go a breath that he had been holding for too long. Then he frowned. "But I could feel her moving and flexing as the waves passed under her."

Hal nodded. "Two of the frames are badly cracked. You couldn't see them until we took up the decking and unloaded the stores. But they would have caused the movement in the hull that you could feel. Shouldn't take too long to put them right."

Jern's shoulders sagged with relief. It was the sort of news he'd been hoping for—although he hadn't allowed himself to hold that hope too strongly. He was superstitious, as were many sailors, and he believed that if he hoped for a good result, it wouldn't happen.

"That's great news," he said now. "Thanks, Hal."

Hal shrugged. "I'm glad it's fixable."

Stig tilted his head to one side, regarding the wounded wolf-ship with a critical eye. "Can you repair her here—on the beach?"

Hal shook his head. "Not properly. We'd have to strip off the planking, take her back to her basic framework skeleton, remove the cracked ribs and shape new ones. Bit of a big task here in the open."

Jern's face fell. He thought Hal had said the ship could be repaired.

Hal patted him reassuringly on the shoulder. "Don't worry. We can do a perfectly good temporary repair here—one that'll get you home again. Then you can find a shipyard to do a proper job." He scratched his chin as he thought about the task ahead. "We'll mend the cracked ribs with a fish," he said. Then, seeing the confused expression on Jern's face, he explained. "We'll shape timbers to fit either side of the rib, then screw them tightly together—like a splint on a broken leg. I'll draw up a template for you so you can shape them. I suggest you do that back at the village below Castle Araluen where there's a good carpentry shop. Then you can bring the pieces back here and screw them in place."

"And that'll hold?" Jern asked.

Hal nodded. "In the short term. Enough to get you home again. But the longer you leave them, the more they'll work loose—and then she'll start flexing again."

He glanced up at the sky. The sun was already behind the hills to the west of the beach and there was a smell of rain in the air.

"It's nearly dark. Let's roll her farther up the beach. I suggest you leave four or five men here to keep an eye on her. I'll ferry the rest of you back to Castle Araluen tomorrow."

As the tide started to come in the following morning, the two dozen sailors from *Wolfbiter* who were accompanying the Herons back to Castle Araluen picked up their weapons, shields and seabags and trooped down the beach to where *Heron* was drawn up on the edge of the water. *Heron* was a much smaller ship than *Wolfbiter*, and there was a few minutes' confusion as they clambered aboard and found space to stow their gear. Then they settled themselves along the center of the deck as Stig and Ingvar shoved the ship off the beach and into the water. There was the usual clatter of wood on wood as the *Heron*'s crew unstowed their oars and ran them out through the rowlocks, then they backed water and the neat little ship slid away from the beach, into deeper water.

Hal threaded his way through the crowd of men sprawled on the decks and took the tiller. He nodded to Stig, who was on the stern oar, and the tall sailor called orders to the rowers.

"Back port. Ahead starboard!"

Under the opposed thrust of the two sets of oars, the ship pivoted neatly in her own length, until her sharp prow was pointed out to sea.

"Ahead together! Pull! Pull! Pull!" Stig ordered, setting the pace for the rowers.

Jern moved to stand beside Hal at the steering platform. He watched appreciatively as the little ship gathered way, the sides of the cove slipping past them with increasing speed.

"She handles nicely," he commented.

Hal smiled at the compliment. "Thanks. We like her," he said. He glanced up at the wind telltale on the mast. It streamed out to starboard. That meant that when they reached the mouth of the cove and turned north, the wind would be dead ahead.

Jern noticed the look. In fact, he had just checked the telltale himself. It was an automatic reaction for any skirl. "Looks like we'll be rowing," he said.

Hal had come to the same conclusion. *Heron*, with her fore and aft sail plan, could tack across a headwind like this, making ground in a series of diagonal runs. But that would mean a lot of sail handling, which would be difficult when the decks were crowded with the extra numbers.

On the other hand, those extra numbers meant they had plenty of men ready to take a turn at the oars. On the whole, Hal decided, they'd make better time if they rowed north to the mouth of the Semath.

"My boys will take a turn at the oars if you want," Jern offered.

Hal nodded his gratitude. "We'll get her clear of the bay first."

He took her a kilometer off the coast, to give himself plenty of sea room. At the moment, the wind was from the north, but that could change without warning and they could find themselves on a lee shore—with the wind setting them back against the land. All skirls were wary of such a thing happening, and it was normal practice to keep the coastline in sight but leave plenty of maneuvering room in case of trouble.

Hal nodded at Jern. *Wolfbiter*'s skirl took a few paces forward and raised his voice to call to his crew.

"All right, boys, why don't sixteen of you take over from the Herons and show them how real sailors row."

After several seconds of sorting out who would row, his men clambered down into the rowing well and replaced the Herons at the oars. With eight men a side, they had two men pulling each one. Jern's first mate, Sten Engelson, took Stig's place at the rearmost oar and called the stroke to get his men rowing in time. Under the increased thrust of the double-banked oars, *Heron* fairly shot ahead, cutting through the water so that a sizable bow wave sprang up and a white wake began to unfurl behind her.

Jesper, who had been manning one of the for'ard oars, came aft and sprawled comfortably on the deck beside Hal's position at the tiller.

"This is the life," he said. "Can we keep them?"

One of the rowers overheard him and grinned up from his bench. "She's a lightweight," he said, heaving on his oar with no apparent effort. "We could keep this up all day."

"Is that so?" Sten called from his bench. "In that case, let's up the pace a little: Pull! Pull! Pull!"

As the rowers pulled faster in time to his increased rate, *Heron* gathered even more speed. There was a long, smooth swell coming from the north, driven before the wind. The ship swooped over the waves, her bow smashing through the tops, sending spray cascading back over the ship, and the men seated on her center decking. Nobody cared. They were sailors and they were used to being wet. The exhilarating speed of the ship's passage more than made up for the minor discomfort of a little water landing on them.

Stig came to join the two skirls at the steering platform.

"I'm with Jesper," he said. "Let's take these people along on all our cruises. We'd never have to raise the sail."

"Your men can certainly handle the oars," Hal said to Jern.

The older skirl nodded. "They're a good crew. But as Lars said, this ship is a real lightweight. They're used to hauling *Wolfbiter* around, and she weighs three or four times as much as this little beauty."

"Well, my men certainly appreciate the rest," Hal told him, nodding to where Ulf and Wulf, the identical twin sail trimmers, were calling good-natured jibes at the rowing crew. In fact, all of the *Heron*'s crew were enjoying the novelty of being rowed, rather than rowing themselves. And they enjoyed the exhilaration of feeling the ship moving so fast. She had never cut through the water like this under oars before.

They powered on up the coast, which lay off their port side like a long, gray-green line. True to the oarsman's word, the *Wolfbiter* crew maintained their cracking pace without any sign of flagging. Long before Hal had originally expected to see it, the mouth of the River Semath opened up on the coast to port. He heaved on the tiller and swung the ship's head through ninety degrees, heading for the broad river.

The swell and wind had been in their teeth up till this point. Now they were coming from almost dead abeam, and the pitching, swooping motion of the ship changed. She began to roll heavily, sometimes dipping her lee-side gunwales underwater.

Hal eyed the river ahead with narrowed eyes. He had originally set *Heron*'s course for the center of the river. But although she was still pointing in that direction, he could see her head was falling off downwind, her line of travel taking her toward the southern bank.

Jern hesitated, not sure if he should call Hal's attention to it. It would be the height of bad manners to advise another skirl without being asked. He relaxed when he saw Hal shove the tiller over, so that the bow angled toward the northern bank. Now the rudder and the oars were pushing her up to the north and the wind setting her down to the south. After a few minor adjustments to the tiller, the two forces balanced and she held a true course down the center of the river.

Hal had seen Jern's momentary indecision. He smiled at him now. "I had noticed," he said.

The rolling motion lessened as they ran in under the shelter of the headlands and the waves died down. There was still plenty of wind, however, and once they had traveled a few hundred meters inland Hal made a sign to Jern.

"Oars up!" the older man ordered, and the eight oars rose, dripping from the water, held parallel to the surface.

"Oars in." They slid inboard with a rattle of wood on wood. The ship continued to move forward, the way gradually dying off her.

"Sail handlers!" Hal called. "Take your stations."

Ulf and Wulf had been waiting for the order. They sprang to their feet and scuttled for'ard, avoiding the butts of the oars as they were hauled inboard.

"Stow oars!" Jern ordered, and there was more clattering as the eight white-oak shafts were raised, then placed into the fork-shaped oar rests that held them running fore and aft down the center line of the ship. At the same time, Ingvar, Jesper and Stefan followed the twins for'ard and took up their position by the halyards on the starboard side.

"Port sail up!" Hal ordered, and the three crewmen heaved

on the halyard, sending the port-side yardarm and sail sliding up the stumpy mast until it clunked into position in the socket that held it in place. As the wind caught it, the sail bellied out for a second or two. Then Ulf and Wulf hauled on the sheets to bring the sail tight. It hardened into a smooth curve, trapping the brisk wind from the north. They heaved in harder and *Heron* accelerated forward. For a moment or two, her lee-side gunwale dipped close to the river surface. Then Ulf and Wulf eased the sheets slightly, just before Hal could call out the necessary order. The ship stood more upright and the water gurgled and chuckled along her side.

Within a few minutes, the white wake was streaming out behind her in a straight line. She had settled on her course and was moving every bit as swiftly as she had under the thrust of the *Wolfbiter* crew's brawny arms.

Jern nodded in appreciation. "Like I said, she's a sweet little craft."

Hal glanced at the banks slipping past them, estimating their speed. "At this rate, we'll be at Castle Araluen in another three hours," he said.

4

MADDIE WAS DREAMING.

She dreamed she was in the marketplace in Castle Redmont's courtyard. Canvas stalls had been set up, selling items of clothing, knives, axes, saddles and bridles, and bolts of freshly dyed cloth. But she was heading for her favorite place in the market— the row of stalls where food was sold.

And in particular, she was heading for the pie stall. She checked her pockets, making sure she had a couple of silver coins. She'd only need one for the savory pie she had in mind, and she'd insist on paying.

All too often, stallkeepers would hand over her purchase and try to wave away her offered payment. "No charge for a Ranger," they'd say, grinning.

But Will had taught her to always pay her way. *We don't accept free food or goods. That way we don't owe anyone anything.*

When she'd queried this, he'd continued. *Imagine that one day you find one of these traders sneaking food or wine from the castle's larder cellars. Or you find them smuggling goods upriver. So you arrest them, and they look at you and say: "But you always accepted the free pies I gave you." You'll be beholden to them. And that will make it harder to do the job you're supposed to do.*

Reluctantly, she'd agreed he was right. It was better for a Ranger to be unencumbered by any sort of debt or obligation. It was why they lived apart from the castle, in their cozy little cabin among the trees. Rangers had to be seen to be impartial, to be influenced by nobody, from the Baron himself to the lowliest pie vendor.

The savory aroma of the pies was stronger in her nostrils now, and her stomach rumbled with anticipation. She took one of the coins out of her jerkin pocket and increased her pace.

A heavyset man heading in the opposite direction barged into her, jolting her shoulder. Not expecting the contact, she dropped the coin. As she stooped to retrieve it, the man buffeted her shoulder again, staggering her. Then he did it again.

"Cut it out!" she said angrily. But he continued to buffet her, shoving her on the shoulder with increasing force.

Then, amazingly, he leaned closer to her and blew his warm breath in her face. She recoiled. His breath wasn't exactly scented like roses. In fact, it smelled strangely of grass and oats.

She opened her eyes and found herself staring into Bumper's long face, a few inches from her own.

"Gedoutof it! Waddaya doing?" she slurred at him, only half awake. Dimly, she realized that, true to his name, her horse had been shoving her shoulder with his head. There was no heavy-set man. Even worse, there was no pie stall. Just her horse and the thick grass where she had been dozing.

By Blarney's perpetual beard, when you sleep, you really sleep, don't you? I've been trying to wake you for ten minutes. I thought you were dead for a moment.

Like all Ranger horses, Bumper was prone to hyperbole. The

bumping and breathing couldn't have been going on for more than thirty seconds. Maddie sat up, rubbing her eyes.

"What do you know about Blarney—or his beard?" she said irritably. Blarney was a minor Hibernian deity Halt had told her about. His beard grew constantly down to his feet, no matter how often he cut it or shaved it. Each night, it would regenerate at full length. As a result, he was constantly tripping over it.

It made him a very bad-tempered minor deity.

Bumper leaned back away from her and tilted his head knowingly. *I hear things. I know things. But for the moment, I thought you'd like to know that there's a ship heading this way.*

Instantly, she came fully awake.

"What? Why didn't you say so?" She tried to scramble to her feet, but caught her left boot in the hem of her cloak, tripped and sprawled on the grass.

Bumper sniggered. *You and Blarney are quite a match, aren't you? So agile. So sure-footed.*

"So shut up," she told him, getting to her feet more carefully and retrieving her bow and quiver from where they had been lying beside her.

Bumper's shoulders shook as he continued to snigger, but silently now.

She shielded her eyes with one hand and peered downstream. Sure enough, there was the pale triangle of *Heron*'s sail, several hundred meters away. The little ship was cutting through the water at a fast pace, driven by the brisk wind on her right-hand side. She frowned. *Right side* wasn't how sailors described it. They had a technical term for it.

"Stuffboard," she said to herself, pulling up her cowl.

Bumper sniggered again, audibly this time. *Stuffboard?*

"Stuffboard. That's what sailors call the right-hand side of their ship," she told him, a superior tone in her voice.

He shook his ears at her. *I think the term you are looking for is starboard.*

She gave in, realizing she could never top him in this sort of discussion. Instead, she began to walk down to the river's edge. He ambled cheerfully behind her.

"Who made you such an expert?" she muttered. But of course, he heard her.

As I said, I hear things. I know things.

"You're a know-all. A know-all and a blowhard," she told him.

He looked mildly pained. *A blowhard?*

She nodded, turning to face him. "A blowhard. And believe me, I know. I just had your oaty, grassy breath in my face and it wasn't any fun."

For once, it seemed, he had no reply. He leaned his head back and stared indignantly down his long nose at her. Then he shook his ears and mane again.

Pleased with her little victory, Maddie hurried down to the river's edge. The ship was only a hundred meters away now. Hoping they had a sharp-eyed lookout on duty, she took a white scarf from inside her jerkin, held it above her head and waved it back and forth.

Perched on the bowpost lookout, Jesper saw the sudden movement on the bank of the river. He was a little disconcerted that he hadn't noticed the person standing there until the white cloth began waving. Whoever it was, they were clad in a green-and-brown-mottled cloak that made them blend into the woodland background. Belatedly, he called a warning to Hal.

"Someone's waving at us! On that grassy bank ahead!"

At the steering platform, Hal, Jern and Thorn had been discussing plans for the repair work on *Wolfbiter*. At Jesper's hail, they swung their attention to the bank.

"What's that he's wearing?" Jern asked.

Hal narrowed his eyes. Like Jesper, he found the figure quite difficult to make out. But he'd seen cloaks like that before. "That's a Ranger," he said.

Jern frowned. "Makes him hard to see," he commented.

Hal glanced at him. "That's the general idea."

Heron was heading straight toward the bank, so there was no need to turn her. Hal called to Ulf and Wulf. "Ease the sail a little." The speed dropped away as they complied.

"He's not very big, is he?" Jern said. Now they were closer, he could see the figure more clearly.

"A lot of them aren't," Hal said. "But don't make him angry. Rangers are incredible warriors."

Thorn had been silent while he scrutinized the slight figure on the bank. Now he spoke thoughtfully. "You know, I don't think that's a man at all. It's a girl."

"In a Ranger cloak?" Hal said, surprised. He'd never heard of such a thing. He looked more carefully. "You could be right." Then the Ranger pushed back the cowl of the cloak and he saw her face more clearly.

"It's Cassandra's daughter!" he said. "Maddie. What's she doing with a Ranger cloak?"

Thorn smiled to himself. "I knew there was something unusual about her."

Even as he had been studying the figure on the bank, Hal

had unconsciously been measuring angles, distance and speed. He called to the twins now. "Down sail!" And the sail slid easily down the mast, where the sail handlers gathered it in and roughly folded it. *Heron* skimmed on over the rapidly shallowing water, and he swung the prow slightly so she would run onto the sand at an angle.

"You're going to stop?" Jern asked. "For a slip of a girl?"

Hal glanced at him for a second, then went back to judging *Heron's* approach to the bank. "That 'slip of a girl,' as you call her, is a Ranger," he said. "*And* she's the daughter of the Princess Regent. I think it might be wise to see what's on her mind."

The bow grated onto the sand, sliding up a few meters. Then, as the way dropped off her, the hull swung parallel to the bank. Instantly, Jesper was over the bow, running a few meters to set the bow anchor firmly into the sand. Maddie nodded to him as he passed her, then walked toward the grounded bow of the little wolfship. The two crews crowded the sides, watching her curiously.

Stig went forward and leaned over the gunwale, offering her a hand. She gripped his wrist and he heaved her effortlessly up and inboard, setting her on the deck beside him.

"Welcome aboard," he said, grinning.

She smiled in return. "I'm glad to see you. I was afraid I might have missed you." She glanced around the ring of curious, bearded faces and frowned. "There weren't this many of you before, were there?"

"We picked up some of *Wolfbiter's* crew," Stig told her.

The little ship's deck was crowded. Maddie estimated that there must be nearly thirty men on board. She smiled inwardly. Thirty Skandians would make a powerful attack force, she thought, if her mother's estimate of their fighting ability was accurate.

She looked around. The press of bearded, muscular sailors obscured her view. She barely came up to shoulder height on most of them. "Where's Hal—your skirl?" she asked, remembering the Skandian term for a ship's captain.

Stig gestured toward the stern. "He's back this way." He waved an arm at the crowding seamen gathered around this strange apparition. Some of them had encountered Rangers before, but none had seen a female Ranger. "Make way, you lot! We're coming through."

The grinning sea wolves parted to let her and Stig through and she followed the tall first mate back to the stern, where Hal and Thorn were waiting, along with a third man she didn't recognize—another of *Wolfbiter*'s crew, she surmised. Hal stepped forward as they approached.

"Welcome, Princess Madelyn," he said. True to Skandian form, he made no attempt to bow. "Is that the right term for you?" She certainly wasn't dressed like a princess, he saw. Beneath the cloak, she had a quiver of two dozen arrows on her belt, balanced by a double scabbard holding a saxe and a smaller throwing knife. Her bow was slung over one shoulder.

"Just Maddie will do fine," she said. "I only do the princess thing at Castle Araluen. The rest of the time, I'm a Ranger— fourth-year apprentice."

Hal noticed the bronze oakleaf around her neck. It was a Ranger's symbol, he knew.

Jern frowned at her announcement. "But you're a girl." There was a question obvious in the statement.

Maddie nodded agreement. She had heard that dozens of

times before. She was used to it by now. "Nice of you to notice. As a matter of fact, I'm the first female Ranger—the first girl to be selected as an apprentice in the Corps."

Thorn shook his head, a huge grin on his face. "I *knew* there was something about you," he said. "That boar you shot—that was no fluke, was it?"

A ghost of a smile touched her lips briefly. "No," she said. "I sort of knew what I was doing. I thought you'd seen through my act."

Thorn smacked his wooden hook into his left palm. "I knew it," he said. "I told these others, *There's more to her than meets the eye.*"

"He did," Hal confirmed. "He said it several times."

"More than several," Stig put in, grinning. "In fact, he became a little tedious on the subject."

"The fact is," Thorn said, "I knew it and none of the rest of you did. No matter how many times I told you."

"Which was a lot," Stig said. But nothing could wipe the satisfied look from Thorn's bearded face.

Sensing he was about to say *I knew it* again, Hal held up a hand to stop him.

"So, Ranger Maddie, what can we do for you?"

5

CASSANDRA WAS LEANING ON THE PARAPET OF THE BALCONY that ran round the tower, surveying the surrounding countryside. She knew that it was too soon for Maddie to return. But she patrolled the balcony each morning, for any sign of activity in the grounds below the castle.

She sensed a movement behind her and turned to see Ingrid, proffering a steaming mug and smiling at her.

"Thought you might like a coffee, my lady," she said.

Cassandra took the mug and warmed her hands around it. In the early morning, the air was still chilly. She took a sip and smiled her thanks.

Ingrid moved forward to lean on the parapet beside her. Since her usual mistress was absent, the young woman seemed to have attached herself to Cassandra, sensing that the princess needed support and assistance. The strain of being in command of their small force was showing on Cassandra's face. She hadn't been sleeping well. Ingrid knew this because she often heard the princess leave her room in the middle of the night to prowl around the balcony, peering into the gloom below to try to sense any movement from Dimon and his men.

"No sign of anyone coming," Ingrid said.

Cassandra shook her head. "It's too early. Maddie would only just have reached the river—if she managed to get away."

The fact that Cassandra voiced the doubt was evidence of the strain she was feeling, Ingrid realized. "She got away," Ingrid said confidently. "If she hadn't, Dimon would have been on the stairs immediately, crowing about it and using her as a bargaining chip."

"That's true," Cassandra said, grateful for the reassurance.

"How long do you think it'll be before she comes back?" Ingrid asked.

Cassandra considered the question. "Assuming the Herons are on time, she should catch up with them in a day or so. Add another two days for them to reach the hill fort. Then, say, two more days to make contact with Horace and come up with a plan. Another day to help them break out. Four more days for them to make it back here. Ten days in all—let's say two weeks to be sure."

"And in the meantime, all we have to do is sit tight here," Ingrid said.

"As you say. We sit tight. And make sure Dimon doesn't catch us out with any more of his tricks."

At that moment, the hammering started and the two women exchanged a quick glance.

"They're at it again," Cassandra said. She turned away from the parapet and hurried around the balcony to the inner side. The hammering was coming from the castle courtyard. But it was obviously on the other side of the keep tower, as whatever was being built was out of their sight.

"What are they up to?" Ingrid said, half to herself. The noise of hammering had begun around midday the day before. It had gone on through the afternoon, then tailed away in the early evening.

"Nothing good. You can be sure of that," Cassandra answered, her brow furrowed. She hated not knowing what Dimon was doing, what he might be planning. She was reasonably confident that they were safe up here in the tower. But *reasonably confident* was a long way from certain. Dimon had proved himself to be devious and ingenious—as witness his successful plan to take control of the castle. And with an enemy like that, it paid to be forewarned of his plans.

Eventually, she shrugged. "I expect we'll find out what he's planning in time," she said.

They stood side by side for several minutes, looking down into the courtyard toward the corner from which the hammering seemed to be coming. For a moment, Cassandra toyed with the idea of climbing down the series of hidden ladders to the cellars, then sneaking out to see what the enemy was up to. But she quickly discarded the idea. It would be too risky. She didn't have Maddie's ability to move without being seen. And there was always the chance that she might give away the existence of the secret stairway to the upper floors.

"We'll just have to be patient," she said, as much to herself as to the young woman beside her.

At that moment, the hammering stopped.

"They've finished building it, whatever 'it' is," Ingrid observed.

"Or they're taking a coffee break," Cassandra replied. But after a few minutes they heard men shouting orders, and then a new sound—the sound of something heavy being dragged across the flagstones. They both leaned forward expectantly, craning over the wall for the first sight of . . . whatever it might be.

The first thing they saw was a team of men—about a dozen of them—hauling on ropes and slowly making their way around the corner of the keep and into the courtyard below. It was obviously hard work—whatever they were dragging, it was something big and clumsy. They could hear the rumbling sound of large wooden wheels on the flagstones, the creak of the ropes and the shouts of the overseers who were in charge, urging the men pulling on the ropes to greater efforts.

Then, slowly, a massive wooden platform began to come rolling into view. As it came into the open, they could see more details: a long, crane-like beam that surmounted the wheeled platform, set on a fulcrum one-third of the way along its length. At its longer end, a cradle of ropes hung down, supporting a leather, bucket-shaped object. They could see an arrangement of cogwheels at the base of the beam, and a large windlass-like structure.

"What is it?" Ingrid asked nervously. Whatever it was, she thought, it boded nothing good for them.

"It's a siege engine," Cassandra replied quietly. "A trebuchet, or a catapult. It's designed to throw large rocks at a building and smash down the walls."

Ingrid looked at her fearfully. "Can it smash these walls?" she asked, looking down at the curved wall of the tower, built in granite and seemingly unbreakable. Then she looked back at the trebuchet. There was something intrinsically evil and threatening about the machine.

Cassandra shrugged. "I'm not sure. The tower is pretty solid. But I guess if they keep at it long enough, it's possible."

She turned as she heard a footstep behind her, to see Merlon emerging from the tower and moving to the balustrade to peer over it. The sergeant seemed unimpressed by the sight of the siege machine below them. That was comforting, she thought. He grunted and spat out into the void.

"What do you think, Merlon?" she asked. "Will they manage to breach the walls with that thing?"

"Won't be easy, my lady. Depends on a lot of things. In the meantime, why don't I get a few of the archers to see if we can slow them down?"

He gestured to the men below, swarming over the siege machine as they dragged it into position. Three of them climbed on board and started turning the windlass. Slowly, the main beam moved up, then back. As it pivoted on its axle, they could see that it was counterweighted by a massive boulder at its shorter end.

Cassandra nodded. Merlon's suggestion made sense. "Good idea. Go get them."

He hurried back into the tower and they could hear him calling orders as he went.

"Once they've wound the beam back against the counterbalance," she told Ingrid, "they'll load their projectile into the bucket at the end of the ropes. Then, when they release the beam, it will swing up and over, and the ropes and bucket will shoot up as well—like a flexible elbow. When the beam stops, the ropes and bucket will keep going like a flail. It'll increase the force of the beam and hurl the projectile up toward us."

Before Ingrid could reply, there was a clatter of feet behind them and three of the archers emerged, moving to line the balustrade. Merlon was behind them. They grinned as he pointed down into the courtyard.

"See that? he said. "It's been made by Dimon and his men. And there are a dozen of his finest, just waiting to throw rocks at us. Why don't you lads see if you can give them something to think about?"

The archers said nothing. But they all drew shafts from their quivers and set them to their strings.

"All together," the senior man among them ordered. "When I give the word."

The massive bows creaked as the three men drew back their arrows, aiming down into the courtyard below.

"Aim low," the senior archer cautioned them. When shooting downhill, he knew, there was a tendency to shoot high. Then, as their aim steadied, he counted down.

"Three, two, one. Shoot."

The three bows thrummed almost as one. There was the usual slithering clatter of arrows leaving the string and passing across the bow stave. Cassandra and Ingrid watched eagerly as the arrows sped away.

"Let 'em have another before they wake up," said Merlon, and in the same instant that the first three arrows struck home, another three were on their way.

Two of the first three shots found their targets. One man fell away from the windlass, an arrow in his upper body. Another, who had been hauling on the ropes to position the trebuchet, went down with a shaft in his thigh. The third shot hit the beam right next to another man and buried itself deep into the timber, quivering with the impact. The man leapt to the far side of the platform, seeking cover.

A few seconds later, the second volley arrived, hissing through the air. By this time, the men on the catapult had become aware of the danger and most had scrambled behind the structure, seeking cover. The arrows screeched off the flagstones, skidding and ricocheting but causing no further harm. As the three archers readied their bows once more, Merlon held up a hand to stop them.

"Wait till you have a good target," he said.

All movement had ceased in the courtyard as the crew of the trebuchet huddled behind its solid timbers. They heard a single voice shouting at them to get back to their positions.

It was a familiar voice.

"Dimon doesn't sound too happy," Ingrid observed. She was grinning.

But Cassandra merely shook her head. "He'll come up with a countermeasure."

And sure enough, as Dimon saw that his impassioned shouting was having no effect, he calmed down and called orders for his men to withdraw. Crouching to avoid further arrows, they scuttled back into shelter behind the corner of the keep tower.

"That's put a spoke in their wheel," Merlon said in a satisfied tone.

Cassandra nodded. "Yes. I imagine now they'll build some kind of shelter over the platform, so they can attack us without being shot in return. But it'll take time," she added. Then she turned to the archers. "Well done, men. You might as well stand down for now."

The three men knuckled their foreheads in salute and trooped back inside the tower.

Cassandra took another look below, at the huge machine now standing alone in the courtyard. From the other side of the keep tower, the hammering began once more. "They're not wasting any time," she said.

"Wonder how long that'll take them?" Ingrid said.

Cassandra shrugged. "Probably a couple of hours. We'll detail someone to keep watch and give us warning when they're ready. In the meantime, we'll need to try to think of a way to stop their little game once and for all."

She leaned over the balustrade, her eyes narrowing as she studied the siege engine more closely. Then she nodded slowly to herself. She thought she could see a way they might be able to do it.

6

MADDIE UNROLLED THE MAP SHE HAD DRAWN BEFORE SHE left Castle Araluen. She had copied it from the large wall map in Cassandra's command center on the ninth floor. She spread it out on the wide bole of a tree stump as Hal, Thorn and Stig gathered round, leaning to look over her shoulder as she touched the map with the point of her saxe.

"This is the Wezel River. It's north of here, as you can see. Maybe twelve kilometers from where we are at the moment. And here, six or seven kilometers east of Harnel village, is an old hill fort, built hundreds of years ago but deserted and derelict in recent times. This is where my father and Gilan are trapped."

"Trapped?" Thorn asked. "Trapped by who?"

Hal grinned. "Shouldn't that be 'by whom'?"

Thorn glared at him. "She knows what I mean." He turned his gaze back to Maddie. "Trapped by who?" he repeated. Then, to make himself totally clear, he added, "Whom has trapped them?"

"A mixed force of the Red Fox Clan and Sonderland mercenaries," Maddie said.

Stig snorted derisively. "Sonderlanders! They'd fight their own grandmothers for money."

Thorn nodded agreement, then added, "Mind you, their grandmothers would probably give them a shellacking."

But Hal held up a hand for silence. "Just a moment, who are these Red Fox people?"

Maddie hesitated. In her enthusiasm, she had jumped right in, she realized. She had a habit of doing that—assuming that her listeners knew what she was talking about before she actually told them. "Maybe I'd better start at the beginning."

Hal nodded. "That would be good."

She gathered her thoughts and launched into a brief explanation of the plot hatched by the Red Fox Clan to lure Horace and Gilan away with most of the garrison and to usurp the throne—and of Dimon's leading role in it. As she mentioned his name, Hal raised his eyebrows.

"Dimon? Wasn't he left in command of the garrison?"

"He had us all fooled," Maddie said bitterly. "Mum and Dad thought he was loyal. They trusted him implicitly."

"I didn't like him," Thorn growled.

She turned a steady gaze on the old sea wolf. "I plan to kill him," she said quietly.

Thorn nodded his approval. "I'll try not to get in your way."

Stig was rubbing his jaw as he thought over what Maddie had told them. "But what does he hope to gain by this treachery?"

"The throne," Maddie said. "He's actually a distant relative of my mother. If he can remove my grandfather, my mother, my father, and *me*, he'll have a legitimate claim to the throne. His plan is to blame the revolt on the Red Fox Clan. Naturally, he'll deny any connection to them—in fact, he'll say that he drove them off, but too late to save my mother. And there'll be nobody left alive to argue the toss. Then he'll make his claim for the throne—all the while looking sad and sorrowful about the whole situation."

She studied their faces as they let this sink in. Then she added, "Unfortunately, there are a lot of people in Araluen who would welcome a return to the law of male succession."

"I always thought your mother was a popular figure," Stig said.

Maddie nodded. "She is. But that's mainly in Araluen Fief and some of the surrounding fiefdoms, like Redmont. Farther north and west, they know little about her. And remember, she's not *actually* the queen yet. So he wouldn't be seen to be replacing her."

Hal was studying the map. He tapped the symbol representing the hill fort.

"So what's Gilan doing getting himself trapped?" he asked. The Herons had worked with Gilan in the past, and they tended to think of him as the person in charge.

"He and my father were tricked. They had reports that there was a small band of Red Fox rebels causing a disturbance up here. No more than thirty or forty, they thought. They took forty cavalrymen and archers with them to nip any possible trouble in the bud. Except when they got here, they found they were facing over one hundred and fifty troops."

"Nasty surprise," Hal said. "Do they know about what's happened at Castle Araluen?"

"We don't think so," Maddie said. "There's no way they could have heard about it. If they had, I think my father would have done something rash like trying to break out of the fort in a direct frontal assault."

"Not a good idea," Hal said. He was studying the map again, as if he could see the opposing forces at the old hill fort.

"No. They're relatively safe in the fort, but if they try to break out, the Red Foxes will see them coming and be ready for them. There'll be no element of surprise, and they'll be outnumbered by three to one."

"Maybe the Red Foxes plan to starve them out. How much food do they have?" Stig asked.

Maddie inclined her head uncertainly. "Not a lot. They took rations for maybe fourteen days. So they must be running short by now."

"They could always eat their horses," Thorn put in.

Maddie raised an eyebrow at him. "They'll never do that. Try telling a cavalryman to eat his horse. That'd be like telling you to eat your ship," she said. She hesitated as she realized how ludicrous that sounded.

Hal grinned. "It's not *quite* the same thing," he said. "But I see your point."

"Stig here could probably eat a ship if he was hungry enough," Thorn said, straight-faced.

Stig looked sidelong at him. He was used to the old sea wolf's teasing. "I'd need a lot of salt," he said.

Seeing that Thorn was about to reply, Hal cut short their banter. "The question is," he said, "what do you want from us?"

Maddie hesitated. This was the crucial point. Her mother had been confident that the Herons would throw in their lot with Horace and Gilan's men. But Cassandra had known them for years. If she were to ask for their help personally, they would almost certainly give it. But Maddie had only met them once before, and she wasn't so sure.

"As things stand," she said slowly, "there's no way for my dad and Gilan to break out of the fort without the enemy seeing them coming and being ready for them. They might win the ensuing battle. My dad is a very capable warrior."

"Gilan's no slouch either," Hal said, and his companions grunted their agreement.

"But even if they did win, they'd lose a lot of men in a straightforward pitched battle like that. They'd be outnumbered and they'd have no advantages on their side. On the other hand . . ." She paused, looking meaningfully at the three Skandians. "If we could launch a surprise attack from the rear, just as Dad and Gilan attacked down the hill, that might tip the battle in our favor."

She paused to see their reaction, and her spirits rose as she saw them nodding.

"I know there are only a dozen in your crew," she said, "but Mum said one Skandian is the equivalent of three normal warriors."

Hal smiled lazily at her. "Why, Ranger Maddie," he said, "are you trying to influence us with exaggerated compliments?"

She flushed, feeling her cheeks redden. "No. I just . . ." She stopped, searching for words, and he touched her arm, letting her off the hook.

"It's all right," he said. "Your mother is right. One Skandian is the equivalent of three ordinary warriors."

"Four if the Skandian is me," Thorn averred.

She smiled at him gratefully. "I can believe that."

"And there's something else," Hal added. "There's not a dozen of us. There are over thirty of us if we count *Wolfbiter*'s crew."

"Would they join us?" Maddie asked. She knew her mother and Gilan were old friends of the *Heron*'s crew. But Jern and his men were a different matter.

Hal shrugged. "I don't see why not," he said. "After all, as the duty ship, they swore an oath of loyalty to the legitimate rulers of Araluen."

"And I've never known a wolfship crew who would refuse the opportunity for a good fight," Stig said.

"*And* I've never known a wolfship crew who'd pass up the opportunity to wallop a few Sonderlanders," Thorn added.

"Let's ask them," Hal said. He rose from his crouched position by the tree stump and started toward the two ships' crews, who were waiting expectantly, relaxing on the grass nearby.

"Listen up, lads," he said, raising his voice. "Maddie here has asked a favor of us. Her father and the Ranger Gilan are surrounded in a hill fort to the north of here by a ragtag group of Sonderland mercenaries and some locals."

There was a growl of subdued anger from the Skandians. As Thorn had intimated, Sonderlanders were not their favorite people.

"How many Sonderlanders?" asked one of Jern's crew.

"About one hundred and fifty. And there are forty Araluens inside the fort. Maddie has asked us if we'll help them. The plan is for us to launch a surprise attack on the rear of the mercenaries while the Araluen troops attack downhill. I've already said my crew will help." He looked at Jern. "And I'm assuming the *Wolfbiter* crew will join us."

Jern chewed his lip thoughtfully before replying. "You're asking us to commit ourselves to a battle on the word of a mere girl? She's hardly more than a child." Some Skandians, regrettably, were conservative in their attitudes as to a woman's place in the world.

Hal's eyes narrowed. "This 'child,'" he said, "is a Ranger. A fourth-year apprentice."

The Herons nodded their heads approvingly. They had dealt with Rangers before. The *Wolfbiter* crew were more doubtful. They had been the duty ship in Araluen for some months, but in that time they'd had little to do with the Ranger Corps.

"So she's an apprentice," Blorst Knucklewhite said. He was one of the rowing crew on *Wolfbiter*. "That means she isn't fully qualified, doesn't it?"

Long on muscle, short on brain, like all rowers, Hal thought. He could see that a demonstration of Maddie's abilities might be called for. He turned to the young Ranger. "See that alder tree yonder?" he asked.

Maddie looked in the direction he indicated. The tree was a good hundred meters away.

"There's a black mark on the bark," Hal continued. "Could you put two arrows into it for us—"

Before he had finished the sentence, Maddie had unslung her bow, nocked an arrow and let fly without seeming to aim. A second arrow hissed away while the first was still in the air. Both of them slammed into the mark Hal had designated.

The crew of *Wolfbiter* looked suitably surprised and impressed. The Herons smiled with an I-could-have-told-you expression. But before anyone could speak, Maddie had dropped the bow and whipped her sling from under her belt, fitting a shot into the pouch in one deft movement. She pointed to the *Heron*, nosed up on the bank forty meters away. The shields of the two crews lined the sides of the ship.

"The shield with the red X," she said. "On the right-hand edge."

Then she stepped forward and whipped the sling up and over her head. The shot flashed away and, seconds later, struck the shield with a resounding CRACK! As she had forecast, it struck on the right-hand edge of the shield, setting it rocking back and forth. By sheer chance, the shield happened to belong to Blorst Knucklewhite.

"Orlog's ears!" he said. "This girl is downright dangerous!"

His shipmates muttered their agreement, while the Herons laughed at the startled expressions on their faces.

Hal knew that Skandians valued skill at arms highly, and Maddie had just demonstrated her ability—and her worth. He turned back to Jern. "This 'mere girl,' as you call her, is the daughter of Princess Cassandra and Sir Horace. And she's apprenticed to the Ranger Will Treaty. If you know your recent history, you might recall all three of them had a lot to do with the defeat of the Eastern Riders when they tried to invade our country some years back. I think we owe them, don't you?"

There was a murmur of agreement from the *Wolfbiter* crew.

Jern held his hands out in surrender. "We'll fight for her," he said. "I just wanted to make sure you knew what you were doing."

7

HORACE WAS SITTING IN HIS TENT OUT OF THE HEAT OF THE noonday sun, sharpening his sword, when Gilan poked his head around the open entrance.

"Isn't that thing sharp enough already?" he said, as Horace rasped away at the gleaming blade.

Horace studied the sword as he worked. It had been made by the famed swordmakers of Nihon-Ja and had been presented to him many years before. The blade was not only sharp, it was incredibly hard. It would put a notch in the blade of a normal Araluen sword. The steel was slightly blue, with wave-like patterns running along it, showing where the separate rods of iron had been beaten together to form it.

"A sword can never be too sharp," he said. "What's on your mind?"

"I've had an idea," Gilan said.

Horace looked up with interest, the whetstone pausing in its rhythmic back and forth stroking of the blade. "Of course, that's what you Rangers do. You have ideas. You think. You plan. Whereas simple warriors like me just look for their next opportunity to whack someone with a sword."

"If you've quite finished," Gilan replied.

"I take it this idea of yours is a brilliant plan to break out of here and send that rabble down the hill packing?" Horace continued. "If so, it's taken you long enough to come up with it."

"It's not exactly that," Gilan said, and Horace feigned a look of disappointment. "But it is related. Come with me."

He turned and stooped under the entrance to the tent, moving out into the bright sunshine. When Horace followed, a few seconds later, the Ranger was already striding toward the north wall.

Horace lengthened his stride to catch up. "So this idea of yours concerns the back of the fort?"

Gilan said nothing. He mounted the rickety stairs that led to the catwalk inside the north wall and climbed to the top. Once there, he moved to the parapet and turned to face Horace.

"It strikes me," he said, "that there may come a time when we want to leave the fort, and possibly launch an attack on the enemy camp." He gestured with his thumb toward the south wall, where the main gate was placed, and the camp that lay downhill beyond it.

"Since we've discussed that idea several times, I wouldn't be surprised," Horace replied. "All we need is a plan—a typically sneaky, underhand, Ranger type of plan."

"And if we were to do such a thing, it would be better if the enemy didn't see us coming—at least not immediately."

Horace nodded. "That would make sense. I'm assuming you're thinking that we might leave the fort via the north side. But, as you can see, there is no gate in this north wall. And not a lot of room on the pathway below it. Certainly not a lot of room for our horses." He gestured down to the track that wound around the fort. At its highest point, it was barely a meter wide. Chances were, if they tried to take horses out onto that narrow dirt track, they would stumble and fall.

Gilan nodded. "I noticed that. My idea is that we build a ramp."

"A ramp?" Horace said.

"A sloping timber walkway that we could lead the horses down," Gilan explained.

Horace gave him an exasperated look. "I wasn't asking for a definition of a ramp," he said. "I was expressing surprise at the idea. Perhaps even admiration."

"We'd have to make a hole in the wall, of course. A hole that we might call a *gateway*," Gilan explained further. "That wouldn't be too hard."

"And where would you see this ramp going?" Horace asked.

Gilan pointed to the next level down on the sloping path. "Down to the next level," he said. At the point he indicated, the pathway was several meters wide, with plenty of room for mounted riders. "We could ride down the ramp to the path, then work our way around the hill and emerge on the other side of the fort, two levels down. We'd be that much closer to the enemy before they saw us."

Horace leaned on the rough timber wall, visualizing such a ramp. "It's a good idea," he said.

"Thank you," Gilan said, with just a trace of smugness.

Then Horace continued. "But there are two problems. One, where will you get the timber for this ramp? There's not a lot lying around."

"You're standing on it," Gilan told him. "We could tear up this walkway, and the stairs, to build the ramp."

"But then we'd have no defensive position if the enemy attacked this side of the fort," Horace pointed out.

Gilan nodded. "On the other hand, if they did attack this wall and made it to the top, they'd be faced with a four-meter drop into the compound below, wouldn't they?"

Horace smiled. He hadn't thought of that. He visualized the surprised look on the attackers' faces as they swung themselves over the top of the parapet and found nothing below them but thin air.

"In addition to that, my archers could engage them from the walkways on the west and east walls, and shoot down any who didn't fall."

"Ye-es," Horace said slowly, now picturing this further concept.

"You said there were two problems with my plan?"

Horace reluctantly abandoned his thoughts of Sonderland mercenaries tumbling to the hard-packed earth below, riddled with arrows. "So I did. The other problem—or problems, to be more exact—is down there."

He pointed down the hill, where the winding path formed a series of steep terraces, to a small group of tents at the bottom. They could see smoke from a cooking fire rising into the air and a figure moving from one of the tents to the fire.

"Unfortunately, our enemy isn't completely lacking in intelligence," he said. "Those lookouts are there to raise the alarm if we do try to leave the fort from this side."

"Actually, I had thought of that," Gilan said.

Horace looked at him. He wasn't surprised to hear it. Gilan wasn't the type to overlook such a basic hole in his plan. "And did you think of a solution?"

"By the time they make their way around the base of the hill to raise the alarm, our cavalry will be in sight anyway."

"You're right," Horace said thoughtfully. "We wouldn't achieve total surprise, of course. They'd still see us coming down the last two-thirds of the hill. But we'd be a lot closer to them than if we were to sortie through the main gate."

"Exactly," Gilan said. "And I can lead the archers out the main gate and down the south side of the hill, while you lead the cavalry at a canter around the track. It won't be a complete surprise, as you say, but it might be enough to panic and confuse them when they see us coming."

"And panic and confusion are our allies in this situation," Horace agreed. He came to a decision and slapped his friend on the shoulder.

Gilan, who was slight of build like most Rangers, staggered a pace or two. "I'm glad you like the idea," he said sourly.

"A trebuchet, you say?" Duncan asked Cassandra. He was sitting up in his bed, which had been placed against the window of his room, affording a view over the parkland below the castle.

Since they had taken refuge in the tower, Cassandra had made a practice of visiting her father and keeping him abreast of events. She valued his comments and advice. After all, he was an experienced commander and one of Araluen's foremost tacticians. She, on the other hand, was new to the business of commanding men in battle.

She nodded now at his question. "That's what it looks like. I've never seen one in real life, but I've seen pictures of them."

He frowned thoughtfully. "And where is it now?"

"It's in the courtyard. Dimon's men abandoned it when our

archers started shooting. I can hear them hammering and sawing on the other side of the keep. I assume they're building some kind of timber shield to protect the crew from our arrows."

Duncan started to throw back the blankets covering his legs. "Well, let's take a look at it."

But she held out a hand to stop him. "Dad, you're a sick man. Don't try to get up!"

"Nonsense!" Duncan said emphatically, brushing aside her protests. "Lying here with nothing to do is making me sick. I feel useless and inadequate. Best thing for me would be to have something to occupy my mind."

He swung his legs out of bed, moving carefully to favor the injured leg, and pulled on a pair of breeches, stuffing his night-shirt into them. Cassandra regarded her father curiously. He seemed to have a new energy about him; he was different from the pale, wan figure she had become accustomed to. There was color back in his cheeks, and although he was still thin, he definitely seemed to have regained some of his old vigor. Perhaps he was right, she thought. He needed a challenge. He needed something to do. Most of all, he needed to feel useful. She helped him rise from the bed. He swayed uncertainly for a moment or two, then recovered his sense of balance.

"Been lying there too long," he said brusquely. "Hand me my stick."

There was a blackthorn walking stick leaning against the wardrobe, and she passed it to him. He leaned his weight on it and took an experimental step toward the door. He swayed again, then beckoned to her.

"Better let me lean on you to start," he said, and she moved quickly to him, letting him put his arm around her shoulders. He beamed at her. "Now lead on."

They made their way to the door leading to the balcony, followed by the curious and delighted looks of those they passed on the way. The soldiers were heartened by the sight of the King on his feet once more, and they murmured greetings and touched their knuckles to their foreheads as he passed. Duncan paused at the door and looked back at them.

"The old dog still has some life in him," he told them, grinning.

He was answered by smiles, and one anonymous voice that called, "Good on you, Bandylegs!" It was the army's private nickname for him, referring to the fact that, after a lifetime in the saddle, he was a trifle bowlegged. He pretended to frown angrily, even though he had been aware of the nickname for many years.

"Insolence!" he snorted, then turned toward the doorway. "Let's take a look at this machine, shall we?"

On the balcony, he released his grip on Cassandra's shoulder and they leaned on the balustrade together, peering down into the courtyard. He was silent for several seconds.

"Yes. It's a trebuchet, all right," he said. "And it looks rather well made. Dimon obviously has an engineer among his men."

He peered more closely, framing his hands around his eyes to help him focus on the trebuchet.

"Hmmm," he said thoughtfully.

She looked quickly at him. "What is it?" she asked.

He pointed down into the courtyard. "The rope they're using. It's coated with tar."

She frowned, not seeing the significance. "That's normal, isn't it?" she asked. "I assume they'd do that to stop it fraying."

"Yes. It's quite normal. But usually the rope on a trebuchet is old and the tar has dried and hardened. This is newly applied. It's fresh." He paused for a few seconds, then added, "And flammable."

Slowly, the significance of what he was saying dawned on her. "So . . . if we were to hit it with fire arrows," she said, "it would probably burn quite nicely."

He smiled at her. "Exactly."

Cassandra turned away to the door. "Merlon!" she called.

The old sergeant appeared almost immediately. "Yes, my lady?" he replied.

She gestured to the interior of the tower behind him. "Get those archers out here again, will you?"

He nodded and disappeared back into the tower room. She could hear him calling out as he went. He reappeared with the archers a few minutes later. Cassandra beckoned to them to join her at the balustrade, then looked expectantly to her father, waiting for him to explain what they had in mind. Duncan took her arm and, limping still, led her a few paces away, then spoke softly to her.

"You're in command," he told her. "You need to tell them what to do. I don't want the men looking to me every time you give an order to see if I approve. You need to appear confident and positive."

Cassandra nodded and moved back to where the archers were waiting. Duncan remained where he was. She pointed to the trebuchet in the courtyard below.

"The rope on that windlass is freshly tarred," she said. "The tar is still soft and wet. That means it's highly flammable."

They all nodded, beginning to see where she was going. "Do

you think you could . . ." Duncan cleared his throat meaningfully behind her, and she recalled what he had said about being positive and confident. "I want you to put a few fire arrows into that rope," she amended. "I want you to set it on fire."

Delighted grins spread across the three men's faces.

"No problem at all, my lady," Thomas, the senior among them, replied.

The others murmured agreement.

"You have a wicked mind, my lady," Thomas continued.

She shrugged, taking the comment as a compliment.

Merlon snapped his fingers at the three archers. "You start preparing some fire arrows," he said. "I'll go fetch a brazier."

8

"IF YOU'RE COMING WITH US, YOU'LL HAVE TO LEAVE YOUR horse here," Hal told Maddie. "We're already overcrowded with *Wolfbiter*'s crew onboard. There isn't room for a horse." He could see Maddie didn't like the idea and he waved an arm around the riverbank. "There's plenty of grass and water here for him," he said. "He'll be fine for a few days."

Maddie hesitated a few seconds longer, than came to a decision. "No," she said. "I'm not leaving him."

She couldn't explain to the Skandian that a Ranger and her horse were inseparable. Already, in recent days, she had left Bumper on his own for too long. She didn't want to make it any longer.

She had no idea what they were going to find at the hill fort, but she and Bumper were a team and she felt more confident when he was with her. Hal raised his eyebrows and shrugged his shoulders at her refusal. In the past, they'd carried horses aboard *Heron*. They could take up planks in the central deck to create a pen. They had even carried several horses at once on occasion. But that was when there was only the *Heron* brotherband aboard. Now, with over thirty men in the crew, with their equipment, weapons and baggage, there was simply no room to do it. *Heron* was, after all, smaller than a standard wolfship.

Maddie strode back to the map, still spread out on the tree stump, and with several rocks holding down its edges. She studied it for a moment, then beckoned Hal to join her.

As before, she used her saxe to point out positions on the map.

"I'll travel across country," she said, indicating a route running northeast from their current position to the hill fort. "It's a good deal shorter than the way you'll have to go—you'll be heading out to the ocean, turning north and then coming inland again when you reach the mouth of the Wezel."

"That's true enough," Hal agreed. "Although we'll probably move a lot faster than you. We've got a lot of extra rowers onboard." He paused, studying the map, mentally measuring the distances involved. Then, inevitably, he checked the telltale ribbon at *Heron*'s sternpost before coming to a decision. "We should reach this point"—he took the saxe from her hand and indicated a position on the Wezel River about five kilometers to the east of the hill fort—"by the end of the day tomorrow. Will you make it by then?"

Maddie nodded. "The map doesn't show any hills or difficult terrain," she said. "That'll give me plenty of time to make that rendezvous. If I get there much before you, I might take a look at the fort and see what we're up against."

"Don't let them catch you," Hal said, without thinking. Then, seeing Maddie's pained look, he added, "Sorry. I forgot. Rangers don't do that sort of thing, do they?"

"We try not to." But Hal's apologetic grin made it impossible for her to take any real offense. "You'd better get going," she said. "I'll see you tomorrow afternoon."

"We'll be there," he said, and turned away toward the river, calling for Stig to get the crews back onboard. She watched Hal striding down the riverbank. There was something in his manner, confident and capable, that lifted her spirits. With allies like these, she thought, she'd have no trouble breaking her father out of the fort.

She turned and walked briskly toward the trees, where Bumper waited for her. She'd unsaddled him when they'd first reached this spot and she hefted the saddle now, heaving it up onto his back, settling it in position and leaning down to tighten the girth straps.

So we're not going on the boat? he asked.

She shook her head. "No room for us. It's full of big, hairy Skandians."

Just as well. I probably get seasick on boats.

"You've never been on one."

That's because I probably get seasick.

She went to reply, then realized that she had no answer to this twisted logic, so she let him have the last word.

Again.

She found a minor road—little more than a rough track, really—heading roughly northeast, and followed it for the rest of the day. The countryside varied between open grasslands and moderately wooded areas. Whenever she came into the open and could see the sun, she checked her direction. It was all too easy for a winding road like this to gradually diverge from its initial path, so that she might find herself inadvertently heading due east, rather than the original direction. She was pleased to see that the road maintained its general heading of northeast, although she determined not to rely on that fact, but to check whenever possible.

She made good time, and around the late afternoon she started looking for a suitable campsite. It would be best to spend the night in among the trees, she decided. She was not too far away from the hill fort and the Red Fox camp. There could well be foraging parties out gathering food or firewood, and she didn't want to run across one of them.

She finally found the ideal spot, a small open glade set about ten meters off the track. She left Bumper in the opening and returned to the track, peering through the trees to see if she could spot him, but he was well concealed. Once it was dark, the glade would be even more invisible to anyone passing by. After all, she had only spotted it with difficulty in the full light of day.

She unsaddled Bumper and hung his bridle over a tree limb. The grass here was thick and lush, and he set about cropping it, grinding it between his big square teeth with a satisfied sound.

Maddie peered up through the canopy of trees to where she could see the sky. It was clear, with only a few small clouds dawdling by overhead. She sniffed the air experimentally. Often, that was the surest way of sensing approaching rain. But the air smelled reassuringly dry, so she decided against pitching her travel shelter and hammock. The thick grass would be soft enough underneath her. And her cloak would keep her warm and dry—and concealed, she thought.

She considered lighting a cook fire but discarded the idea. The smell of woodsmoke would linger for hours and be a sure giveaway, if anyone was searching the area, that someone was camped here. Instead, she ate a frugal meal from her travel rations: smoked meat, dried fruit and flat bread.

The lack of a fire meant no coffee, of course, and for a moment she nearly relented. Then she realized that the smell of brewing coffee would be even more of a giveaway than woodsmoke. Smoke might come from an accidental fire. Fresh brewed coffee could only indicate someone nearby. Reluctantly, she washed her meal down with fresh water from a nearby creek, filling her canteen from the same source. Will had taught her that it was always wise to top up your fresh water supplies whenever possible. Having experienced the taste of water left too long in the wood-and-leather canteen, she understood the sentiment.

"You'll owe me for this, Dad," she said quietly.

Bumper looked up from his grazing. *You said?*

"Nothing. I was talking to my dad."

The little horse appeared to look around the glade. *Who is not here.*

"I know that. I was speaking rhetorically."

He inclined his head, peering down at her where she sat cross-legged on the grass. *I'm not sure that's the accurate meaning of rhetorical.*

"So bring me up before a magistrate and charge me. It's close enough to what I had in mind," she said.

He shrugged—insofar as a horse could be said to shrug—and put his head down once more, teeth busily cropping and tearing at the grass, jaws grinding.

It had been a long day's ride, and once the sun set, she settled back, head on her saddle and folded saddle blanket, and rolled her cloak around her.

Her bow was unstrung, hanging in a tree close by—the damp night air would play havoc with a tensioned bowstring—but her sling was coiled loosely around her right wrist and several lead shot were arranged on the grass beside her saddle. In addition, her saxe and throwing knife were within easy reach.

"Keep your ears open," she said to Bumper. If anyone approached during the night, he would hear them or smell them and give her plenty of warning. He snorted agreement and she closed her eyes and was almost immediately asleep.

She was awoken by the predawn chorus of birds. She lay on her back for a few seconds, enjoying the joyous sound and stretching luxuriously. A gray light filtered through the trees, and there was a thick ground mist. A few meters away, the dark shape that was her horse moved quietly about the glade, keeping watch, as he had done all night.

"Did you get any sleep?" she asked. She knew that he could be asleep and still hear or sense someone approaching. He snorted and nodded his head.

She rolled out of her cloak, stretching once more and groaning slightly as she rose to her feet. As ever, the old wound in her hip twinged slightly after several hours of being immobile. She rubbed it absentmindedly and contemplated the day. Once the sun rose, this mist would clear and it would be another fine day, she thought. That was all to the good. She didn't enjoy traveling in the rain.

The previous afternoon, she had collected sticks and twigs to use as kindling, and a couple of larger deadfalls, hiding them from the dew under the low branches of a leafy bush. She dragged them out now and started building a fire. The smell of woodsmoke and coffee wouldn't be a risk for her now, as she was moving on from this spot. There would only be a problem if there was somebody in the immediate vicinity, and she knew that, if that were the case, Bumper would have warned her.

"Nobody around, is there?" she asked, striking her flint with the edge of her saxe.

Would have told you if there were.

She got the fire going and filled her small coffeepot from the canteen, setting it in the edge of the fire to boil. When it was bubbling cheerfully, she tossed in a handful of coffee and stirred the pot with a green stick. The delicious aroma filled the air and she smiled in anticipation. She had caught the Ranger's curse of addiction to coffee. She might manage to spend the evening without it, but mornings were a different matter.

She filled her mug with the fragrant liquid, spooned in honey and stirred it vigorously. Then, sitting by the fire, hands wrapped around the mug, she drank deeply.

"Oh, that's good. You don't know what you're missing," she told her horse, after several more sips.

Bumper shook himself. *By the same token, you don't appreciate the rich flavor of fresh green grass.*

She concealed a shudder at the comparison. "That's true. Funny that didn't occur to me."

She ate more of the flatbread from her pack and a handful of dried fruit and nuts. They would keep her going until about midday. But the coffee was the real restorative. She checked the pot, found another half cup still in it and poured it into her mug.

When she finished, she rinsed her mug and tossed the dregs of the pot onto the fire. She repacked her things, kicked dirt over the now-smoldering fire and saddled Bumper. She took her bow down from the tree limb where it was hanging and strung it. The air was dry now and the string wouldn't suffer—and, as she had been repeatedly told by Will, *An unstrung bow is a stick.*

She swung lightly up into Bumper's saddle. Now that she had been moving around for some minutes, the stiffness in her hip had faded.

"Let's go," she said. "I want to take a look at this hill fort."

9

THE FIRST FIRE ARROW STREAKED AWAY. THE OIL-SOAKED rag wrapped tightly around its warhead created a hissing sound as it whipped through the air. It left a thin trail of gray smoke behind it as it flashed down to the trebuchet. But Thomas, the archer, hadn't allowed enough for the extra weight and drag of the burning cloth and the shaft fell short of its target, smacking into the timber decking of the trebuchet platform.

"You missed," said Dermott, one of the other archers.

Thomas eyed him balefully. "You try then."

Dermott dipped his arrow into the flaming brazier Merlon had set on the balcony beside them. Waiting until the rag was fully alight, he leaned over the parapet, drew and released. Again, a thin trail of gray smoke was left behind it. The arrow struck true, burying itself in the coils of tarred rope that wound round and round the windlass. But it was buried too deeply and the flame was extinguished before it could spread to the rope.

"Hah!" Thomas said scornfully.

Dermott, who was considerably the younger of the two, went red in the face and cursed quietly. Then, realizing who was standing beside him, he nodded his head apologetically to Cassandra. "Your pardon, my lady."

She shrugged. "I've heard worse from my father," she told him. The archers grinned and Duncan snorted indignantly. Then she looked at the third archer, standing ready by the brazier. "Third time's a charm, Simon."

He nodded, dipped his arrow into the flames, waited a few seconds to make sure it was burning properly, and then took his shot.

Like its predecessor, the arrow smacked into the coils of rope around the windlass. But this time, the flame, which had been subdued by the wind of its passage, flared up again. The watchers on the balcony gave little cries of triumph and waited.

After several seconds, they were rewarded by the sight of flames creeping across the tarred rope. The tar burned with a black smoke, and the flames quickly grew in intensity. Then they reached the point where a single strand of the rope ran up to the trebuchet beam. The flame licked upward, burning more fiercely on this exposed section of cordage, which had better access to the air around it. Thomas nocked another arrow and stepped toward the brazier, but Cassandra held out a hand to stop him.

"Wait. We may not need it."

Flames were now running freely along the entire length of the rope. And, as the tar burned away, they began to eat into the fabric of the rope itself. Suddenly, with an audible *TWANG*, the rope, which was under tension, gave way and the beam whipped down and hit the timber block that acted as a stop when it recoiled. There was a massive crash and Cassandra was sure she heard a splitting sound as well. A moment later, she saw she was right, as the beam sagged at the point where it crossed the axle.

"Oh, well done!" said Duncan. "Well done indeed!"

"You've cracked the beam," she said triumphantly. "That'll hold them up."

A moment later, the sound of hammering ceased and several men ran out from behind the keep into the courtyard to investigate the crashing sound from the trebuchet. There were cries of anger and frustration as they saw the damage. Then they summoned more of their companions to drench the smoldering rope with buckets of water and help drag the damaged machine back behind the keep tower.

Cassandra eyed her three archers, who were watching the confusion below with enormous satisfaction. "Are you waiting for something in particular?" she asked.

"Sorry, my lady!" said Thomas, and he and his two companions nocked, drew and shot at the confused crowd below.

Two men went down. One of them stayed down. The other hauled himself to his feet, holding on to the framework of the trebuchet, an arrow through his lower leg. As the archers released another volley, the men in the courtyard below scuttled to take shelter behind the trebuchet, crouching on the side farthest from the south tower. Arrows continued to hiss furiously about their ears as they inadvertently showed themselves for a second or two. Then there were no more targets visible, and the three archers stopped shooting without further orders.

Someone below began shouting commands, and the trebuchet began to move slowly as the men sheltering behind it seized hold and began to shove it back toward the corner of the keep tower. It was awkward going, with all the pushing happening on one side, and the siege machine moved crabwise, slewing away from the direction they wanted. Then three more men raced out from the cover of the keep and grabbed the towing ropes that still trailed behind the platform.

"There!" shouted Cassandra, pointing suddenly. The archers had been fixated on the trebuchet itself, waiting for one or more of the men behind it to move incautiously and expose himself to an arrow.

At her cry, they shifted their attention to the newcomers, sending arrow after arrow hissing down into the courtyard. But they were rushing and they shot without proper care. The iron-headed arrows struck sparks off the cobblestones and skittered past the men on the drag ropes without hitting any of them.

Cassandra cursed softly in her turn now. She realized that she was used to the shooting of archers like Gilan and Will and Halt—men who could aim and shoot in a fraction of a second and invariably hit their targets. The garrison's archers were good. But they were nowhere near as good as Rangers.

As the old saying went, Most people practice till they get it right. Rangers practice till they never get it wrong.

Under the double impetus of the men on the drag ropes and those crouched on the far side of the siege engine, pushing on the frame, the trebuchet rolled faster and faster. Within twenty seconds or so, the men on the drag ropes were concealed by the corner of the keep. More of their companions joined them once they were under cover, and the trebuchet disappeared around the corner of the tower.

All the while, the three archers peppered the trebuchet with arrows, but to no real effect. The only reward for their efforts was the sole figure lying unmoving on the flagstones.

And the burned rope and cracked main beam of the trebuchet.

Thomas lowered his bow, realizing there were no further targets on offer. He was displeased. He felt he and his men hadn't acquitted themselves too well. And they had failed under the gaze of their princess.

"Not very good, I'm afraid," he said, and the other two mumbled in agreement.

Cassandra shook off the disappointment she had felt and waved away their apologies. "You did your best," she said.

Thomas shook his head. "We can do better than that," he avowed. "We *will* do better than that next time. Trust me."

It galled him that he had let her down—at least, that was how he saw it. Cassandra was a popular leader with the men. She was fair-minded and generous in her praise when they served her well, and as she had just demonstrated, she was unruffled and considerate when they were less successful. On top of that, she had impressed them with her skill and leadership as they had fought their way back up the stairs to the eighth and ninth floors. And she had shown an ability to think quickly and effectively in the fighting on the stairway.

She was no mere figurehead, they all knew. She was a courageous and clever leader and an excellent tactician. She had effectively countered every one of Dimon's moves so far, and they had developed a blind faith in her continuing to do so until help arrived. And now that her father was advising her, their confidence grew even stronger.

They stood, lining the parapet beside her, as the hammering began again from below.

"Not much we can do here," Cassandra said after several

minutes had passed. "You men might as well go back inside and get some rest. I think we'll be busy again in a few hours."

Dejected, they trooped back inside the tower to their quarters. Cassandra and Duncan remained on the balcony.

"How long do you think we've held them up?" she asked.

Duncan pursed his lips thoughtfully and considered his answer before replying. "They'll need to replace that beam. And wind new rope onto the windlass. And then they'll have to mount those shields they've been hammering away at. The beam shouldn't be too much trouble. All they'll need is a sapling cut down and trimmed. It doesn't have to be squared off. I'd say we've got three hours—maybe four—before they're ready to try it again."

She nodded. "That's pretty much what I thought," she said. She leaned down, resting her chin on the parapet, listening to the hammering and the occasional shouted order from below.

"Well, let's see what Dimon does next," she said.

Her father laid a hand on her shoulder. "Whatever it is, you'll find a way to counter it," he said.

She looked up at him, uncertainly. "You think so?" she asked.

He smiled at her. "I know so."

It was closer to four hours before the sound of hammering and sawing stopped again. Duncan, still weak after his long convalescence, had returned to his room and was sleeping soundly. A few minutes later, Cassandra heard shouting from behind the keep tower, and the familiar groaning rumble of the trebuchet's big wooden wheels moving across the flagstones.

"Merlon!" she called, not taking her eyes away from the corner of the keep tower. Slowly and ponderously, the trebuchet reemerged, now transformed.

The beam had been replaced. As Duncan had predicted, the enemy had used another large sapling, smaller branches cut but not as neatly trimmed this time. The windlass, what she could see of it, was now wound with white rope—with no sign of the flammable tar that had made it vulnerable to fire arrows. But now the entire platform was shielded by a two-piece inverted V-shaped roof, which protected the platform below from archers high overhead. There was a gap between the two halves of the roof that allowed room for the beam to rise and fall as it was cocked and then released.

The big weapon was being pushed along by men sheltering on the far side of the platform. Cassandra could catch fleeting glances of them, but they offered no easy targets for arrows from the south tower.

Merlon frowned as he watched the ponderous machine move out into the courtyard. There were large rocks piled on the platform, between the two front wheels—obviously ammunition for the catapult. The three archers had come out with the sergeant and they moved restlessly around the balcony, trying without success to find an angle where they could sight a target among the men tending the machine.

"I think he's got us foxed this time," Cassandra said. She frowned. Dimon wasn't going to make the same mistake again. Now they would find out how effective his siege machine might be.

"Should I wake your father, my lady?" Merlon asked. She considered the suggestion, but shook her head. Duncan needed to rest. Once they saw what Dimon had in mind, she might rouse him for advice. But until then, it was better to leave him.

Under the commands of whoever was in charge—she

assumed it was Dimon—the trebuchet was wheeled around until it was facing the tower. The front of the framework was also covered by wooden panels, shielding the men as they moved about the platform. Guided by the unseen commander, the trebuchet moved ponderously back and forth until it was aligned. Then a figure darted out from under the sheltering roof and hefted one of the large sandstone rocks piled on the platform, scuttling back into the shelter of the roof before anyone could take a shot at him.

The watchers on the tower heard a massive creaking noise as the windlass was turned and the rope began to stretch. Then the counterweighted end of the beam began to inch its way up, as the longer end was hauled back down. There was a pause when the counterweight reached its uppermost position.

"They'll be loading that rock into the sling now," Merlon said under his breath.

After several seconds, they heard a sudden shouted order. The counterweight dropped, slamming into the timber stop on the deck of the platform, and the longer arm whipped upward. When it reached the apex of its travel, the rope sling swung out behind it, the weighted canvas pouch describing an arc as it whipped upward.

As the rope came to the end of its arc, the massive boulder was hurled from the canvas sling and hurtled up toward the tower.

10

MADDIE RODE STEADILY THROUGH THE MORNING, PAUSING AT intervals to allow Bumper to rest.

After several hours, she reached the banks of the Wezel. The river ran fast and deep, and she knew she'd have to look for a ford.

She checked her map and then the surrounding countryside, finding the deep bend in the river they'd picked as a rendezvous point. It was a half a kilometer to the east. The hill fort was approximately five kilometers west of her current position.

"Might as well look closer to the fort," she muttered, and turned Bumper's head to the left, riding westward along the riverbank in search of a place to cross.

In less than a kilometer, she found a spot where the river widened. The current ran more slowly in consequence, and she could see the sandy bottom, barely a meter and a half below the river surface. Checking upstream and downstream to make sure she wasn't observed, she urged her little horse into the river. At first, the water reached barely to Bumper's knees. But after ten meters or so it rose rapidly, until it was just below the saddle.

"Steady now, boy," she crooned. "Take it easy."

If the water level continued to rise at the rate that it had, she would be swimming before too long—and the prospect of a night in wet clothes didn't appeal to her. Under her cautious urging, Bumper went on, a pace at a time. The water came up a few centimeters more, then stopped rising. With increasing confidence, Bumper strode on, sending wide, V-shaped ripples out across the placid surface.

"Take it easy, I said," she ordered.

He shook his mane at her. *I'm fine. I can see where I'm going.*

She was about to argue when she realized he was right. Logically, if the water grew deeper, the current would flow more slowly. Bumper could feel the river bottom underfoot and sense the strength of the current against him, so he could tell by the force of the water whether the river was growing deeper or shallower. After a few more meters, the water level fell until it barely reached his belly.

Told you so.

"Just keep walking—slowly," she told him. If the water suddenly became deeper, she wanted plenty of time to stop him and to keep herself relatively dry. Bumper snorted derisively, but he moved more slowly and more carefully.

Then the water was shallowing rapidly and he bounded forward across the sand bottom, showering silver spray into the air as he made his way toward the far bank.

And here we are.

He trotted the last few meters through water that was now only ten centimeters deep, pausing as his feet touched dry ground to shake himself massively. Water cascaded in all directions. A lot of it landed on Maddie.

"Did you have to do that?" she asked.

Bumper craned his head round to make eye contact. *Not really. Just felt like it.*

Not for the first time, she wondered what it would be like to have a horse who wasn't fond of practical jokes. She brought him to a halt and, taking her feet from the stirrups, removed her boots one after the other and poured the water out of them. Her tights would have to wait until later. She wriggled uncomfortably in the saddle, feeling the wet cloth squishing against the leather.

The terrain here was similar to what she had been traveling through for most of the previous days: thickly wooded areas interspersed with open meadows and grasslands. She stood in the stirrups and surveyed the ground on either side. There was no sign of any movement, no sign of people.

She nudged Bumper around so that he was pointing west and set him to a slow canter along the cleared land of the river-bank. Later, when she judged they were closer to the hill fort, she would reduce the pace to a walk to keep the noise down. As it was, the horse's hooves thudded softly on the thick grass under-foot, making barely any sound.

It was a warm morning, and with the wind of their passage, her clothes quickly began to dry. They were still damp, but not uncomfortably so. The squishing had stopped, at least. After a while, the trees closed right down to the riverbank and she had to swing north, looking for a game trail or a farm track to follow. She found one that meandered through the trees in a general westerly direction. The ruts made by generations of farm cart-wheels passing this way were all too obvious.

After several kilometers winding through the tree trunks, stooping low in the saddle to avoid low-hanging branches, she checked the reins softly.

"Ease down a little, boy," she said in a low voice. They had made good time and the hill fort must be close by now. That meant that the Red Fox Clan's camp must be getting closer too and, for all she knew, there might be hunters or foragers from the camp moving through the woods, searching for small game. They continued on at a reduced pace. Then she stopped Bumper altogether and swung down from the saddle.

You're leaving me here?

"'Fraid so. I might have to take cover in a hurry. Bit hard to do that with a walloping great horse along."

He sniffed derisively but, for once, let her have the last word as she gestured for him to move off the track they had been following and to conceal himself among the trees.

"Don't go anywhere. I won't be long," she told him.

She unslung her bow and ghosted down the track. Her feet made barely a sound on the soft ground. After years of training with Will, it was second nature for her to set them down carefully and softly, no matter how fast she was moving, avoiding twigs and deadfalls in her path, sensing those she didn't see and stopping herself from placing any weight on them. That long practice meant she could move this way at a normal walking pace.

Every so often, she paused, turning her head this way and that to see whether she could hear anyone else moving along the track or among the trees to either side. She kept her cowl tossed back on her shoulders so she could hear more clearly. There was nothing but the normal forest sounds—birds chirping in the undergrowth, small creatures scuttling to avoid her through the leaf mold that formed the forest floor, and the occasional whispering rush of a larger animal—perhaps a badger or a fox—as it paralleled her trail through the trees.

The trees began to thin out until she could see for a hundred meters to either side as the forest gradually gave way to grassland. Eventually, she emerged on a wide meadow that sloped away uphill. She stopped within the tree fringe, concealed in the shadows, and checked the open ground ahead, searching once more for any sign of people moving. She must be close to the Red Fox camp by now, she reasoned.

And as she had the thought, two figures appeared over the rim of the hill above her, striding down the slope toward the spot where she stood.

The temptation to duck back into the cover of the trees was almost overpowering. But she knew it would be a fatal mistake to do so. Movement would draw their eyes to her in an instant. They might not see who she was, but they would know that someone had moved and had retreated into the shadow of the trees. And if she were seen to retreat, she would be seen as a possible enemy. After all, if she was a friend, or another member of the Clan, there would be no reason to move into concealment.

Heart pounding as they approached, she stood frozen in place, against the trunk of a large oak. She was in shadow, and the cloak draped around her, concealing her form, blending with the mottled bark of the oak tree. Her cowl was up—she had pulled it up when she reached the more open ground—and her face was hidden in its shadow. Now the only course she had was the one that had been drummed into her brain repeatedly over the past three years by her teacher and mentor.

Trust the cloak.

She followed the path of the two approaching men, moving only her eyes to keep track of them. At first, they had seemed to be heading straight for her, but now she could see that they were veering off to her right. They would pass close by the spot where she stood—barely four meters away—if they maintained their present direction.

That should be far enough, she thought. *Should be*. The words echoed in her brain. Briefly, she wondered what she would have done if they had continued straight toward her. Probably, her best course of action would have been to inch slowly around the tree, moving so slowly and so gradually that the movement would be almost imperceptible. She was glad it hadn't come to that. Movement was the last course open to her. It was better to stay stock-still, wrapped in the cloak, blending into the background.

She could hear the men talking now. At first, their voices were a low mumble, the words indistinguishable. But, as they drew closer, she began to make out what they were saying.

". . . why we should bother with an attack. We can simply wait them out. They must be short of food by now."

"The general says it's to keep them off balance, to keep them guessing. We've hit them from the front, so tomorrow night he wants a raid on the north wall. Get behind them. Make them edgy."

"Waste of time, I say."

"Maybe not. We've not tried anything for a few days. Who knows? We might catch them napping and put an end to this whole thing."

"Or we might not. And those archers are too good to mess around with. We've lost too many men already. Now he's risking another forty."

"That's why he wants a night attack. What they can't see, they can't shoot."

"I suppose that's right. Still, first chance I get, I'm pulling back. Dark or not, one of those archers is a Ranger. They can hit their target in the dark. They're demons, some folk say."

In spite of the situation, Maddie smiled to herself. It had been some time since she had heard anyone voice that sentiment. A lot of simple country people in Araluen believed that Rangers were some kind of dark wizards, able to appear and disappear at will. And their skill with a bow was close to legendary. As with anything that people didn't fully understand, it became exaggerated the more it was discussed. The man near her obviously believed that members of the Corps could see in the dark.

The voices faded as the two men moved in among the trees and continued on their way. She frowned thoughtfully, remaining still until they were long gone. The Foxes were obviously planning a night raid for the following night. And on the back wall of the fort. The man might be right. They might catch the defenders off guard. Night battles were always uncertain affairs. It would be useful if she could get some kind of warning to her father about the planned attack.

Deciding that the men were well out of sight by now, she continued up the hill, moving in a low crouch across the long grass as it waved in the moderate breeze.

There was a natural rhythm to the movement of the grass and the shadows of the clouds that drove across the sky. She matched that rhythm, blending into the very fabric of the countryside. The cloak made her a difficult mark to spot, and her smooth, steady approach helped her fade into the background around her. She had seen Will demonstrate this kind of movement many times and she knew it worked. Often, she had lost sight of him, even though she knew exactly where he was and where he would reappear. After training with him for three years, she was confident in her ability to cross relatively open ground and remain unnoticed.

Not unseen. A watcher might see her. But he wouldn't be aware of what he was seeing.

She sank lower to the ground as she approached the crest of the hill, until she was almost doubled over, the long grass reaching up to conceal her.

Finally, she dropped to her hands and knees, then onto her belly, moving forward under the impetus of her elbows and knees, virtually invisible in the gray-green grass.

Her eyes came level with the crest, and she slid forward another meter to see more clearly. There, below her, the hill sloped down again to a flat field where the Foxes had their camp. There must have been at least fifty tents pitched by a small stream that ran through the meadow, tumbling down from the hill beyond. Men moved back and forth among the tents, but without any sense or appearance of urgency. Smoke rose from their cook fires and the waft of grilling meat came to her.

Somewhere, someone was repairing a piece of armor or a weapon, and she could hear the ring of a hammer on steel. Interestingly, she noted, the Foxes had posted no sentries on this side of their camp. They weren't expecting any enemies to appear from behind them.

And that might come back to bite you, she thought.

Then she raised her eyes and let them travel up the far hill, taking in the terraced path that ran round and round it, spiraling upward to the wooden fort at the very top. She could see figures on the parapet as the defenders kept watch on the camp below. A large lump formed in her throat as she focused on one, leaning on the parapet to one side of the main gate. It was too far to make out his features, but the body language—the way he leaned and then the way he moved as he took a few paces to the side—was unmistakable. She knew in that instant that she was watching her father.

"Hello, Dad. I'm here," she whispered, her voice husky.

11

〰〰〰〰〰〰〰〰〰〰〰〰〰〰

INSTINCTIVELY, THE FIVE PEOPLE WATCHING FROM THE BALCONY ducked below the parapet as the massive rock flew upward. Cassandra braced herself for the sudden impact of the rock striking the wall of the tower. She heard a strange whirring noise, but no sound of rock striking rock. She made eye contact with Thomas, who was crouching beside her. The archer shook his head, puzzled.

Then Merlon laughed and they looked at him as he slowly stood from his crouched position.

"They missed," he said. "They missed us clean. The shot was off line to the right and way too high. Even if it had been on line, it would have sailed way over the tower."

The others straightened and watched as the men below prepared the trebuchet for another shot. The rope around the windlass creaked loudly as it was wound tight and stretched. Slowly, the weighted end of the beam crept up once more. This time, the engineer in command didn't wait until it had reached its maximum elevation. It was only three-quarters of the way up when he called a halt. One of the crew dashed forward to retrieve a boulder, which was then loaded into the sling.

A few random creaks sounded from the tensioned rope. Then a figure holding a long shield emerged from behind the machine and backed away to check the alignment. Instantly, the three archers let fly and all three shafts slammed into the shield. The man staggered a pace or two but was unharmed. Seeing that their first three shots were ineffective, Cassandra ordered her men to cease shooting.

"No sense wasting arrows," she said. "Wait till there's a proper target."

The man behind the shield began calling orders and, slowly, the trebuchet began to inch its way to the left. Finally satisfied that it was correctly aligned, the man moved back into cover.

A resounding crash echoed around the courtyard as the trebuchet was released once more. The beam swung down, slamming into the stop, allowing the rope sling to continue the arc and hurl the boulder clear. Again, the watchers on the balcony ducked behind the shelter of the parapet. This time, they heard the rock as it whirred overhead. It was on line but still too high, and it flew above the tower and disappeared down the hill beyond the castle.

There was another long pause as the machine was reloaded. More creaking of ropes, more groaning of timber under stress. This time, however, the men tending the trebuchet wound the windlass until the counterweight was only halfway to its maximum height. Two first shots had flown clear over the tower. Less impetus was needed if the rock was going to hit its mark.

This time, the crash as the trebuchet's beam hit the stop was noticeably less. As before, Cassandra and her men dropped into cover.

She felt a vague tremor beneath her feet as the rock, under

vastly reduced power, hit the tower somewhere below them. She stood and leaned over the parapet to see the effect. There was a litter of sandstone rubble on the flagstones at the foot of the tower, obviously all that was left of the projectile, but no sign of any damage to the structure itself.

"I think I see their problem," she said slowly, speaking to the sergeant. "They're too close to the tower."

Merlon nodded. Normally, trebuchets were deployed at long range, hurling their projectiles in a high parabola so that they came smashing down into their target in a more or less horizontal arc. But here, the catapult was barely thirty meters away from the tower and it was difficult to bring the flight of the projectile lower so that it struck the building. The tendency was for each shot to fly over the tower and go crashing into the parkland below, hundreds of meters away.

If the engineers reduced the arc of the beam by not winding it back fully, as they had just attempted, the shot flew with reduced power and barely scratched the surface of the hard stone of the tower.

"Not only that," Merlon said, "but they've got it mounted on a mobile platform. Every shot throws it off line." Normally, trebuchets were a static installation, with their legs set solidly in the ground.

As if in answer to his observation, the trebuchet hurled another rock at them, this time under full tension. This rock flew too high once more and was off line as well. The group on the balcony barely bothered to duck.

There was a long pause, with no sign of activity from below. They could hear the men talking, but they were too far away for the listeners to make out any words. Occasionally, a voice would be raised in anger, and Cassandra assumed that belonged to the artilleryman in charge. Then there was movement around the base of the throwing beam.

"Archers!" Cassandra called, and the three men nocked and drew. But the inverted V-shaped roof impeded their aim, and they lowered their bows, frustrated. Cassandra shielded her eyes with her hand and peered at the trebuchet. She could see some detail through the slit in the protective roof. Three men were working on the timber stop that the butt end slammed into at each shot.

"They're raising the stop," she said.

Merlon nodded thoughtfully. "That way, they can wind the windlass to full tension," he said. "The arm will swing up faster when they release—it'll be under full stretch. But the new stop will halt the movement a lot sooner. It will cause the sling to whip over earlier than before. They'll get a lower flight path and greater speed."

"Let's see what happens," Cassandra said, as the work around the butt end of the beam was finished and the men moved back to their positions. Another stone was loaded and the windlass creaked and groaned, rope and timbers straining as they wound the counterweight up to its maximum position.

"We might need to take cover this time," Cassandra muttered, and her companions crouched until only their eyes were above the parapet.

CRASH! The beam jerked upward, noticeably faster this time, with the counterweight raised to its highest position and the rope stretched taut as an iron bar. The stop brought the shorter end of the beam to a juddering halt, and the rope sling swung up and over, hurling the rock loose.

But again, the shot was off line. Dimon's men had forgotten to adjust the alignment after the previous shot and the rock flew wide. Had it been on line, Cassandra noticed, it would have smashed into the tower several meters below their vantage point.

"Looks as if he's got it worked out," she said.

But Merlon held up a cautionary hand. "Maybe not completely."

Dimon's artillery commander, still covered by his long shield, stepped gingerly out into the open and supervised the realignment of the trebuchet. The hardwood wheels squealed on the flagstones of the courtyard as the crew heaved the big machine around, a few centimeters at a time. Watching from the balcony, Cassandra could see that the arm was perfectly lined up with her position. Her pulse pounded a little faster as she saw the throwing arm being hauled back to full cock. Then another rock was loaded into the sling.

CRASH!

The trebuchet released and she had a momentary sight of the rock hurtling through the air, seeming to fly straight at her. She dropped below the parapet once more, pressing against the granite as she waited for the impact.

SLAM!

This time, she felt the stone thud into the tower, seemingly just at her feet. Then she heard a patter of falling masonry below, and her heart skipped a beat. Had the projectile smashed the stones of the tower? It seemed impossible that it could do so with one shot, but she had heard the sound of rocks falling to the flagstones below.

Hesitantly, she raised her eyes over the parapet, then, realizing that it would be several minutes before the trebuchet could hurl another rock, she leaned over to survey the damage.

There was a light brown mark on the gray rock of the tower, about two meters below the point where she stood. She frowned.

Beside her, Merlon let go a short bark of laughter. "Sandstone!" he said, as she looked at him curiously. "They're shooting sandstone rocks."

"So?" she asked. "What else would they be shooting?"

"Well, granite if they could get their hands on any," Merlon told her. "The walls of the tower—of the whole castle, in fact—are granite. Hard, durable granite. The rocks they're throwing are sandstone. It's much softer and weaker than granite. It'll never do any damage to the walls. It won't even scratch them. The rocks will just shatter when they hit the tower wall. They'll never break through that way."

He was grinning contentedly, but Cassandra was still doubtful.

"If they keep on throwing rocks and hitting the tower repeatedly, surely that will weaken it?" she asked.

Merlon shook his head. "Not so long as they're throwing sandstone rocks. I'd say they fetched them from the quarry below the east wall of the castle, down beyond the tree line. But no matter how many they hit us with, or how hard they throw them, the result will be the same. The rocks will simply shatter into a hundred pieces. They'll be in more danger down in the courtyard from falling chunks of sandstone than we'll be up here."

Heartened by the fact that they had just hit the tower, the trebuchet crew were already winding the beam back. The ropes and timbers groaned under the strain and another rock was fitted into the basket. They heard a shouted order.

SLAM! Then . . . *CRASH!* The boulder hit the tower again, this time a little off to one side. It shattered, and the pieces ricocheted off the curve of the wall at an angle. Once more, there was no sign of damage to the tower, other than a sandstone-colored blemish on the gray granite.

"Sooner or later, they'll have to wake up to the fact," Cassandra said. "Once they hit us three or four times in the same spot and cause no damage, they must see it's useless."

"They may. But of course, their shooting up till now has been pretty haphazard. So far they've shown no sign of being able to hit us three or four times in the same area."

"Granted. But what if they decided to start throwing granite boulders at us?"

Merlon smiled. "That's my point. They can't. There's no granite within a hundred leagues of here."

"But the castle is built of granite. Where did . . . ?"

He stopped her with a wave of his hand. "Yes, it is. And they exhausted all the local supply of the stone when they built it. Think how much rock went into these five towers and these massive walls. Best get down," he cautioned, glancing down into the courtyard where the trebuchet was ready to shoot.

They both crouched below the parapet and heard the sound of wood on wood that told them the trebuchet had hurled another rock. Then there was a thud as it struck the tower below the parapet, followed by the sound of falling rocks hitting the courtyard flagstones.

"I suppose they could start tearing down one of the other towers to get granite boulders," Cassandra suggested.

Merlon considered the idea, then shook his head dismissively. "It'd be awfully hard to break down any of these walls," he said. "Nobody who's laid siege to the castle in the past has managed it. They're pretty solidly put in place, then mortared tight. It'd take days. Weeks, more likely. And even if they managed it, the individual building blocks in these walls are too big for the trebuchet. They'd have to break them down into smaller pieces."

"Could they do that?"

He laughed. "Have you ever tried to break granite slabs down into smaller pieces, my lady?"

"Can't say I have. I take it it's not easy."

"It's a job masons hate. And they have the skills and special tools to do it. I doubt if that lot"—he gestured with a thumb over the parapet—"could get it done in a month."

"How do you know all this, Merlon?" she asked.

He smiled knowingly. "I've been in the army a long time, my lady. I was at the siege of Castle Mollegor with your father many years ago. Before you were born, that was. Served with the artillery then, as a matter of fact."

"So I take it we can just sit tight and let Dimon waste his energy trying to smash granite with sandstone?"

"That's about it, my lady. Take it easy and let his men wear themselves out with all the cranking and loading and heaving on ropes. We'll set someone to keep watch on this side of the tower, just in case. Of course, our lads could take the odd shot at them from time to time to keep them guessing, but we may as well put our feet up until Dimon realizes he's flogging a dead horse."

12

MADDIE WAS BACK AT THE RENDEZVOUS POINT BY THE RIVER when the *Heron* arrived that afternoon. While the crew began setting up a camp among the trees, she consulted with the command team—Hal, Thorn and Stig.

"I plan on going through the enemy lines tonight to get a message to my father," she told them. She had drawn a sketch of the positions of the camp and the hill fort, and it was spread out on the ground between them. They sat in a semicircle around it.

"Is that wise?" Hal said cautiously.

She looked up at him. "It's necessary. The Red Fox Clan are planning a surprise attack tomorrow night and I want to warn him about it."

Thorn scratched his beard thoughtfully. "Your father has no idea you're coming?" When she nodded that he was right, he continued. "Well then, aren't you taking a risk that if you go sneaking up to the fort they'll see you and put an arrow through you? I mean, I know you're a Ranger, and you can appear and disappear at will, but if you want to make contact, you'll have to reveal yourself and you might get shot before they realize who you are."

"That's assuming that you can get past the enemy sentries in the first place," Stig put in.

"That won't be a problem," she said. "Their discipline is slack and the sentries are merely going through the motions. As for getting shot by Dad's men, I don't plan on going all the way to the fort. I'll work my way halfway up the hill and shoot a message arrow into the timber frame above the gate. They'll see it tomorrow morning."

There was silence as they considered her plan, all of them staring at the sketch of the hill fort and enemy camp that lay between them. Hal finally looked up, studying her appraisingly.

"Well, as you keep telling us, you *are* a Ranger, so presumably you know what you're doing," he said.

She nodded acknowledgment. He was impressed by her quiet confidence. When she said she could get through the enemy lines without trouble, she wasn't boasting. It was a mere statement of fact.

"There's just one point," he continued. "I'm coming with you."

She opened her mouth to argue, but he cut her off. "I'm not coming up the hill with you. I'll stop here." He indicated the ridgeline behind the Red Fox camp. "I need to take a look at the ground we'll be fighting on."

It was a reasonable idea, she realized, and she nodded.

Hal touched the crossbow lying on the grass beside him. "Plus I can give you cover when you're coming back out, just in case things don't go exactly to plan."

"When do things ever not go according to plan?" Thorn asked innocently. They all grinned. As the old saying went, once a fight started, all plans went out the window.

"I'll want to start up the hill after midnight," she said. "The moon will be up by then."

Hal looked at her curiously. "I would have thought you'd want no moon while you were sneaking through their lines?"

But she shook her head briskly and indicated the sky above them. "There's a good bit of scattered cloud about today. Once the breeze gets up tonight, that'll mean a lot of shadows moving across the hill, and that'll make it easier for me to stay hidden. I won't be the only thing moving."

Stig grinned at his oldest friend. "You were right," he said. "She *does* know what she's doing."

Maddie let her gaze wander over the three cheerful Skandians. It was all very well to joke and make light of things, she thought, but there was something she wanted understood.

"One final point," she said, locking eyes with Hal. "I'm in charge. When we're on your ship, I defer to you. But this is my kind of operation. This is what I'm trained for. So if I tell you to do something, do it straightaway, without arguing. Clear?"

"Perfectly," Hal said. She was right. On board a ship, he expected instant obedience to his orders. But tonight, they'd be in her field of expertise.

Maddie smiled at him. "Good. Now we may as well try to get some rest. It'll be a long night." She paused, then added: "Can your man Edvin have a meal ready for us an hour after dark?" She knew Edvin was the cook on board *Heron*.

Hal nodded. "You're as bad as Stig," he said. "He's always thinking of his stomach."

"That's precisely what I'm doing," she told him. "An empty stomach has a tendency to rumble and growl. Not a good thing to happen when you're only a few meters from a sentry."

Hal was impressed. "I wouldn't have thought of that."

She smiled at him. "I was caught that way during my first-year assessment tests," she said. "It's an embarrassing way to be discovered and you can't stop your stomach from doing it."

"I certainly can't," Stig admitted. "Mine roars like an angry bear when I'm hungry."

"Which is most of the time," Thorn observed. But, like Hal, he was impressed by Maddie's attention to detail. The moving cloud shadows and the need for a full stomach were things he never would have thought of either. He remembered his first suspicions about this girl when they had gone hunting in the forest below Castle Araluen. *There's more to her than meets the eye.* He realized how right he had been.

She folded up her map and put it in an inside pocket in her jerkin, then rose to her feet, dusting stray blades of grass from her knees. The Skandians followed suit, Thorn groaning softly as he rose.

"Feeling your age?" Hal teased the old sea wolf, who glared at him.

"Feeling my knees is more like it," he said. "Just as well I'm not coming with you tonight. The Foxes would hear them creaking from half a kilometer away."

They set out around the ninth hour, making their way along the farm track Maddie had scouted earlier in the day. They walked one behind the other, with the Ranger some three meters in the lead. Hal paid strict attention to her hand signals, freezing in his tracks when she indicated he should do so, then continuing when she gave the all clear. Her senses for this sort of action were more highly developed than his. She heard tiny sounds that he would never have picked up, stopping and waiting until she had identified each one and determined there was no danger lurking ahead of them. Once, she held up a hand to stop him, then, a few seconds later, pointed down and to the left. Peering in the direction she indicated, he saw a large gray-and-white badger shoving its way through the undergrowth, regarding them with a distinctly bad-tempered expression. Used to the sounds and sights of the open ocean and the movement and surge of the waves, Hal felt out of place in the dim forest, surrounded on all sides by the sound of small creatures scurrying out of their way. But he could tell that Maddie was in her element, and he trusted his safety to her guidance.

They emerged from the trees at a wide, well-grassed meadow that sloped gently upward. From the sketch she had drawn, he knew the enemy camp would be over the crest. She paused and pointed to her nostrils. He sniffed and could smell woodsmoke. He nodded, indicating that he understood her signal. Then she pressed her hand, palm down, toward the ground and sank to her knees. Reasoning that she wanted him to do the same, he copied her movement. She began to work her way through the long grass, moving at surprising speed and making virtually no sound whatsoever. He followed her, moving more clumsily and slowly.

She glanced back and saw he was falling behind, so she reduced her pace, allowing him to catch up.

He realized that she was staying low in case the enemy had posted sentries on the ridgeline. There had been none there earlier in the day, she had told them, but the enemy might have grown more cautious once night fell. In any event, it made sense to assume that they might have. Hal continued slowly up the hill, glancing left to right along the crest. Then he remembered her instructions, issued before they left camp: *Don't look up. Your face will reflect the moonlight and they'll see you more easily.* Hurriedly, he dropped his gaze and lowered his face, crawling upward, intent on the ground directly in front of him. If there was a sentry there, Maddie would see him, and her face was obscured by the deep cowl on her cloak.

But there was no guard positioned on the crest. He frowned. The enemy were obviously overconfident—and none too efficient. That was all to the good, he thought. It would make them all the more susceptible to panic when they were attacked unexpectedly from behind.

He heard a low hiss and looked up cautiously. The crest was only a few meters away and Maddie had sunk to the ground, crawling on her belly for the remaining distance. He copied her, dragging himself forward through the grass on his elbows, until he was lying prone beside her, peering down at the enemy camp.

Her sketch had been surprisingly accurate, he saw. The tents were pitched haphazardly at the bottom of the slope, forming an untidy huddle, dotted here and there with the red glow of campfires. To one side, closer to the small creek that ran through the bottom of the shallow valley, there was a group of four larger pavilions. Presumably these belonged to the commanders of the army. Several of them were lit from within by lanterns, even at this late hour. The light glowed through their canvas sides. A sentry stood outside one of them, slouching under the front awning, a spear in one hand.

Hal touched Maddie's elbow and pointed, then mouthed the word *Commander* in her direction. She nodded her understanding. Then she held up her hand to him, palm out-ward, in an obvious signal: *Stay here.*

He nodded in turn, and after waiting several more seconds, she slid on her belly over the crest and began to snake her way down through the knee-high grass, angling off to the east, and away from the command tents. That made sense, he thought. The Foxes would tend to keep a closer watch around their offi-cers' tents. He tried to watch her progress, but after she had gone twenty meters or so, he lost sight of her as a moving bank of cloud shadow drifted across the hill. Several minutes later, he thought he saw a slight movement farther down the hill, but couldn't be sure if it was her or not. He shook his head in admi-ration. She was good at this.

Moving silently, Maddie snaked her way down the hill, aiming to the right-hand side of the cluster of tents. She paused every twenty meters or so to survey the ground ahead of her and gradually picked out the sentries on patrol. There were half a dozen in all, moving slowly back and forth on beats along the base of the hill, where the ground flattened out before beginning to rise once more to the fort.

None of them seemed too alert, and all of them were looking up the other hill, toward the fort. Naturally, that was the direc-tion from which they expected danger to come. She slipped across the shallow stream at the base of the valley. It was only three meters wide and twenty centimeters deep. But, on her belly, she was thoroughly soaked. She sensed movement to her left and slid her eyes sideways. One of the sentries had deviated from the path he had been following so far and moved across the creek, angling upward toward the first terrace of the path that wound up to the fort. He would pass close by her current position, she saw. Slowly, she lowered her head and lay still, her body and legs concealed in the long grass, covered by the cloak.

She could hear his boots swishing in the long grass now. He was only a few meters away.

All I need is for him to tread on my hand, she thought bitterly, pressing her face into the soft, wet grass, willing him to move on. The swishing footsteps stopped, almost beside her, and for a dreadful moment she thought he had spotted her. Then she heard him yawn and she relaxed. A yawning man was not an alert one. All of a sudden, she had a terrible urge to yawn as well. She fought it down, clenching her teeth until her jaws ached. Then, finally, the sentry moved away and she felt the tension drain out of her. When she sensed he was at least ten meters away, she allowed herself to succumb to the yawning reflex, but managed to stifle any sound as she did so.

Yawning, she thought. That was something she had never considered. Maybe all sentries should be taught to yawn from time to time. The man continued to move away from her, and she resumed her uphill progress, moving faster as he disappeared around the curvature of the hill. She slid on her belly onto the first terrace, formed by the spiraling track. There was less cover here. The track had been constructed from rammed earth and small stones, and the long grass on the face of the hill didn't grow as thickly here. Waiting for a cloud shadow to pass over her, she scurried across the bare track and onto the next slope, huddling down among the sheltering grass once more.

The track formed five levels, or steps, as it spiraled around the hill, and she planned to go up to just beyond the third level. Measuring distances that afternoon, she had judged it to be about eighty meters from the fort itself—an easy distance for her bow. But the shot would be uphill, and it would be difficult to judge accurately in this uncertain light. She continued up the slope, waiting for cloud cover before she crossed the track and worked her way upward. She began to angle across to the left, to bring her more in line with the gateway above her. She had started on the extreme right-hand side of the hill.

She reached the third level, crossed the track and slipped back into the cover of the long grass. She paused for a second or two, then rolled on her back, surveying the hill below her, and the enemy camp, ensuring that none of the sentries were looking in her direction. When she rose to her feet to shoot, she would have the dark green mass of the hillside behind her, so she wouldn't be obvious to those below. But the movement might draw attention, and she wanted to be sure she wasn't being observed.

Still on her back, she slowly loosened the fastening of her cloak and shrugged out of it. Her bow was slung across her left shoulder below it and she unslung it now, then re-donned the cloak. Waiting for another cloud shadow to cross the hill, she rose slowly to her feet and crouched at the uphill edge of the track, waiting to see if there was any outcry or any sign that she had been spotted.

Silence.

She reached into her quiver and selected the arrow she had prepared specially that afternoon. It had a ten-centimeter length of white ribbon attached just ahead of the nock. She set the arrow on the string and, making sure the ribbon could run freely, stood up, drew, aimed and released. The arrow hissed away from the bow, the white ribbon streaming out behind it. As she had remarked earlier, shooting uphill in poor light made ranging uncertain. The ribbon arrow was a way of checking the distance and the elevation she'd need. The ribbon was too light to cause any real resistance, so it wouldn't affect the flight of the arrow. But when it struck the timbers of the hill fort, the strip of white would be visible, hanging down from the shaft and showing her where her shot had fallen.

Just to make sure, she had prepared two ranging arrows, but now she saw she wouldn't need the second. Her first shot had hit the palisade, almost two meters below the rim. She could see the white strip of ribbon against the dark bulk of the fort. It fluttered sideways in the light breeze, the movement making it easier to see. The range had been fractionally longer than she'd estimated. Now she took her message arrow from the quiver and nocked it. Drawing back, she adjusted her aiming point to send this arrow a little higher than the first, then released.

This time, the arrow struck the palisade just below the rim. She nodded, satisfied. It should be visible there the following morning, she thought. She dropped into a crouch once more.

"Time to get going," she muttered to herself.

13

HORACE AND GILAN WERE ON THEIR ROUTINE DAWN WALK
around the palisade. They patrolled each morning, making sure
that nothing had changed in the enemy camp below them and
that there was no threat forming up in the valley.

As had been the case for the past few days, there was no sign
of any unusual movement in the Red Fox camp. The normal
cook fires had been stirred into life, and smoke spiraled up from
them at various points around the camp. Horace looked hungrily at them. His stomach wasn't used to the reduced rations
they'd been eating. As commander, of course, he could have told
his orderly to provide him with a full meal, but he refused to do
that. He ate what his men ate. No more.

He looked now to the east, where the sun was just tipping
over the horizon. The clouds above it formed a fabulous rose-
colored display.

"Beautiful," he murmured.

"What's that?" Gilan said beside him.

He gestured to the eastern sky. "The sunrise. It's beautiful."

But Gilan shook his head and leaned over the parapet. "No.
I mean, what's *that?*" he said, pointing over the edge. Horace

moved to join him. There was an arrow embedded in the timber of the wall just below the top of the palisade. And another, a meter below it, with a strip of white ribbon attached to the nock.

Gilan reached over and carefully worked loose the nearer of the two, holding it up for Horace's inspection.

"It's a message arrow," he said in a quiet voice. "A Ranger's message arrow. There's a Ranger down there somewhere." He looked up from the arrow, peering into the valley below, searching for any sign of the person who had shot this arrow up the hill. Then, realizing if it had been a Ranger he wouldn't be anywhere in sight, Gilan turned his attention back to the arrow, sliding open the hollowed-out message chamber and removing the tightly rolled paper inside. "Or there was," he corrected himself, "sometime during the night."

Horace was pointing to the other arrow, with the strip of fluttering white ribbon. "What about that one?"

Gilan was intent on safely extricating the wafer-thin message slip that had been in the arrow. Without looking up from his work, he replied. "It's a range finder," he said. "That's a Ranger arrow as well."

Horace moved to look over Gilan's shoulder as he started to unroll the message. "Who shot it there?" he asked.

But Gilan continued to work the message slip. It was a delicate job. If he tried to do it too quickly, he risked tearing the flimsy paper.

"Don't know yet," he said, frowning. "Can't see the signature."

"Don't you Rangers all have your own special fletching?" Horace asked. "Can't you tell from that?"

"Do you expect me to know the fletching colors for fifty Rangers?" Gilan asked. "Do you think I can keep them all in my head?"

But he realized that there *had* been something familiar about the fletching on the two arrows. He stopped work on the message slip and studied the arrow again.

"Red and white, with a black cock feather," he said to himself. The cock feather was the feather that stood out at right angles to the bow when the arrow was correctly nocked. The other two vanes were red, with a strip of white. "Red and black are Will's colors," he said slowly. "The white strip indicates his apprentice."

He looked up at Horace, realizing the significance of what he had just said. The tall warrior's eyes were wide-open.

"Maddie?" Horace said.

"Maddie," Gilan confirmed.

Horace stepped quickly to the wall, peering down into the valley below for a sight of his daughter.

Gilan put a hand on his arm. "She won't be there now," he said gently. "She would have shot this last night."

"Well, what does it say, for pity's sake?" Horace demanded, and Gilan went back to unrolling the message slip. His friend waited in a frenzy of impatience, wanting to rip the flimsy paper from his hand and tear it open, but knowing that he might destroy the message that way.

Finally, agonizingly slowly, Gilan had the message slip unrolled. He read the opening line.

"It's for you," he said and proffered the message slip to Horace, who refrained from snatching it just in time. "Don't tear it," Gilan said in a warning tone. Horace ignored him, but calmed himself and handled the message carefully, spreading the curled paper out to read it. The writing was tiny but very neat and legible.

"'Dad,'" he read aloud, "'I'm in the forest with thirty Skandians. Be aware that the Foxes are planning a surprise raid on your north wall tonight with forty men. We need to talk. I'll come to the east wall tomorrow night, at two hours past midnight. Put a yellow lamp above the main gate if you get this message. Maddie.'"

He looked up at Gilan, who was grinning broadly.

"That's one heck of a girl you've got there," the Ranger Commandant said. "Where the blazes did she find thirty Skandians?"

Horace shook his head. He looked out at the valley again, a little wistfully. His daughter was out there, somewhere. He wished he could see her. Wished he could talk to her.

"Hal and his brotherband were planning to visit," he said. "But there are only a dozen of them."

"Well, thirty Skandians will be very useful if we decide to break out of here," Gilan said.

Horace nodded slowly, then looked round at the far wall. "That's true. But first we have to take care of this surprise attack tonight."

"Which isn't going to be a surprise anymore," Gilan said. "Thanks to Maddie."

"That should make them stop and think," Horace said. It was mid-afternoon and they had completed their preparations for the attack. The two stairways that led up to the north-wall walkway had been removed, as had the first three meters of walkway at either end. In the compound below, they had set sharpened stakes into the ground, pointing up at an angle to deter attackers from jumping down—although the four-meter drop should accomplish that.

"We'll post your archers at the northern end of the east and west walkways. When the enemy come over the parapet, they'll find themselves trapped and exposed to your men's arrows. If they try to jump down, they'll either impale themselves on those stakes or break an ankle or two."

Gilan nodded. "Sounds good to me. How do you plan to light those beacons?"

Horace had set three braziers full of oil-soaked wood on the walkway, spaced evenly along it. The plan was to ignite them once the Foxes were trapped on the walkway, backlighting them and making them clearer targets for the archers.

"I'll place a burning torch on top of each one, with a cord reaching to the east and west walls, and down into the compound itself. Once they're on the walkway in numbers, we'll pull the cords and tip the torches into the braziers. They should blaze up immediately."

Gilan shrugged. "We could always use fire arrows to light them," he said.

"Fire arrows aren't totally reliable. They can go out while they're in the air and then you have to shoot again. This way, I'll be sure we can light them up immediately."

Gilan was silent for a moment or two, studying the preparations and trying to see if they had missed anything. Finally, he nodded approval.

"As you say, that should give them a nasty shock. We're lucky Maddie was able to warn us about the attack." He paused. "Why do you think they decided to do this now? After all, they simply have to wait us out."

"Several possible reasons," Horace told him. "They probably want to keep us on edge, wondering where and when the next attack might come. That could lead to our making mistakes. Plus, they're planning to surprise us. If they did, they'd probably kill a lot of us, and they know we can't afford to lose any men. And finally, there's always the chance that the attack might be successful and they might drive us out altogether."

"But now, the surprise will be on our side."

"Yes indeed. I must say, it's very useful to have a Ranger in the family. I can't wait to see her tomorrow night and hear the news from Castle Araluen."

While the preparations had been made for the defense of the fort, Horace had spent a lot of time prowling the south rampart, peering into the valley, studying the trees and the long grass, hoping for some sign of his daughter. He persisted in spite of Gilan's assurances that if Maddie didn't want to be seen, she wouldn't be.

"She'll be back in the trees somewhere, well hidden," Gilan told the tall warrior.

Horace nodded gloomily. "I know. But it's galling to think that she's out there somewhere, probably watching us, and I can't see her."

"She's very good at staying hidden. Unless you tread on her hand," Gilan said with a smile, remembering Maddie's indignation when she had been caught during her third-year assessment. Horace wasn't familiar with the story and frowned at him. But the Ranger Commandant waved his unspoken question aside. "It's a long story," he said.

Horace grunted. Intent on his daughter's being nearby, he was only half listening to Gilan anyway. Then he gathered his thoughts and focused. He'd see Maddie tomorrow night, he thought. Tonight, he had a raid to repulse. The shadows were starting to lengthen as the sun slipped down behind the trees in the distance, and he remembered a detail that he had to attend to. He looked around and beckoned a trooper over to him.

"Yes, sir?" the soldier said.

Horace indicated the framework over the gate in the south wall. "When the sun goes down, I want a yellow lantern placed above the gateway," he said.

The man looked puzzled. "A yellow lantern, sir?"

Horace nodded. "Yes. Either wrap the lantern in yellow cloth, or paint the glass yellow. It has to be up there at sunset. Clear?"

"Yes, sir. Yellow lantern on the gate. I'll attend to it, sir." He actually had no idea where he'd find yellow cloth or yellow paint, but he was sure the quartermaster would find a solution to the problem. That's what quartermasters did, after all. He saluted and hurried away to the store house.

"That's the joy of command," Gilan said. "You don't have to worry about the details, you just tell a soldier to make a yellow lantern."

"Don't know why Maddie insisted it had to be yellow," Horace grumbled.

Gilan grinned at him. "She's a Ranger. And we like to make things difficult for the rest of you."

"Well, she's certainly learned that lesson," Horace agreed. He cast one more look over the arrangements at the north wall. His men were just setting the torches in position on the three braziers, and running cords to the vantage points he had selected. It was the final detail, he realized. Once it was dark, the torches would be lit, then replaced when they burned down.

"Wish she'd told us *when* they plan to attack," he said.

Gilan shrugged. "My guess is they'll want darkness, so it'll be after the moon has set. That'll be around two hours before dawn." The enemy weren't skilled at the art of concealment, he knew. They wouldn't realize the value of moving cloud shadows. Instead, they'd opt for the obvious—total darkness.

"May as well get some sleep while we're waiting," Horace replied, and they turned for their tents.

14

At Castle Araluen, the regular dull thud of rocks hitting the tower had continued throughout the afternoon. From time to time, the sound and vibration through the floor of the tower ceased as the attackers exhausted their supply of rocks and sent for more.

Cassandra had set lookouts to keep watch on the results of the battering. Aware that any shots that hit above the parapet would scatter broken sandstone shards in all directions, she cautioned her watchers to stay behind the curve of the wall for each shot, venturing out to inspect the results in the lull while the trebuchet was reloaded.

Initially, she would check every fifteen minutes or so herself. But as time passed and there was no apparent damage done to the hard granite walls, she relaxed and waited for her observers to report to her.

The constant impact of boulders against the wall had woken Duncan, and he sent a servant to ask what was happening. When she told him, he smiled grimly.

"He won't scratch these walls with sandstone rocks," he said.

"He's wasting his time trying. But as long as he keeps it up, he's not trying something more effective. Just keep your heads down out there."

She sat with Merlon at the big table on the ninth floor. The sergeant was nursing a mug of ale—a small mug, in view of their limited supply.

"You've been on the other side of this sort of thing," she said. "Any thoughts on what he might try next?"

Merlon pursed his lips thoughtfully, thinking back to his days in the artillery. "Well, if I were him, and I could see the rocks weren't doing any good, I might try fire bladders."

"Fire bladders?" Cassandra asked. "What are they?"

"You fill pigs' or cows' bladders with oil and pitch and put a burning wick in them. Then you throw them instead of rocks. The idea is, they hit the wall and burst, letting the burning oil run everywhere. The pitch makes it stick to anything it touches. Or anyone."

"But the walls won't burn," Cassandra pointed out.

Merlon nodded. "No. But if he lobs them so they hit above the balcony, the burning oil could run down the wall and through into the tower itself. The floor might burn."

"But we could always extinguish it," Cassandra pointed out. "Remember we have the water cisterns in the roof."

"True. But some of our men could be burned, or some of our supplies or equipment. It wouldn't bring down the tower, of course. But it might make things very unpleasant for us. And then we'd have to flood the ninth and eighth floors, which would be a nuisance as well."

"Hmmm," said Cassandra thoughtfully, picturing the

possible scene of confusion and damage. "Do you imagine he might try that eventually?"

Merlon shrugged. "I would."

It was another hour before the regular, slow-paced barrage of rocks against the wall ceased.

One of Cassandra's soldiers, who was currently on watch, came running into the tower from his vantage point on the balcony.

"My lady," he said urgently, "you'd better come see this."

Cassandra had been dozing in an easy chair, her feet propped up on a low bench. She stood, stretched herself and followed the trooper outside. The problem with being besieged, she thought, was that one's life fluctuated between long periods of boredom and short moments of sudden fear and uncertainty.

The soldier went to the parapet and pointed to the courtyard below. Leaning over, Cassandra could see several men carrying what appeared to be glossy bags, filled with something. Looking more closely, she recognized the bags as animal bladders. The bladders were stacked at the front of the platform, where the rocks had been stowed earlier. But they had been moved back slightly, so that the archers on the balcony couldn't get a clear shot at them. Now one man hefted one of the bladders and carried it to the sling, while the rest of the crew wound the trebuchet back. The loader heaved the full bag—which wobbled and surged in his hands, indicating that it was full of liquid—into the sling. Then another man stepped forward with a burning rope's end and held it down to the bag. A thin trail of smoke curled up where he lit the wick.

At that moment, the trebuchet released with its usual crash

of timber on timber. The sling whipped over on its rope and the bladder soared up toward them. Cassandra ducked below the cover of the balustrade.

It was a good shot. The trebuchet crew had had a lot of practice perfecting their aim.

Cassandra started in fear as the bladder struck the tower, half a meter above the door, and burst. Almost instantly, there was a roar of flame as the oil and pitch ignited, and a flood of fire erupted over the balcony, some of it clinging to the walls, while the rest dripped down and spread tendrils of flame over the floor. Some of it made its way under the door, and she heard cries of alarm from inside the tower as men rushed to extinguish them.

She suppressed a sudden jolt of panic as she assessed this new danger—one she had never encountered before. She wasn't sure how to cope with it. Logic told her that the flames couldn't do any permanent harm to the structure of the stone tower, but the oil and pitch formed a sticky, burning coating on anything it touched. If such a projectile hit one of her men, or even burst close to him, she realized, he would face an agonizing death—or at least horrific injury.

And if several of those dreadful missiles happened to hit the wooden door, and coat it with their sticky, flaming contents, they could well burn it down, opening the way for more damage inside the tower rooms.

She ran to the door and shoved it open. She was relieved to see that the fire inside had been extinguished, and she shouted for Merlon. The old soldier had been supervising the men who had put out the fire. He moved to her side, coughing with the smoke that swirled about the room.

"Get buckets full of water and keep them on hand here," she ordered. She glanced up at the narrow, unglazed windows on either side of the door. "And stuff those windows with wet blankets." For a moment, she considered flooding the floor with water from the roof cisterns, but discarded the idea. It would take hours to soak the floors thoroughly, and that would deplete her precious water supply. Better to use buckets to drench any fire that started up.

Merlon saluted and hurried away to obey her orders, shouting for others to follow and help him. From the courtyard, she heard the slam of the trebuchet as it released another projectile. She slammed the door shut and leaned against it. After a short pause, she heard the *SPLAT!* as a bladder hit the walls outside and burst. A yellow-red glow showed through the windows and under the door, and she could smell the vile stench of the burning oil and pitch.

Panic rose in her once more, the fear like a hand squeezing her chest. She fought it down, waited for the light of the flames to subside, then opened the door again. There was a patch of viscous, burning fuel on the balcony flagstones, beneath the left-hand window. More flames dripped down from the wall above it. She beckoned to the first of the soldiers who arrived, carrying two buckets of water.

"Here!" she shouted, pointing, and he dashed forward, set one bucket down, and hurled the contents of the other on the flames. She was relieved to see that the sudden flood of water smothered the burning fuel. The water hissed and bubbled and steam and smoke swirled around the balcony. But the fire was out.

"Back inside!" she ordered, then moved to the balustrade to

watch for the next shot. Her instincts told her to seek safety inside the tower, but she knew she would have to observe the results of each shot, and call for help when and if it was needed.

From the courtyard, there was a ragged cheer as the trebuchet crew heard the startled shouts of the men in the tower and finally sensed some reward for their efforts. The windlass creaked as they set to with a will, winding the arm back for another shot, moving with renewed enthusiasm. Cassandra resumed her position at the parapet, watching as another bladder was loaded into the sling.

Again, the trebuchet released, and again she retreated to shelter behind the tower.

SPLAT!

The fire bladder burst against the balustrade wall, just under the balcony this time, and burning oil and pitch cascaded over onto the flagstones, in the spot where she had been standing. There was more cheering from below.

An idea was forming. As the crew began to cock the trebuchet once more, she hammered on the door and called into the interior of the tower.

"Thomas! Dermott! Simon! Out here, please!"

The three archers appeared a few moments later. She beckoned them over to the wall and pointed downward. They followed her pointing finger nervously. They had seen the sudden shower of burning oil that had spread through the doorway.

"Watch while it throws, then run like mad for the back of the terrace," she said.

The trebuchet gave off its distinctive *SLAM!* as the arm crashed down and the sling whipped up and over. Cassandra waited until they could see the bladder hurtling toward them.

"Take cover!" she shouted.

She and the three men dashed around the tower to the shelter of the rear of the balcony. This shot was high and off line. The bladder struck the curve of the tower and failed to burst, deflecting off to one side, then falling into the courtyard below, where it set off a blaze of smoke and flame.

She beckoned the three archers back to the parapet. There would be a longer delay between shots this time as the trebuchet was realigned. She pointed down to the space behind the weapon.

"When they release it, the sling with the bladder in it swings out behind the arm," she said. "Did you see it?"

"Yes, ma'am," Thomas said and the others nodded.

"If you could hit the bag with an arrow just after it leaves the sling, you'd burst it and shower them with their own burning oil," she said.

Thomas frowned. "It'd have to be a good shot," he said doubtfully.

But she punched his arm in encouragement. "You can do it," she said. "You just have to anticipate the moment when it leaves the sling. And if all three of you shot at the same time, you'll treble your chances."

Thomas lost the doubting look and looked at his two companions. "What do you say, lads? Is it worth a try?"

Typically, it was young Dermott who answered. "We can do it, Thomas. Leastways, if you can't, I can!" His eager grin robbed his words of any offense.

The third archer, Simon, was nodding. "Worth a try, Thomas."

The three of them readied their bows and stepped up to the parapet. Cassandra watched as the trebuchet crew finished realigning their weapon and began to crank back the arm once more.

"As soon as you shoot, run like blazes for cover," she warned them, realizing how appropriate her choice of words was for the situation.

The three archers watched intently, their bows half drawn. The sling was loaded, the throwing arm finished its last few centimeters of movement. They heard the commander below call the release.

SLAM!

Thrum! Thrum! Thrum!

The three archers released their arrows at the spot where they estimated the fire bladder would appear in a second or so. In spite of Cassandra's warning, the three men all waited to see the result. The arrows streaked through space a fraction of a second early. Then the fire bladder was on its way as all three missed.

"Run!" yelled Cassandra, suddenly aware that she had become fixated on the target. They all crouched and ran for cover.

SPLAT!

This time, the bladder burst against a narrow slit window to the right of the door, sending a shower of burning oil cascading inside the tower. Merlon's men hadn't blocked the window with wet blankets yet; and they heard more shouting from inside, the sound of running, stamping feet and the splash of water as buckets were emptied over the flames. Black smoke billowed from the slit window. She saw a dripping blanket being stuffed into the aperture. Again, the men below cheered.

Thomas caught Cassandra's eye. "Timing was off," he said. "Next time we'll stagger our shots. I'll count them in."

She nodded. Instead of all three firing at the same time, if they shot one after the other, they would increase the chance that one of them might intercept the bag of oil. They resumed their position by the parapet, bows ready, arrows nocked.

Thomas spoke to his companions. "I'll shoot on one. You on two, Simon, and you on three, Dermott." They nodded their understanding.

The men below could see the archers' heads watching over the parapet, and they greeted them with cries of derision and contempt. They had seen the roils of black smoke and the showers of flame left by their shots, and they felt they had finally gained the upper hand in this contest. They might not be able to burn the tower down, but they could certainly make things unpleasant for those holed up inside.

The windlass creaked and groaned as the arm was wound back. A fire bladder was loaded into the sling and the fuse was lit.

"Ready . . . ," said Thomas, and the three bows came up.

SLAM!

"One . . . two . . . three!" Thomas shouted and the three bows spat their arrows out into the space below them.

Thomas's arrow missed. Simon's arrow, released on the count of two, flew straight and true and intercepted the distended bag of oil. Instantly, as it burst, the bag seemed to disappear in midair, replaced by a shapeless, spreading mass of brown liquid. Dermot's arrow flashed through the spreading cloud.

Then the burning wick ignited the volatile liquid and transformed it into a cloud of flame, dropping onto the trebuchet, spreading across the timbers and the rope, reaching under the mechanism with its burning tentacles of fire. Flames set in and the fire took hold, fed by the oil and pitch and racing across the dry wood of the trebuchet and its platform. Smoke and flame billowed up. Cassandra noticed four oil bladders still stacked at the front of the platform and a tendril of flame creeping its way across the timber floorboards toward them. The crew, who had been making a halfhearted attempt to quell the flames, noticed the impending danger too. One of them cried a warning, and they all turned and ran headlong from the trebuchet, heading for the keep tower. The flames reached the stacked oil bladders.

For a moment, nothing happened.

Then there was a fierce *WHOOSH!* of flame, and all four bladders went up, almost simultaneously. Huge writhing coils of smoke billowed into the air as the flaming oil ran all over the framework of the trebuchet, setting it alight in a dozen places. There was no stopping it now, and the fire crackled and snapped as it ate into the timber.

"Oh, well done," Cassandra said quietly.

The three archers were at first surprised by what they had achieved. Then they took to slapping one another on the shoulder as they watched the fire engulf the trebuchet.

An hour later, Dimon's siege machine was a smoking, blackened wreck.

15

Once it was fully dark, Horace and Gilan crouched on the southern walkway, with only their heads showing above the parapet. There was a lot of ambient light in the hill fort behind them, with several cook fires preparing food and at least a dozen torches and braziers providing light and warmth for the garrison, and they had no wish to be seen silhouetted against it by those below.

It was just after the eighth hour when Gilan touched Horace's arm and pointed to his right. "There," he said softly. "See them?"

Horace followed the direction in which Gilan was pointing, squinting to see more clearly.

"Look a little to the left or right," Gilan advised him. "Your peripheral vision is better in the dark."

Once Horace did this, he could make out what Gilan had seen. Half a dozen men were moving surreptitiously out of the camp, heading for the distant tree line. He was watching them when he felt Gilan's hand on his arm once more. This time, the Ranger was pointing to the eastern side of the enemy camp. Sure enough, another small group was moving out, crouching as they went. If he and Gilan hadn't been expecting it, Horace thought, they probably wouldn't have noticed. The campfires in the Foxes' camp had been built up unusually high tonight, and the glare they created tended to dazzle a watcher's vision and mask any movement.

"They're trying to be inconspicuous," Gilan said. He was whispering, in spite of the fact that the would-be attackers were well out of earshot. "My guess is they'll circle round in a wide loop and regroup at the base of the north side. There go another lot." He indicated the west side once more.

He stepped back from the parapet and rose from the crouch he had been maintaining, rubbing the small of his back to ease the slight stiffness there.

"They'll have to make their way across to the trees, where they'll be under cover," he said. "I figure it'll take them at least an hour and a half, maybe two hours, to work their way round to the northern side of the fort," he said. "Let's go check things on the north wall."

They climbed down the stairs and made their way across the compound to the north side. The entire contingent of archers was there, along with ten of the troopers, waiting for orders. The remaining cavalrymen were keeping watch on the south wall.

Horace stepped forward. "Right, men. Eight of you take the western walkway. Gilan will join you there. The rest of you can join me on the eastern side. The signal to start shooting will be when we ignite the three beacons here on the north side. Understood?"

There was a low mumble of understanding from the archers. The split was uneven, with eight on the west wall and twelve on the east, because Gilan would be joining the western group, and his skill as an archer was equivalent to two or three of the others.

Horace addressed the ten troopers who were assembled. "It'll be your job to deal with any of the enemy who manage to make it down from the walkway and avoid the sharpened spikes there. They may try to rope down," he told them. "Use your lances for preference. Don't let them get into close quarters."

The cavalry lances were designed primarily for use on horseback, but their long reach would make them ideal for this sort of defensive action.

"May as well get to your posts now," Horace continued. "We don't expect the attack to start for several hours. Gilan's guess is that they'll wait for the moon to set. So you can sleep at your posts, as long as you leave one man awake and on watch. And keep your weapons handy. All right, get moving."

There was a stir of movement as the three forces moved to take up their positions, the archers climbing to the walkways on the eastern and western sides of the fort, where they would have a clear shot at the northern walkway as the raiders came over the parapet. They settled down, leaving one of their number to keep watch. The others lay on the walkway or sat with their backs to the palisade. They were professionals, and long experience in the army had taught them to take any opportunity to sleep that arose. Within a few minutes, most of them had dozed off.

On the ground level, the ten troopers settled down as well. Horace and Gilan walked to the north wall. They had left a ladder in place, and the two friends climbed it now, moving to the parapet to study the hill below them. As yet, there was no sign of the raiders forming up.

Horace grunted impatiently.

"They'll still be working their way around the east and west sides," Gilan told him.

"All the same, I wish I knew where they are and what they're doing," Horace replied. "I'd like to know when they're ready to start up the hill."

"I was thinking the same thing," Gilan said and, for the first time, Horace noticed that he had a coil of rope looped over his shoulder. "So I might slip down there and keep an eye on things."

As he spoke, he moved to the right, to the midpoint between two of the torches burning in the braziers. They were small torches and the light they cast was uneven, leaving a patch of shadow at the middle, where the light didn't quite reach. Gilan looped the rope over three of the pointed logs that formed the palisade and eased his upper body over the wall.

"You're going down there?" Horace asked.

Gilan grinned at him. "That's the general idea. We want information and this is the best way to get it."

"But what if you're seen?" Horace asked.

Gilan's grin turned to a long-suffering look. "Oh, please."

He rolled over the top of the wall, holding the rope tight and avoiding letting his silhouette show. Then he lowered himself quickly down into the darkness. "I'll whistle when I'm back," he called softly. "Stay there and wait for me."

And he began to ghost his way down the hill, moving swiftly through the long grass. Horace was able to follow his progress for a minute or two. Then he was distracted briefly by the cry of a night bird. When he returned his gaze to the spot where he had last seen Gilan, there was no sign of him.

It took Gilan fifteen minutes to reach the base of the hill. He was guided by the campfires of the observers who were posted there. He angled away from them so he would be approaching out of the darkness. Mindful that the raiders would also be approaching from below, he stayed several meters uphill. The last thing he wanted was for one of the Foxes to stumble over him. When he saw one of the sentries pacing nervously by the campfire, five meters away, he dropped into cover and lay still, watching and listening.

He lay there for half an hour before he heard movement. Looking up, all the while making sure to keep his face in the shadow of his cowl, he saw a group of six men making their way toward the campfire from the eastern side. A few minutes later, another small group came into sight, this time slipping in from the other side. He heard a voice, pitched low but obviously annoyed, from one of the men in the first group.

"Where have you been? You took your time."

"We had farther to come than you," came the reply. "The trees were a good fifty meters farther away, and the tree line fell away to the west."

The first man replied with a surly grunt. Obviously, he wasn't mollified by the explanation. "We don't have all night," he said. "The moon will set in an hour and I want to start up the hill once the light has gone down."

As he spoke, a second group arrived from the western side, then another from the east. That made about twenty-five men assembled here, thought Gilan. According to Maddie's note, there would be forty in the attacking party, so there would be more to come. He saw that he was a good ten meters up the hill from the point where the raiders were assembling. Slipping down to his belly, he crept closer, until he was barely five meters away. As he moved, he heard two more groups arrive, to be greeted in lowered voices by those already in position. Allowing that there might be more than six in each party, that probably meant they were all now assembled.

A moment later, the first voice spoke again, confirming the fact. "All right. We're all here. The moon will set in about forty minutes, and that'll be our signal to move. Where are the rope carriers?"

Six men held their hands up and stepped forward. Gilan could see that each one had a large coil of rope around his shoulders.

"Good," continued the leader. "Space yourselves out, ready to go up the hill. Move slowly. We don't want anyone spotting us too early. Luckily, they've got those torches on the wall up there, and they should dazzle their night vision a little."

The assembled men turned to look up at the fort. Gilan froze as they did, realizing he was now in their field of vision. The temptation to drop his head into cover was almost irresistible. But Gilan had been doing this sort of work for many years now, and he resisted it, staying still as a rock. As their leader spoke again, the heads turned back from the fort toward him and the moment was over.

"Once you get to the top, drive those stakes into the ground and anchor the ropes. The rest of us will use them to get to the top without slipping or falling. Stay as low as you can while you're climbing, and don't make a sound. Check that your weapons aren't loose or likely to rattle."

There was a small flurry of movement among the assembled group as they checked that swords were secure in their scabbards and axes were slung tight across shoulders. There was a low chorus indicating that all was well.

"Take a look at those sentries patrolling the walls." Again, all faces turned upward, and again, Gilan froze in position.

"Time your movement for when they've just passed that center torch and turned back. Their eyes will be dazzled for a few minutes and their night vision will be pretty much ruined. When they reach the torch at either end, stop moving."

He looked around the assembled men. "We've got four ladders?" Again, men raised their hands. "Last man up in the four middle groups, make sure the rope is tied to a ladder, then we can haul them up when we're ready. They should slip easily through this long grass. The ends are bowed upward to help them move freely."

Gilan squinted to see the shape of the long ladders that rested on the ground near the men who had raised their hands. He was glad Maddie had warned them. Things might have been a bit sticky otherwise. The attackers had clearly thought through their plans carefully, and they might well have broken the Araluens' defenses if they hadn't been forewarned.

The leader continued. "Once we've made it to the wall, get over as fast as you can. There should be a stairway at either end. Head for that and get down into the fort itself. Kill anyone you see. If we panic them, this might end up being more than a nuisance raid. With a bit of luck, we might rout them completely and put an end to this nonsense."

He paused to let this sink in. "All right, get some rest if you can. We've only got an hour to wait. No moving around. No talking and, above all, no lights. Just lie still. Get some sleep if you can—but if anyone snores, I'll kill him."

There was a low mutter of laughter.

"I mean it," he said, and the ripple of laughter died away.

Time for me to go, Gilan thought. Lowering his head, he squirmed silently around until he was facing uphill again and began to silently snake his way up to the fort.

16

"THEY'RE COMING," GILAN SAID SOFTLY. HE AND HORACE were crouched on the northern walkway, staying low to keep their heads from showing in the torchlight as they watched the hillside. Two sentries patrolled their usual set paths behind them, meeting in the middle of the wall, turning and walking back to the ends. As they had been ordered to do, the sentries ignored the two leaders crouched against the logs of the palisade.

The moon had set, but there was still plenty of light from the stars, and Gilan had seen the first surreptitious movement of men crawling up the grassy slope.

There were six of them, spaced out evenly along the length of the wall, and they moved carefully and slowly. They were good, Gilan thought, but not up to a Ranger's standard of unseen movement. He nudged Horace with his elbow.

"See them?"

The tall warrior whispered in reply. "I've got them. Mind you, if you hadn't told me what to expect, I might have missed them."

The men continued upward, knotted ropes uncoiling behind

them. They were nearing the top of their climb when Horace whispered to the two sentries as they met in the middle of the walkway.

"Get down now."

"Yes, sir," one of them replied. As he and his partner crouched and headed quickly for the ladder, Horace and Gilan stood up and continued to patrol in their stead. Once, just to make it seem more realistic, Gilan paused and leaned over the wall. He noticed that the six men all froze, lying still on the grass. Then, apparently satisfied, he resumed his beat along the wall. When the rope bearers reached the base of the wall, they would be out of sight, unless Horace or Gilan leaned over the parapet to see them. But, knowing what to listen for, the two Araluens could hear the slight sounds made by the men as they carefully worked their wooden stakes into the soft earth—stakes that would anchor the ropes for the rest of their party. There was a low sound of movement in the grass as those below tested the ropes, making sure they were secure. Then the rest of the raiding party began to climb the slope.

Gilan and Horace turned back inward and patrolled back to the middle. As they met, Horace spoke softly.

"They're stopping when we're on the inward leg, just as you said they would."

"They'll start again when we turn back," Gilan reminded him. "Keep a careful eye on them now. They'll be pulling the ladders up soon."

Senses keenly attuned, they heard the sounds of the attackers gathering at the foot of the wall. Then a soft slithering sound told them that the ladders were sliding upward through the grass, their up-curved ends acting like sled rails as they came.

The raiders knew that they were hidden from sight at the base of the wall and they pressed in close, readying the ladders, moving as silently as they could. When they had the four ladders poised and ready to place against the walls, their leader abandoned all attempt at secrecy and shouted the order.

"Ladders!"

The four ladders thumped against the top of the wall, and men started running up them.

Horace bellowed a warning. "Attack! Attack on the north wall!"

They could hear the rattle of feet on the assault ladders as men swarmed up and over the top of the palisade. The two defenders raced down their own ladder, then grabbed it and hurled it clear of the walkway. At the same time, Horace bellowed another order.

"Beacons! Now!"

On the north wall, the three torches that had been sitting on top of the braziers were tipped onto the oil-soaked wood. There was a brief pause, then a flash of flame as the wood took fire.

The light flared up, revealing a mass of some twenty men on the walkway. Instantly, the archers on the east and west walls drew, aimed and shot. A storm of arrows slammed into the attackers as they bunched together. Four of them went down immediately. The others fanned out left and right as more men rolled over the top of the wall to join them. The backlit figures raced for the ends of the walkway, expecting to find stairs down into the compound below. Instead, they found a three-meter gap between them and the east and west walls and a sheer drop below them, with no way down.

More arrows slammed into them as they hesitated. More

men went down. The others huddled behind their shields, staggering under the impact as the powerful bows slammed their arrows into the metal and wood. Then their leader, realizing what had happened, shouted a new order.

"Get the ladders! Get them over this side!"

Covered by their comrades' shields, his men reached up and hauled two of the attack ladders over and inside the fort, letting them slide into the compound below the walls. Their leader ran to be first down one of the ladders. But, five paces short of it, he was struck by an arrow and hurled back against the rough timbers of the palisade. His men, however, followed his orders and began to pour down the ladders in a solid stream.

"Damn! I didn't think of that!" Horace muttered. He had been heading to join the archers on the eastern wall, but now he stopped as the raiders began to clamber down the ladders into the fort. The ten troopers left to face them moved forward with their lances ready. But they'd only ever been intended as a mopping-up operation, and the Foxes surged forward, deflecting the lance points with their shields, battering and hacking at the lances with swords and axes.

Once the lances were deflected, their length became a disadvantage, and the troopers hurriedly discarded them, struggling to clear their swords from their scabbards.

"Gilan!" shouted Horace. "Come on!"

The Ranger Commandant had been heading for his own assigned post when he heard Horace's call and turned to see the struggling mass of men at the base of the wall. As more of the raiders came down the ladders, the archers on the east and west walkways were forced to stop shooting, for fear of hitting their own men.

Drawing his sword in his right hand, and his saxe in his left, and muttering a low curse, Gilan dashed forward to join Horace.

The two warriors stood shoulder to shoulder, facing the attackers as they gathered at the foot of the ladders. For a moment, the raiders hesitated, studying their enemies, then they surged forward. Their choice of opponent seemed simple. On their left was Horace—tall, muscular and wearing mail armor and helmet, armed with a long, gleaming sword and a round buckler. Many of them recognized the Kingdom's foremost knight. To their right was Gilan—slim and agile, armed only with a sword and a saxe. The attackers veered toward him, sensing he was the easier target.

It was a mistake. Horace might have been the champion knight of the Kingdom, with a long reputation of victories in battle and single combat. But Gilan was an expert swordsman. As a boy, he had trained under the legendary swordmaster MacNeil, and he had maintained his skill with the weapon ever since—the only Ranger who was permitted to carry a sword.

He was blindingly fast. In addition, he was agile and light on his feet. Now, as the first two raiders moved to attack him, he advanced to meet them. His action was unexpected. Most men facing two advancing opponents would instinctively retreat. For a moment, they were startled, but then they recovered quickly.

The first lunged at him with a sword. He was on Gilan's left side, which the Red Fox warrior felt was relatively unprotected. Without even looking at him, Gilan caught the sword blade on his saxe and deflected it downward, maintaining contact and jamming the longer blade against the ground. Even as he nullified this threat, his own sword darted out at the attacker on his right. He had seen a gap between the man's shield and his shoulder.

Gilan's sword, gleaming blood-red in the smoky firelight, struck like a viper, driving into the man's upper body, piercing the chain mail there. The swordsman gasped and stepped back, stumbling as he did so. In the same fraction of a second, Gilan freed his sword and swung in a diagonal overhead cut at the man on his left. The stroke went home and the man fell to his knees, crying out in pain and shock. Then he toppled sideways.

In the space of a few seconds, Gilan had dispatched two of the raiders. Their companions realized their mistake too late and began to back away. Gilan's speed and accuracy had caught them by surprise, and none of them wished to face the Ranger.

But now it was Horace's turn to engage and he surged forward. He was big and powerful, and every bit as fast as Gilan. He slammed his shield into one man, sending him sprawling, and taking down one of his comrades as he went. Then Horace brought his razor-sharp, super-hard sword whistling down in an overhead stroke. The man it was aimed at raised his own sword in defense and was horrified to see Horace's sword slice through his blade as if it were soft wood.

The man screamed and fell, mortally wounded. But Horace barely paused. He continued his charge into the enemy ranks, his sword flashing from side to side in a deadly series of arcs, his buckler deflecting and blocking the blows aimed by his opponents, or slamming into shields and sending their owners flying, seemingly without his needing to think about it.

Then Gilan joined in again, cutting and thrusting with blinding speed, and the two of them mowed down the attacking force like harvesters cutting down a crop of wheat. Men stumbled and fell. Shields splintered, sending pieces of wood and leather spinning in the air.

And the enemy turned tail, heading for the ladders that had given them access to the fort. They bunched at the foot of the ladders, the rearmost men turning to face the two deadly attackers, the first to reach the ladders scrambling back up to the northern walkway.

Even the Araluen troops were stunned by the deadly efficiency of the two companions. They stood back, knowing they weren't needed, watching in awe as the invaders fell away beneath the two flashing, whirling swords.

"Let 'em go," Horace called finally, and he and Gilan lowered their swords as the panicking raiders pushed and shoved one another out of the way to reach the relative safety of the walkway.

Relative safety only. Once they reached the timber platform, they were exposed once more to the deadly shafts from the archers. The first few to arrive there, thinking they were finally safe from the two grim swordsmen below, neglected to keep their shields up. They paid for the mistake with their lives, falling, riddled with arrows, to the rough planks.

The leader of the attack, who had been hit by an arrow when he led the initial charge toward the ladders, lay slumped against the parapet, his vision slowly fading as he watched his men stumble and stagger to the two ladders remaining on the outside of the wall. Those who didn't make it in time to avoid the congestion there simply hurled themselves over the parapet, preferring to risk the fall rather than the deadly hail of arrows from the east and west walkways.

Horace leaned on the hilt of his sword as the last of the attackers fled over the wall. He took his helmet off and pushed his mail coif back off his head, letting it fall in folds around his neck. He didn't exult in the mayhem he and Gilan had caused among the attackers, but he knew that their swift and brutal action had been necessary. The attackers had been on the verge of gaining the advantage as they swarmed down into the compound. Had that happened, the result might have been very different. If he and the Ranger Commandant hadn't intervened and broken the attack, the Red Fox Clan might now be pressing for their surrender, with Horace's men scattered dead on the sandy compound floor. He looked to his left and met Gilan's steady gaze. He sensed that the Ranger was sharing his thoughts.

"Good work," he said quietly.

Gilan nodded. "I might say the same to you."

It had been some time since the two had fought side by side against a ruthless enemy like this. Horace watched as Gilan wiped his sword blade clean on the cloak of one of the fallen men. "I'd forgotten how fast you are," he said.

Gilan gave him a faint smile. "I'd forgotten how terrifying you are," he said. "What did the Nihon-Jan call you—the Black Bear, wasn't it?"

"That was more to do with my appetite than my battle skills," Horace replied. Then he turned away as a sergeant approached and saluted. "Yes, Nilson?"

"Casualty report, sir. We lost two troopers when the enemy first got to the compound floor. Three others are slightly wounded. No casualties among the archers, of course."

"Of course," said Horace. The archers hadn't been engaged in the hand-to-hand fighting, and the enemy hadn't had any long-distance weapons. "How did the opposition make out?"

"Not so well, sir. I've counted a dozen dead and another eight wounded. Some of those who made it back over the wall were probably wounded as well."

"That makes it a costly raid for them, doesn't it?" Horace commented. "And to think they were planning on whittling down our numbers." He indicated the scaling ladder, still leaning against the inner side of the walkway. "Better get some men onto the north wall to keep an eye on them, Nilson. Not that I expect them to be back in a hurry. Pull their ladders up and inside. We may as well use them."

"Yes, sir." The sergeant saluted again and turned away to organize a watch on the wall.

Horace wiped the back of his hand across his forehead and spoke to Gilan. "I'll call a truce tomorrow morning," he said. "We'll let them have their wounded men back. We don't have the men to guard them or look after them."

He leaned back, stretching stiff muscles, and rubbing the small of his back with one fist.

"Then, tomorrow night, we'll see what Maddie has to say about matters," he said.

17

VIKOR TRASK, COMMANDER OF THE BESIEGING FORCE, LOOKED at the sorry group of men slumped on the ground before him and scowled.

They were the survivors of the ill-fated raid on the hill fort the previous night. They were battered and bleeding, some with multiple wounds roughly bandaged by their companions. All of them sat with their eyes downcast, not wishing to meet his gaze.

When they had straggled back into the Red Fox camp in the early hours of the morning, Trask refused them permission to return to their tents and rest. Furthermore, he forbade his healers to help them with their wounds. Instead, he made them stay here, on the rough assembly ground in front of the camp, without warmth or shelter, without firewood or food. Grudgingly, he allowed some of the other men in camp to bring them water, but that was all.

"Let them think about how they've failed me," he told one of his lieutenants, when the man protested at the cruel treatment of wounded, exhausted men.

Trask was a Sonderlander, and the leader of the group of mercenaries who had answered Dimon's call for assistance. By dint of the fact that his Sonderlanders made up the majority of the besieging force—there had been one hundred and ten of them in the original group, compared with forty-three local recruits—he had been placed in command of the combined force.

But he was not a good commander.

He was an experienced fighter, having served as a mercenary on the Iberian peninsula and in several campaigns in Gallica. But in those battles, he had been under the command of capable local leaders, who would determine the tactics to be used and set him with simple tasks to carry out. Never, in those battles, had he sought to study or analyze the tactics his commanders were using, or why they might be using them. Trask was a blunt instrument. His favored method in battle—indeed, his only method—was a frontal assault that relied on overwhelming numbers to be successful. He was inflexible and unimaginative, two fatal flaws in any field commander. Worse, he was a vain man, and he failed to recognize his own shortcomings.

Early in this campaign, at the aborted river crossing, he had been wounded in the arm by an arrow. It was only a slight wound, and it was largely due to his being unused to fighting against archers. Trask had known that Araluen, unlike any of the other western countries, employed a large contingent of archers among their fighting men. But in his opinion, archers were skulking cowards, who would sneak around the outskirts of a battle, shooting men from cover, then fading away at the first sign of a real attack. Although many of his men carried hunting bows, Trask had no comprehension of the power and range of the Araluen war bow. Nor did he have an idea that a force of twenty trained archers could put a storm of sixty or eighty arrows into the air in under ten seconds, with the last arrows already launched before the first volley struck home.

A good commander, knowing he was facing an Araluen force, might have inquired about the capacity of Araluen archers to sway a battle and devised tactics to nullify them. But Trask, as has been stated, was not a good commander.

He glared now at the bedraggled men huddled on the hard, dusty ground before him.

None would meet his gaze. They knew what was coming. His idea of leadership was to hector and rant at the men he commanded when they failed to do his bidding. They may have tried bravely to overcome the enemy—and indeed, many of them had. But that counted for nothing with Trask. They had not just failed. They had failed *him*. And that he took as a personal insult.

"Cowards!" he roared at them now, unable to restrain himself any further. "Cowards and poltroons. You failed me! I set you a simple task and you failed! Can any of you offer an excuse for that?"

Nobody stirred. Nobody met his furious gaze. They all knew that if they tried to explain how they had been ambushed, stranded on the walkway and decimated by the archers, he would simply brush aside their explanations and scream more insults and abuse at them. That was his way. That had always been his way.

He looked around the haggard faces, seeking one in particular—one he could pin the blame on.

"Where is Bel?" he demanded. Ruka Bel had been the commander of the raid. Indeed, he had planned the whole thing. He was a young officer among the Sonderlanders. Unlike his leader, he was a clever tactician, capable of making a plan and then adapting to unexpected situations when the battle was joined.

And there were *always* unexpected situations in any battle.

"Where is he?" Trask screamed. He needed someone to blame for the debacle and Bel was the logical choice. If the attack had failed, it was because the leader of the attack had failed. Trask strode among the survivors, shoving them, pulling their downcast faces up to his to identify the man who had betrayed him. But there was no sign of Ruka Bel.

"He's dead," a voice told him, and he whirled to face the direction from which it had come.

"What do you mean, dead?" It was a stupid question. But Trask was a stupid man.

"He was hit by an arrow as we were trying to get down into the compound," a second man told him.

"So you left him?" Trask accused them. "You deserted your leader?" He could hardly use the dead Bel as a scapegoat—but Bel could become an instrument with which he could berate and accuse these sad excuses for soldiers.

"He was *dead*," a third man said. There was a hint of rebellion in his voice, as if he realized where Trask was heading.

"So you say. And you're lying. A single arrow wouldn't kill a man like Bel. He was a true soldier! A hero! And you deserted him. You ran! You turned tail and ran! And you left your leader wounded and bleeding when you did."

There was no reply. None of them would meet his gaze. He glared around at them, and as he did so, his gaze fell on one of his servants, making his way through the crouching, huddled men. The servant held up a hand to signal Trask.

"What is it?" the commander asked roughly, beckoning him forward.

"General, there's a flag of truce over the fort, and one of their commanders is standing outside the gate."

A flag of truce? Trask felt an unexpected surge of hope. Perhaps Bel's raid—he already thought of it as Bel's raid, not his own—had caused more damage, more casualties, than they had thought. If the Araluens were suing for terms, perhaps he could salvage something from this disastrous expedition.

For, angry as he was, Trask could sense the mood of his men. They were dejected and morose. The fact that his treatment of them might have had a lot to do with this didn't occur to him. He knew mercenaries needed victory in the field if they were to maintain their enthusiasm and commitment. But this small force of Araluen regulars had thwarted him at every turn. Unless he could do something to change his run of defeats, his men would begin melting away, deserting into the thick forests that surrounded them.

He hurried through the camp, his anger at the failed attacking force put on hold for the moment. Reaching his pavilion, he shaded his eyes and peered up the hill. As his servant had said, there was a white flag flying over the gateway, and a tall warrior, dressed in armor and wearing a sword, stood on the upper terrace of the hill. Beside him stood another figure, dressed in drab green and gray, wearing a strange mottled cloak and carrying one of those accursed longbows. It was those last two items that identified him. He was one of the mysterious Rangers of Araluen, Trask realized. He'd heard of them but, typical of the man, he knew little about them, other than a few fanciful rumors and legends.

One of his men was standing close by and staring up the hill at the two figures, his mouth slightly open.

"Get me a white flag!" Trask demanded. The man dashed

away and returned a few minutes later with a large white cloth fixed to the top of a spear shaft. "Come with me," Trask ordered. "You too," he added, indicating two of his staff.

With the white flag standing out in the morning breeze, he began to trudge up the hill, his feet slipping from time to time on the long, smooth grass. As he began to make his way upward, the two men at the top of the hill started down.

The two groups were separated from each other by two of the terraces when Horace held up his hand for Trask to stop.

"That's far enough!" he said.

Trask hesitated, then pointed to the white flag his soldier held. "You can trust us," he said. But Horace laughed in reply. Trask tried again. "If we talk here, we'll have to shout to make ourselves heard."

"So shout," Horace said. In fact, that was the reason he had called on them to stop. He wanted the enemy leader to be forced to speak loudly, so the surviving prisoners in the fort would hear what their commander said.

Trask shrugged, realizing that his enemy was not going to give in on this point. He also realized that the second man, the Ranger, had an arrow nocked to his bow, although he kept the weapon lowered and hadn't drawn it back. But if Trask tried to move farther up the hill, it would take only seconds for the man to draw and shoot, and Trask knew that he would be the Ranger's first target if a fight started. As he had the thought, his wounded arm throbbed painfully, and he rubbed it.

"I assume you want to discuss terms for surrender?" Trask called.

Again, Horace gave a short laugh. "Do you want to surrender?"

The Sonderlander reacted indignantly. "Of course not! I mean *your* surrender!"

Horace shook his head contemptuously. "Not today, I think," he said. "But I want to discuss our prisoners. We have a dozen of your men, some of them injured. We're willing to return them to you. They need medical treatment."

"So you'll burden *me* with them?" Trask asked him.

Horace raised his eyebrows in surprise. "They're *your* men," he pointed out. Such exchanges were quite normal between opposing forces—although, in this case, Trask had none of Horace's men to exchange for his own.

Trask said nothing, aware that the men with him would overhear and that, if he abandoned their wounded, word would go round the camp in minutes.

"I also thought you might want to take the bodies of the men who were killed, so they can be buried properly," Horace said. "We're willing to give a working party free access. They'll need to be unarmed, of course."

Trask hesitated for a long minute. If he refused this chance to provide decent burial for his dead, he knew it would be an unpopular move with his men. Reluctantly, he nodded. "Very well. I'll send ten men—ten unarmed men—to gather the bodies for burial."

"And the prisoners?" Horace pressed.

But Trask shook his head. "You can keep them! They're cowards and failures!" he snapped.

Horace smiled grimly and dropped his hand to the hilt of the long sword at his side. "You're welcome to step up here and see if you can do any better," he invited.

But Trask wasn't having any of it. He touched the bloodstained bandage around his upper arm. "I'm wounded," he said.

"Of course you are," Horace said with a grim laugh. "Very well: ten men, unarmed. Have them up here in an hour. They may need a cart to take the bodies down."

He paused, waiting for a response, but Trask said nothing. Horace allowed a faint smile to touch his lips. "You may go now," he said and, turning his back on the Sonderland leader, he began to retrace his steps up the hill.

The Ranger remained facing Trask, the arrow still ready on his bow, his eyes watchful. With a muttered curse, Trask turned on his heel and began to work his way back down the hill, slipping and sliding as he went.

Inside the fort, Horace climbed to the walkway, where one of the captured mercenaries had been standing near the gate, watching the scene below.

"You heard what your leader thinks of you?" Horace said.

The man's lip curled in contempt. "I heard."

Horace pointed to the compound below, where the other survivors were gathered inside the gate. Four of them, the more seriously wounded, were on makeshift stretchers.

"You're free to go," Horace told him. "You can rejoin your comrades, or head for the coast. It makes no difference to me."

"We could stay and join you?" the mercenary suggested.

But Horace shook his head. "I don't think so. Once you turn your coat, it can become a habit. I'm not sure I could trust you."

Ten minutes later, the gate opened and the prisoners began filing down the hill, the less seriously injured carrying their comrades on the stretchers.

18

DIMON LEANED AGAINST THE WINDOWSILL AND PEERED UP at the south tower, a scowl marking his usually handsome features.

He was in a bedchamber on the top floor of the keep. The squat, solid central tower was several floors lower than the four graceful, soaring towers set at each corner of the castle and connected by the high curtain walls that ran between them. From this vantage point, he could look up to the balcony running around the top of the south tower, below the pointed, conical roof that surmounted it.

He had been here for over an hour, keeping watch on the comings and goings above him while he thought about his next possible course of action. As he watched, he could see Cassandra's men patrolling the balcony regularly, keeping an eye out for any possible movement in the compound below.

Twice, he had seen Cassandra herself peering over the parapet. Each time, his lips had drawn back in a snarl and he had cursed quietly. He had become fixated on the princess. She had proven to be a more capable opponent than he expected. He knew she had a reputation from her younger days—a reputation for courage and leadership. But he assumed that the tales of her previous exploits—in Skandia when she was a teenager and later in Arrida when she had delivered the ransom that set Erak, Oberjarl of the Skandians, free from captivity—had been carefully embroidered and exaggerated over the years by sycophantic admirers and hangers-on. There was no shortage of such people in a royal court, he knew.

But it appeared that her reputation was well founded. She had reacted quickly and effectively to his seizure of the castle, leading her people to their virtually unassailable position in the south tower.

He had tried to drive her from her refuge by brute force. But her blocking of the stairway rendered that attempt unsuccessful— and expensive in terms of the lives of his men. The trebuchet seemed to be a good idea, until he realized that the sandstone rocks it could hurl were virtually useless against the hard granite walls of the tower. He had hoped that the fire bladders might have broken the morale of the defenders in the tower—or at least caused casualties as they spread their sticky tendrils of flame among the men and equipment holding out on the ninth floor.

And for a while, it seemed that they might have the desired effect. The sudden showers of fire that they unleashed on the defenders were causing alarm and panic. He had witnessed that from this same window.

But then the inexcusable carelessness of his men in leaving the supply of fire bladders piled on the platform of the trebuchet led to disaster. The blackened, twisted wreckage in the courtyard below attested to that fact.

He could build another siege machine, but that would take

days. And his men would be wary of manning it. He had lost several to arrows from above, and another two had been badly burned when the stockpile of fire bladders had ignited and exploded. But the bigger problem facing him was time.

Each day, he climbed to the castle wall and scanned the horizon to the north, looking anxiously for any sign of approaching troops. There had been no reports from the north, where Horace's force was trapped in the hill fort. And that meant that Horace's position was secure—as was Cassandra's here at Castle Araluen. If the mercenaries surrounding the fort had broken through and defeated the defenders, they would have been quick to send word. In this case, no news was bad news.

He didn't deceive himself that Horace and Gilan would stay confined. They were too skillful, too clever and altogether too experienced in battle for that to happen. Sooner or later, he realized, they would break free and head south again.

And even if they didn't manage to force their way out, the Sonderland troops wouldn't stay in place indefinitely. Mercenaries fought for profit—for the pay they received and for the plunder they could take from defeated enemies, whether it was weapons, valuables, armor or ransom money. And if they weren't getting them—and, even worse, could see little prospect of doing so—they would soon melt away and find richer fields to conquer.

So he knew that the longer he took to winkle Cassandra out of her defensive position, the greater the chance became that Horace and his force of disciplined, highly trained troops would arrive back here to set her free. Time was running out.

He racked his brains as he stared at the tall, impregnable tower facing him. He had tried force and Cassandra had defeated him. He had tried to trick her, promising to set her and her cursed brat of a daughter free, telling her that the hill fort had fallen and Horace was dead. And he had tried to batter the tower down, and then hurl fire and devastation at the tower with his trebuchet.

And each time, Cassandra had countered his attempts to oust her.

Now there was only one course that he could think of. He shook his head bitterly, looking again at the terrace above him, hoping to catch some sight of the woman who had become his enemy and his bane. But there was no sign of her, and he turned away, heading for the door and the stairway that led to the lower floors of the keep.

Cassandra was in the storeroom with Ingrid, taking inventory of the supplies of food that were available. The fresh food that had been stockpiled here was almost gone. But there was plenty of salted and smoked and dried food left—enough to last them for months.

"We've plenty of flour," Ingrid told her. Maddie's former maid had taken on the job of quartermaster, organizing meals for the defenders. "See, we can bake fresh bread each day. No butter. But we have enough oil for at least a month."

"Try to organize it so we vary the meals each day," Cassandra told her. "Dried and preserved food can become monotonous, so keep changing it up."

Ingrid nodded. She had developed a good working relationship with the soldier who had taken on the duties of chef. Thank goodness he wasn't a real chef, the girl thought. She couldn't have coped with a chef's overbearing manner and readiness to take offense at any sign of someone else interfering in his work.

"I'll talk to Proctor," she said. "We'll come up with a schedule so we don't serve the same meal too often."

"That'll help. You could also—"

"My lady! You need to come quickly!" Whatever else Ingrid could do was forgotten as a soldier pushed open the storeroom door, saw Cassandra, and called to her. She turned away from the racks and shelves of barrels and jars facing her.

"What is it?" she asked.

The man gestured roughly in the direction of the stairwell. "It's Dimon," he told her. She had instructed all her men to refrain from calling their enemy "Sir Dimon" or using any other honorific. "He says he must talk to you."

"Must he indeed?" Cassandra said mildly. For a moment, she considered sending a message back to the rebel leader, along the lines of his taking a flying leap into the moat. Then she realized that such an action would serve no good purpose.

"I'll come," she said to the soldier at the door. "Keep on with the inventory, Ingrid. We'll go over it tonight and plan a schedule of meals." She smiled to herself. Such were the duties of a leader: count barrels of beans and bacon and flour one moment; talk to the enemy commander the next. I suppose one never gets bored with a life like this, she thought.

"Very well, my lady," Ingrid said. She took the list and the charcoal pencil Cassandra had been using and continued with the stocktake while Cassandra led the way to the stairwell.

"Did he say what he wanted?" she asked the soldier.

But he shook his head. "No, my lady. Just to talk to you is all."

She went down the interior stairs to the eighth floor, then

headed across to the doorway leading to the spiral staircase that ran the full height of the tower. There was a soldier on duty there, watching and listening for any sign that the enemy might be trying to bridge the gap in the stairway. He nodded to her as she approached.

"Dimon is on the stairs, my lady," he said.

Cassandra, ever wary of treachery from the former guard commander, peered carefully around the stone wall. She could see the stairs winding down below her, and the timber wall blocking the gap where her men had removed a three-meter section of steps.

"Dimon?" she called experimentally. She heard movement on the steps below. Presumably someone had gone to fetch the traitor. A minute or so later, she heard his voice. As ever, the sound of it made her blood surge with hatred.

"Is that you, Cassandra?"

"Who did you think it might be?" She found it hard to maintain a civil conversation with Dimon. He had lied to her and tried to trick her on so many occasions that she approached any conversation with him with total suspicion. When he didn't reply, she sighed and called down the stairwell, "Yes. It's me. What did you want?"

"I want to talk to you," came the response.

"You seem to be doing that. Stop beating around the bush and tell me what you want."

There was another long pause, then he said, in a dejected voice, "I just want to say that you've won."

She took a half pace back, startled by his admission. This was the last thing she had expected to hear. Threats, yes. Another ultimatum, or perhaps a proposal for a truce. Yes. But an admission of defeat? She shook her head, looked at the two soldiers standing beside her. They looked as puzzled as she was. One of them, the one who had come to fetch her, frowned and shook his head.

"I've won?" she repeated. She was caught unprepared by the statement. She had no answer for him other to repeat what he had told her, and wait to see what he proposed now.

"I've tried everything I could. I should have thought of this damned tower, should have remembered how impregnable it can be. But you've outthought me at every turn. Everything I've tried, you've had a counter for. And now I'm done."

"And so . . . ?" she queried. This defeated tone was totally unfamiliar to her. She didn't trust it. She was searching for the trick in his words, thinking furiously to see what deception he might have in mind.

"I'm out of time, Cassandra. It's as simple as that. Any day now, Horace will be back with his men, and that'll be the end for me. So I'm getting out while the getting is good."

"You told me he was dead," she said accusingly.

There was a long pause before he replied. "I was lying. You knew that. Or at least, you suspected it."

She frowned, thinking furiously. Had he just given something away when he said Horace would be back any day? Had Horace broken out of the hill fort? She temporized. "You're inside the castle. You could hold him off for months if you want to," she said.

He gave a short bark of laughter—but the sound was devoid of any humor. "Do you think that's what I want? To be captive here in the castle while he mobilizes the army and begins a real siege? To be trapped, with no way of escaping? No. I know when

I'm beaten. I know when it's time to throw in my cards. If I go now, I've got a chance of reaching the coast and getting out of this country."

"Where will you go?" she asked. She was genuinely puzzled by this sudden change of heart. All she could think was that Horace *had* escaped and Dimon was panicking as he waited for her avenging husband to appear over the horizon. The more she thought about it, the more it made sense. Horace was a fearsome warrior and he would make a terrifying enemy—particularly of a man who had betrayed his wife and then tried to kill her. If Horace was on the loose, and heading south, Dimon would be well advised to show a clean pair of heels, as soon as possible.

"Sonderland," was the surprising reply. "They can always use troop commanders. I'll join them as a mercenary. Don't try to come after me. And tell Horace not to try to track me down. The Sonderlanders look after their own."

"I imagine they do," she said, still trying to see beyond his words, still searching for the trick that she felt must be concealed here. Why tell her he was leaving if he didn't, actually, leave?

"So you've come to congratulate me, have you?" she said after a pause. Again she heard the bitter laugh echo in the stairwell.

"No. I've come to tell you you've won. But you've been lucky. If my men hadn't left those oil bladders stored where you could set fire to them, it might have been a different story. I would have rained fire on you from that trebuchet until you and your men were burned to cinders. I'll be pulling out tomorrow with my men. You can watch us go. But don't feel too smug about it. One day, I'll come back. And I'll finish what I started. Maybe not tomorrow. Maybe not next year. But one day, when you least expect it."

"Good of you to warn me," she said dryly.

"It's not a warning. It's a promise. And I want you to live in fear of that day, never knowing when I might be back."

This bitterness, this vitriol, was more like what she expected of Dimon. She shook her head, wondering. Could he really mean what he was saying? Was it really all over? Her aversion to Dimon was so strong that she doubted the truth of his words. But then, she thought, she'd find out tomorrow. If he was genuine, she'd see him and his men leave.

"And that can't come soon enough," she said to herself. He obviously heard her voice but couldn't make out the words.

"What did you say, Cassandra?" he called.

"I said 'good riddance,'" she replied.

19

Maddie crouched below the wall of the hill fort, craning her head back to peer up at the palisade. Close in to the wall as she was, she couldn't see any sign of sentries moving on the walkway above her. But she could hear the regular tramp of their feet as they patrolled back and forth.

She had circled out to the west, taking a wide detour around the Foxes' encampment before angling back in to climb the hill. She could have taken a more direct route, and gone through the camp itself, trusting to her training and skill to remain unobserved by the sentries who patrolled the camp. It would have been quicker, but there was also risk involved. One careless movement, one piece of bad luck—or one person treading on her hand—and she might have been discovered. And she had learned now that bad luck was a factor that had to be considered in a situation like this. If there was a risk-free way, or at least a way with less risk, then that was the path she would take.

As she got closer to the fort, she had to take extra care not to be sighted by the sentries on duty. They would be more alert and more efficient than the men patrolling the camp at the base of the hill. They were professionals and they were highly disciplined. And she knew the archers were all good shots.

In addition, they were commanded by her father and Gilan—and neither man would tolerate any slackness or inattention to duty. So she had moved with extra care up the last two terraces to the base of the fort. In her note, she had told her father to expect her, but she had given herself plenty of time and she sensed she was a little early.

She sat down, leaning her back against the palisade wall, and considered her position. If she made any kind of noise, the men on the walls might overreact before they knew who she was. Finally, an idea occurred to her. She cupped her hands around her mouth and imitated the call of a curlew, making the sound three times. The pacing feet patrolling the wall above her stopped immediately. She heard voices whispering urgently. Wrapping the cloak around her, she leaned into the wall, keeping herself as inconspicuous as possible. After a few moments, she heard soft footsteps above—approaching from the corner where the west and south walls met and where, she assumed, the stairs that led up from the compound would be situated. More whispered voices, and this time she made out the word *curlew*. Then Gilan's voice called softly from almost directly above the spot where she was huddled.

"Maddie? Is that you?"

"It's me, Gilan. I'm early, I think."

She stood and moved out from the wall, where she would be more visible from above. Craning her head back, she could make out three heads silhouetted against the starlight, leaning over the palisade—Gilan and the two sentries. She saw Gilan turn to one of the other men.

"Tell Sir Horace that his daughter is here," he said. The man nodded and moved away rapidly. Then Gilan leaned over the palisade once more.

"Rope coming down," he called softly. A few seconds later, a rope hit the long grass beside her with a swishing sound. She seized hold of it and began to climb the palisade wall, leaning her weight back against the rope and walking herself up the logs until she reached the top. Gilan and the remaining sentry reached out to meet her, lifting her over the top of the palisade and setting her down on the planks of the walkway.

The Ranger Commandant embraced her warmly. "If you'd waited a second, we would have hauled you up," he said. "How do you like our lovely home?"

She disengaged herself from his embrace and looked around. "I've seen better," she said, grinning at him, happy to see him well and obviously unhurt. "Can't say I care for your neighbors."

"I'm not fond of them myself," he told her, then added, "You know, we're quite a way from the sea here."

She inclined her head, a little puzzled at the comment. "You are?"

"Yes. Quite a way. Not a lot of curlews around here, as a matter of fact. They're marsh birds, you know. And they aren't nocturnal."

"I did know that," she said.

"In which case, I'm wondering why you chose to imitate a curlew's call by way of announcing yourself."

"Oh, that. Well, my bird calls are so good, I thought if I did a bird like an owl or another night flyer, you might think it was a real bird and not realize it was me. I suppose I should have organized a signal to let you know I was here."

"As it was, a very bad imitation of a curlew seemed to do the trick," he told her.

She bridled a little. "It was an excellent imitation. I heard one of the sentries say the word *curlew*."

"What he said to me was, 'There's someone outside the wall doing a very bad imitation of a curlew.' Having heard your bird calls, I immediately knew it must be you."

Any further discussion of Maddie's avian imitations was precluded by the sound of running feet. She looked up to see a tall figure running toward her along the walkway and allowed herself to be swept up in her father's embrace.

"Maddie! Maddie!" he cried. "How are you? Are you all right? What are you doing here?"

"I'm fine, Dad, fine." She laughed, managing to wriggle free and looking up at his face. "We heard you were trapped here and I brought the Skandians to help break you out."

"Your note said there were thirty of them. Where did you find so many Skandians?"

"The Heron brotherband visited Araluen, and they got word that the duty ship had been damaged and was on the shore. I recruited both crews to help."

Horace shook his head, perplexed. "But how did you know? And how's your mother? Is everything all right at Castle Araluen?"

And at that point, she realized that her father had no idea what had happened at the castle, no idea of Dimon's treachery. She took both his hands and looked steadily into his eyes. "Take a deep breath, Dad," she said, and the serious tone of her voice told him that she had bad news.

"Is Cassandra—" he began, but she hushed him.

"She's fine. Now, no questions for a few minutes while I bring you up to date."

She spoke quickly and concisely, telling them of Dimon's betrayal of Cassandra and his leadership of the Red Fox Clan. As she described his duplicitous entry into the castle, Horace's eyes glittered with rage and he began to exclaim angrily. But she squeezed his hands firmly and shook her head, stopping him.

She described how she had moved in and out of the castle, using the secret tunnels built so long ago.

As she mentioned this, Gilan nodded. "I might have known you'd find them."

She glanced at him. "Just as well I did. I was able to infiltrate a Red Fox Clan meeting and discover that Dimon was their leader; that you were trapped here by a much larger force than you'd anticipated; and that he planned to occupy the castle and kill Mum and anyone loyal to her." She didn't elaborate on the hair-raising pursuit through the forest when she had escaped the vengeful Red Fox members. She sensed that, if she did, her father would interrupt her, seeking reassurance that she had come to no harm.

"But Mum was too quick for him. She gathered a small force of troops and archers and retreated to the south tower."

Horace raised his eyebrows. "Of course. The last refuge."

"She's perfectly safe there. When Dimon tried to force his way up the stairs, she and her men sent him packing. They've removed the last section of the staircase so he can't get to them. It's a secure position, with plenty of food and water. But of course, they can't go anywhere."

"Rather like us," Gilan said heavily.

"Except she doesn't have thirty wild Skandians ready to help her break out of the trap she's in," she said.

Horace rubbed his chin thoughtfully. "Exactly where are these Skandians?"

Maddie pointed vaguely down the hill to the south. "They're camped a few kilometers away, in the forest, close to the river." She looked at Gilan. "Hal sends his regards, by the way, as do Thorn and Stig."

The Ranger smiled. "Nice to know they're close by," he said. "You did very well to convince them to help us."

She shook her head. "They didn't need convincing. Once they heard that Mum was in trouble, they were keen as mustard to help. And the crew of the other ship were just as happy to throw in with them." Again, she didn't mention the minor detail of having to prove herself to the crew of *Wolfbiter*. That wasn't important now.

It occurred to Horace that they had been standing on the walkway for some minutes now while Maddie provided all this information. He gestured to the compound below, and the fire burning outside his and Gilan's tents.

"Let's move somewhere more comfortable and continue this. I imagine you'd like a cup of coffee to warm you up, Maddie?"

He saw her teeth flash in the dim light as she grinned at him. "I'd kill for one."

Gilan patted her shoulder affectionately. "Spoken like a true Ranger," he said.

They walked down the stairs to the compound, Maddie arm in arm with her father, who kept throwing bemused glances her way. He was trying to come to terms with the fact that his daughter had turned into a seasoned, skilled Ranger and warrior. The realization didn't come easily as, like all doting fathers, he still thought of his daughter as twelve years old. There was a camp table and two canvas chairs set up outside Horace's and Gilan's tents. Gilan quickly fetched another and they all sat. He beckoned to an archer, standing guard.

"Make us a big pot of coffee, please," he said. As the man nodded and turned away, Gilan thought of something. "No need to skimp," he said. "Use full measures. We'll be getting out of here soon." Over the past week, Horace's rationing edict had applied to coffee as well as the food available.

The man grinned. "Yes, sir!" he said eagerly.

Then Gilan turned back to the others. "So, what's our plan?"

In reply, Maddie reached inside her jerkin and produced the map she had drawn of the immediate area. She spread it out on the table, and they all leaned forward to study it.

"Your mapmaking has improved," Gilan said. "This is a lot better than you used to do."

Maddie smiled at the praise. "Thanks," she said. "I have been working on it." She decided not to mention that this was her fourth attempt. Knowing that her Commandant would be seeing it, she had discarded the previous three versions as not being good enough.

Horace sighed. "Can we stop treating this as an apprentice assignment and get on with it?" he asked, and they both looked suitably chastened.

Gilan made a courteous gesture. "Please go ahead," he said. Horace was the overall commander, and their tactics and deployment would be his to decide.

Horace looked at his daughter. "Where will you be during the battle?"

"Hal has asked me to stay back behind the fighting," she said, and Horace nodded approval. Maddie hadn't argued with Hal's suggestion. With her slight build, she knew that a pitched hand-to-hand battle would be no place for her, and as Hal had pointed out, there was a more valuable role she could fulfill.

"One of their brotherband is called Ingvar," she said. "He's huge and evidently an amazing warrior. But he has limited peripheral vision, and Hal suggested I should stay in the rear and cover his back, in case some of the enemy get behind him. They have a girl named Lydia who usually fills that role, but she didn't come on this voyage. Apparently she's a dead shot with an atlatl."

Gilan raised his eyebrows. "That's putting it mildly. I've seen her throw."

"All right," Horace said, bringing them back to the main subject. "I plan for us to exit the fort through the north wall.

"We'll make our way down the hill. The first time the enemy see us, we'll be two terraces lower than they expect—almost halfway down. That should give them a surprise. I'm assuming they'll form a shield wall. That will be their logical step. I'm going to lead ten troopers off to their right wing, ready for a flank attack. The right wing of the shield wall will angle round to face us. Gilan will be in the center, with the rest of the cavalry and all the archers. The archers will start to lay down an arrow storm, forcing the Foxes to get into cover behind their shields. Then they'll move downhill. That's about the time we'll want your Skandians to get involved, coming over this ridge behind the enemy camp." He touched the tip of his dagger to the point on the ridge from where she and Hal had observed the camp.

Maddie studied the map and the relative positions Horace

had sketched out. "With any luck, they won't see us until it's too late," she said.

Horace nodded. "The enemy will have their eyes on us. That's part of the reason I'll move out to their right—to distract their attention. Have the Skandians walk down the hill until they're spotted, then turn 'em loose. We'll hit them from three sides at once. That should put the wind up them," he said.

It was a simple plan, but Maddie had learned that simple plans were the best. There was less to go wrong—and something *always* went wrong.

"Looks good to me," she said.

Gilan concurred. "Me too."

Horace looked from one to the other, making sure neither of them had any reservations. Then he nodded. "Right. Let's talk about timing," he said.

20

Castle Araluen had been quiet for the past day. There had been no attacks on the stairwell, no new machines to threaten the defenders. There had been no sign of Dimon, no further word from him since his admittance to Cassandra that he had given up and would be leaving for Sonderland.

Nevertheless, Cassandra refused to let herself be lulled into a sense of false security. Recent events had taught her to distrust Dimon implicitly. She sensed he was up to something and that his capitulation was a sham.

As a result, she insisted that her men maintain the high level of vigilance they had assumed from the start of the siege. She had Merlon and several other senior soldiers checking constantly on sentries, ensuring they weren't slacking off and allowing the apparent lack of activity from the enemy to make them careless. And she kept a watch over Merlon and the others herself, ensuring that they remained at the highest possible level of attentiveness as well. She discussed the situation with her father, grateful for any advice he might offer.

"Stay patient," he told her. "This is the hardest part of a siege. It's easy to remain alert when you're under attack. But it's different when nothing happens hour after hour. Your senses become dulled and your attention can wander."

As a result, she set and maintained a regular schedule of patrolling for herself, striding around the terrace that surrounded the south tower, checking the castle yard below, inspecting the keep for any sign of activity through its windows, and studying the other three towers and the battlements on the curtain walls that joined them. Then she would descend to the eighth floor and check the sentries at the stairwell, studying the wooden barrier that barred the way to the lower stairs for any sign that the Foxes had attempted to damage it or degrade it.

She would break that schedule at irregular intervals—as the mood took her—and begin extra impromptu inspections. It was all too easy, she realized, to become complacent with a fixed schedule. Changing that at random was necessary to maintain focus on her surroundings and the movements of her enemies. It also kept her own men on their toes. If they had no idea when or where she might appear to check on them, they had little choice but to stay alert at all times, not just those times when they knew she was scheduled to inspect them.

It was mid-morning and she was on one of her surprise inspections, starting at the balcony around the ninth floor, when she saw it.

From the lofty observation point, she had an excellent overview of the main gate and drawbridge. They were set in the southeast wall of the castle, down to her right, enabling her to keep track of the comings and goings below.

It was the noise that first drew her attention. There was a low rumbling sound from the gate. She realized that the massive drawbridge was being lowered. The upper part of the wall hid the actual bridge from her sight, but the noise was unmistakable.

"Listen to that," she said to Ingrid. The girl had taken to accompanying Cassandra on her rounds, ready to take notes of any slackness in the defenders or any actions that might need to be taken. There was usually very little note-taking to be done.

"They're opening the gates," Ingrid said. Then she pointed down into the courtyard. "Look there, my lady."

The stables were set on the northeast wall, where their view was slightly blocked by the keep tower. As Ingrid pointed, a double file of horsemen began to trot out into the courtyard, their horses' hooves clattering on the flagstones. The men were dressed in the same uniforms they had worn when they first infiltrated the castle, with helmets, chain-mail overshirts and red surcoats. Their round shields, painted red with a yellow X, were slung on their backs. They all carried their long lances stepped into the holding sockets on their right stirrups, so that the shafts were held vertically.

Cassandra estimated that there were about forty in the party, although she noted with grim satisfaction that their numbers were fewer than they had been when they first arrived. Their attempted attacks on the stairs and with the trebuchet had thinned their ranks somewhat.

As the riders trotted toward the gatehouse in a double file, they were joined by another mounted man, cantering his horse to take the lead. Even from this distance, Cassandra could see that he had resumed the fox mask that he had worn days before, concealing his identity.

"Dimon," she said quietly, as the lead rider clattered under the massive archway, the rest of his force following behind him in two files.

Ingrid grunted in reply. "Looks like he meant what he said," she observed, a note of surprise in her voice.

Cassandra made no reply.

The two files of horsemen were hidden from sight for several minutes. Then they reappeared on the grassy field outside the walls, and wheeled right to head downhill to the forest, with Dimon in the lead. Cassandra and Ingrid moved around the terrace to keep them in sight. As the men rode out of the shadow of the walls, the morning sun struck their helmets, setting them gleaming.

"My lady," said Ingrid slowly, after a minute or so. "Do you notice something odd about those riders?"

Cassandra peered more carefully, trying to see what the girl might be referring to. After several seconds, she shook her head. "Not that I can see. What is it?" She realized that Ingrid's eyes were younger than hers and her vision was sharper. She sighed inwardly. One of the penalties of growing older, she thought.

"Their helmets are gleaming in the sunlight . . . ," Ingrid began.

Cassandra turned to look at her, frowning, not seeing the significance of the remark. "Helmets tend to do that. They're metal, after all."

Ingrid nodded, but then pointed at the mounted men. "But their spearpoints aren't," she said.

Cassandra jerked her eyes back to the troopers. Ingrid was right. The sunlight danced and gleamed off the bobbing helmets. But there was no matching reflection from the heads of the lances they all carried.

Which could only mean that the spearpoints weren't metal.

"And look at the way they're all sitting," Ingrid continued. "They're slumped, with their left hands on the pommels of their saddles, not on the reins. All of them. And some of them don't look as if they're completely at home on horseback. They're bouncing around like sacks of potatoes."

"What are you saying?" Cassandra asked, although she had already half guessed the answer.

"They're tied on." Ingrid sounded much surer of herself, as if her initial doubts had been dispelled. "Their left hands are tied to their saddle pommels. Their right hands have been left free to hold their spears—except they're not spears. They're just long sticks. Those men are prisoners," she said, with growing conviction in her voice. "They're not Dimon's troops."

Cassandra nodded slowly, looking at the girl admiringly. "Which means Dimon's troops are still inside the castle," she said.

"Yes. And I'll wager that man leading them out isn't Dimon. I'll bet he's still inside as well."

"So he wants us to think he's gone . . ."

"Which means we'll come down from the tower . . ."

"And find him and his troops somewhere down there, lying in wait for us. Well spotted, Ingrid." Cassandra laid her hand on the younger woman's shoulder. At that moment, a soldier came onto the terrace, holding a message bag in his hand.

"My lady, we just found this on the stairs. Must have been thrown up past the barrier earlier this morning."

He handed the bag to Cassandra. It was a small weighted canvas sack, designed to hold a written message and be thrown over battlements or other defensive positions. She took out the single sheet of vellum inside, glanced at the seal and broke it, unrolling the message.

"From Dimon," she said unnecessarily. Then she handed the sheet to Ingrid, after reading it herself.

Farewell, Cassandra. Do not try to follow me. I have taken several of your people with me as hostages and they'll suffer if you do. The others are in the dungeons below the keep. They're probably running low on food and water as I saw no reason to feed them.

Remember to keep looking over your shoulder. I'll be back one day, when you least expect it.

D.

Ingrid read the message aloud, the folded the sheet again.

"Clever, isn't it?" Cassandra said. "He warns me not to follow, tells me he has hostages, and threatens me for the future. And buried in there is the message that our people are imprisoned, with no food or water—more or less as an aside."

"Designed to have you hurrying down the stairs to the dungeons to set them free," Ingrid said, nodding slowly.

"Exactly. And somewhere down there, I'll find Dimon and his men, armed and ready to attack us." She shook her head. "He's a treacherous snake, isn't he?"

"He's using your own good nature against you," Ingrid said. "He knows that you wouldn't leave your people short of food or water." She paused, then added, "On the other hand . . ."

"On the other hand what?" Cassandra asked.

Ingrid seemed reluctant to answer, but eventually she spoke. "On the other hand, I could be wrong about the spearpoints and the riders. Maybe he *has* left and maybe there *are* prisoners in the dungeon who need food and water."

Cassandra studied her worried face for a few moments, then replied. "Well, there's one way to find out."

Ingrid looked at her in alarm. "You're not planning on going down the stairs?"

Cassandra smiled and shook her head. "No. I'm definitely not planning that."

On the ninth floor, Cassandra moved to the secret door where Maddie had entered from the hidden stairs that ran down to ground level. She stopped to take a lantern from a hook, lighting it with a taper from a box over the fireplace. She slipped the latch and opened the door, peering in.

For a moment, her head swam as she looked down into the black depths. The lantern illuminated only the first five or six meters and she had a dislike of cramped, dark places. Steeling herself, and with a quick, nervous grin to Ingrid, who was standing by, watching anxiously, she stepped in and began to descend the ladders that led to the dungeons.

She moved slowly, testing each step before she placed her full weight on it. Maddie had mentioned that one of the rungs had given way beneath her weight when she had initially climbed up and Cassandra had no wish to go plummeting down through the darkness.

As she passed the main stairway between the seventh and eighth levels, she could see a dim light where her men had removed the section of stairs. Then the darkness closed in again.

There were observation holes on the platforms at each floor and, as she reached each one, she would move toward it, keeping the lantern shielded, and listen. Then she'd put her eye to the spyhole and look. For the first four floors, she heard and saw nothing. Then, at the level of the fourth floor, she heard a low murmur of voices. Putting her eye to the spyhole, she studied the room inside the tower. This was the level where the arched stone bridge connected the south tower to the keep. It was the most likely point of egress if she and her men were to vacate their sanctuary.

At least, that appeared to be what Dimon thought. A large group of his men, fully armed and armored, were lounging on the floor inside the big, open room, talking in low tones among themselves as they awaited developments. As she watched, a knowing smile forming on her lips, the door from the bridge opened and Dimon himself strode in. He looked around angrily.

"Keep your voices down!" he hissed, and the mumble of conversation died away.

That won't last, she thought. As soon as Dimon left, the conversations would start up again. You couldn't keep soldiers from talking—usually grumbling about their lot.

Dimon prowled restlessly round the room. He stopped by one of the troops, a sergeant by his insignia. "Any sign of them yet?" he asked.

The sergeant shook his head. "No, my lord."

Dimon swore softly. "Well, stay alert. They'll be coming down soon. Send someone for me when you hear them coming. Get your men out of sight and let them come into the main hall here. Then surround them. But wait until you see Cassandra. I want her taken."

"Yes, my lord."

"And raise that drawbridge again. I don't want to risk having it down if Horace suddenly turns up."

The sergeant frowned. "Won't they realize we're still here if the drawbridge is up?"

Dimon shot an exasperated look at him. "They can't see the bridge itself from the tower," he said. "Raise it slowly, so they can't hear you doing it." He whirled angrily on the men lounging behind him, talking quietly among themselves. "Keep the damned noise down, for pity's sake! We're supposed to be long gone."

The men fell silent and Dimon stalked away, heading for the bridge that led to the keep.

"*My lord* indeed," Cassandra said in a low, sardonic voice. Then she began slowly climbing back to the ninth floor.

21

DAWN WAS NEARLY BREAKING BY THE TIME THEY FINISHED discussing their plans for the coming battle. Maddie joined Gilan and Horace as they made their usual pre-dawn patrol around the palisade, paying particular attention to the goings-on in the Red Fox camp below the south wall. Everything seemed normal, with the camp awakening and fires being stirred into life. Gilan glanced at the red ball of the sun rising over the forest in the east, then jerked a thumb down at the enemy camp.

"Maybe you'd better stay here until dark," he said. "You might be spotted going back down the hill in daylight."

Maddie snorted. "You don't have a lot of faith in my unseen movement skills, do you?"

He smiled at her. "It's just that people will be moving around down there and there's always the chance someone might tread on your hand," he said.

She rolled her eyes at him. "I'm never going to live that down, am I?"

He grinned. "I shouldn't think so."

"Well, I'll have you know, when I was escaping from the Red

Foxes after I heard them plotting in the old abbey, somebody *did* step on my hand, and I still wasn't discovered."

Horace looked between the two of them, a slightly puzzled look on his face. "Why would anyone step on your hand?" he asked.

Gilan waved the question aside. "It's just a Ranger thing," he said.

Horace sighed. After years of adventuring with Will and Halt, he was used to being palmed off with that answer, or something like it, when they wanted to leave him out of a joke. He regarded his daughter now, seeing her hiding a grin.

"That sort of thing isn't very respectful," he said. "I can't do anything about Gilan, but I am your father, after all."

She tried, unsuccessfully, to stop grinning. "And highly respected, too," she said in her most dutiful daughter voice.

"Hah!" said Horace skeptically. Then a thought struck him and he brightened. "It just occurred to me," he said, "if we're breaking out of here in the next few days, we don't have to ration the food any more. I can finally have a decent breakfast."

With that cheerful thought, he hurried through the rest of their morning patrol and then climbed down the stairs and headed across to the cookhouse to give the duty cooks the news.

For the first time in a week, Horace enjoyed a proper breakfast, sighing with contentment as he mopped up the last scraps of food with a piece of toasted flat bread, then leaning back to savor his coffee. Maddie, who had joined them for breakfast, pushed her chair back, stretched her arms above her head and yawned.

"I might get some sleep," she said. "I was up all last night and it looks as if I'll be up again tonight as well."

"Use my tent," Horace told her. "It's got a good soft bed."

"Of course, as a Ranger, she could sleep quite comfortably on the hard ground, wrapped in her cloak," Gilan said.

Maddie looked at him sidelong. "I *could* do that, as you say. But it's not obligatory," she replied.

Gilan raised his eyebrows. "I could make it an order."

She smiled sweetly at him. "And I would ignore it if you did."

Gilan sighed. "My authority seems to be slipping. Young people just don't have the respect they used to. When I was young, I never would have spoken to my Commandant with such disrespect."

"But things were so different in the olden days. I've often wondered, how did you manage before they discovered fire?" Maddie said.

Gilan decided to quit while he was behind. "Get some sleep," he said.

Maddie rose, grinning, then yawned and headed for Horace's tent.

Gilan glanced at the big warrior, who was smothering a yawn of his own. "What about you? You were up half the night as well."

"I'll take your tent," Horace said. "You can sleep on the hard ground, rolled in your cloak. You're a Ranger, after all."

Maddie slept till mid-afternoon and awoke refreshed and hungry. She and her father had an early supper, then, once it was fully dark, she slipped over the east wall and slid down a rope to the grassy path below. She looked up and saw two heads craning over the palisade. She waved a hand in farewell.

"Bye, Dad. Bye, Gilan," she called softly. "I'll see you tomorrow."

"Bye, Maddie. Take care," her father called in reply. In the darkness, he could still see the quick gleam of her teeth as she smiled up at him.

"I always do," she said, then she slipped over the edge of the terrace and began to make her way down the hill. Gilan and Horace stayed, watching her. Before too long, Horace had lost sight of her completely. Gilan kept her in sight a little longer, but only because he could anticipate which way she would go in the moving shadows.

"She's very good," he said to Horace. "Will has taught her well."

"You're all very good," Horace said. "I can never see any of you once you start sneaking around."

"Sneaking around?" said Gilan in a hurt voice. "We prefer to call it 'unseen movement.'"

"Call it what you like," Horace said. "To me it's sneaking around."

They moved to the south wall to keep an eye on the enemy's camp, watching to see if there was any sign that Maddie had been spotted. But there was no sound of alarm or outcry and, after an hour, Gilan touched Horace's sleeve.

"She'll be through their lines by now," he reassured his friend. "Let's get something to eat."

It was the best way he could think of to stop Horace worrying about his daughter.

Maddie skirted the Red Fox camp on the eastern side, moving in a wide semicircle to reach the slope running up behind it to the southern ridge. Staying in a crouch, she moved uphill, using the long, gently swaying grass for cover. Once she reached the spine of the ridge, she rolled over to the far side, avoiding silhouetting herself against the night sky. She lay still for a few moments, listening and watching to see if there were any patrols moving in the valley below, on the south side of the ridge.

There was nothing.

Lying on her belly, she looked back to the hill fort, straining to see if she could make out her father and Gilan on the ramparts. But the darkness defeated her. She could see the glow of the campfires inside the compound, but that didn't give enough light to identify individuals on the wall. A little sadly, she turned away.

"Bye, Dad," she muttered.

Continuing to move carefully, she went down the slope, then up the far side until she reached the cover of the tree line. Then she stood upright and jogged through the forest, her bow strung and ready in her hand, toward the Skandians' campsite.

As she approached the camp's central fire, she was pleased to see that Hal had set a proper watch, with a ring of sentries set well outside the reach of the firelight. Each man stood in the shadow of a tree, where he was not immediately visible. Anyone without her skill at remaining unseen would have been spotted and challenged before he could get close to the campsite.

Nor had Hal concentrated his sentries on the side nearest the enemy camp, as a lot of commanders would have done. His sentries covered the relatively safer western perimeter as well, even though it might have been reasonable to assume that there was no danger likely to come from that direction. She nodded approvingly. Danger, she knew, could come from any direction.

She worked her way carefully through the trees until she was five meters from one of the sentries. He was carrying a spear and one of the Skandians' big round shields, and she had no wish to come up on him unexpectedly and risk being speared. She stayed behind a tree and called softly.

"Hello? It's me, the Ranger."

The sentry, who had been leaning on his spear in an at-ease position, immediately stiffened into a ready posture and dropped into a crouch, shield up, spear pointing outward, eyes searching the darkness ahead of him.

"Who's there? Where are you?" he called, keeping his voice low.

"I'm behind a tree, close by you. Now lower your spear and I'll step out into the light. Just don't do anything I might regret. I told you. I'm Maddie, the Ranger."

He continued to probe the darkness, but still saw nothing. After a few seconds, he lowered the point of his spear and stood up from his crouch.

"All right," he said. "Step out and let me see you. But no tricks."

Pushing her cloak and cowl back, she stepped quietly out into the open, her bow slung over her shoulder and both hands extended to the sides to show that she carried no weapons. She saw the man relax as he recognized her.

He shook his head. "By Orlog's earlobes, you startled me!" he said, an admiring tone in his voice. "How did you get so close without me seeing you?"

She shrugged. "We're trained for that sort of thing," she said. "All right if I come forward now?"

"Yes! Yes! By all means," he told her, beckoning with the

hand that held the spear for her to move toward him. She did so, being careful not to move too quickly, letting him get a good look at her.

"Sorry about that," she said. "But I couldn't really blunder through the trees for everyone to hear, could I?"

He grinned at her. "No. I suppose not. Just don't tell the others that I never saw you till you called out. I'll be a laughingstock."

She smiled. "It'll be our secret," she said. "Where's Hal?"

"He'll be in that smaller tent on the left," he said, pointing again with the spear. Most of the men slept in a large tent consisting of a tarpaulin stretched over a center ridgepole. Hal, as the leader of the force, was entitled to a tent by himself and, knowing how much his comrades snored, he inevitably took advantage of the fact. Maddie nodded her thanks and set out toward the camp. A few of the Skandians looked up at her curiously as she passed, no doubt wondering where she had sprung from. She nodded greetings to them and continued on her way, unchallenged.

As she came closer to the smaller tent, the flaps were thrown back and Hal emerged, bending from the waist to negotiate the low opening. He saw her and his face lit up with a smile.

"You're back," he said. "We wondered where you got to."

"Gilan thought it would be better if I waited till it was dark before I came back," she said.

He nodded. "Very wise. So did you set a time for the attack?"

"Tomorrow, mid-morning. Does that give you time to get ready?"

"Plenty. The men are getting bored sitting here doing nothing."

"Good. We'll set out just after dawn so we're in position in plenty of time." She glanced at the small cook fire and the battered coffeepot resting in the glowing embers beside it. "Now, if you'll pour me a cup of coffee, I'll go over the plan with you."

22

THREE DAYS PASSED BEFORE DIMON'S PATIENCE, ALREADY worn thin, finally gave out.

It hadn't been an easy time for him and his men. Forced to stay quiet and give no sign that they were still concealed in the castle, they had been largely confined to the big room on the fourth floor of the south tower, where the arched bridge connected to the keep. Conscious that Cassandra and her men commanded a clear overview of the courtyard and the bridge, they couldn't access the keep tower or the courtyard without being seen from above.

Nor could they move along the battlements to the gatehouse or the east tower. Those were also exposed to view from above. Plus, they needed to be on hand to intercept Cassandra and her men when they attempted to leave their refuge in the south tower.

So they waited impatiently, keeping as quiet as possible—for any sound might carry up the stairwell to the floors above. It created an intense strain on Dimon and his men. They crept around as quietly as they could. At night, they could show no light through the lower windows, in case it was seen from above.

Any dropped weapon or utensil was met with a whispered savaging from their commander. As a result, tempers frayed and nerves were stretched to breaking point. Fights and quarrels broke out, but the demand for silence and stealth meant that these couldn't be resolved, so bad blood among the attackers grew by the day.

From time to time, either Cassandra or Ingrid would climb stealthily down the hidden stairs and peer through the spyhole at the fourth floor. The young lady's maid enjoyed this activity enormously. She derived great pleasure from the sight of the Red Foxes trying to remain silent.

"They're like great clumsy oxen," she told Cassandra, with a broad grin on her face. "They tiptoe around, tripping over their own huge feet. And if anybody makes a noise, he gets yelled at by Dimon for his carelessness—in a whisper, of course."

Cassandra smiled in return. "Which usually makes more noise than the original offense."

Ingrid nodded. "It seems nothing is louder than someone trying to curse in a whisper," she said. She thought for a few seconds. "When should we let him know that we're aware he hasn't left?"

Cassandra shook her head. "We won't. Let him figure it out for himself. The longer he sits waiting for us to come down, the more time Horace and Maddie have to get back here and give him a nasty surprise." She smiled to herself. She might be a prisoner in the tower, but for the moment, Dimon was every bit as confined as she was. The fact appealed to her sense of irony.

Finally, however, Dimon admitted to himself that his ruse had failed. Eschewing any further stealth, he crossed the bridge to the keep and climbed to the highest floor, standing by the window from which he had previously observed his enemy. He leaned out, studying the ninth-floor balcony above him. There was nobody visible there, so he cupped his hands around his mouth and shouted.

"Cassandra!"

He withdrew, wary of the archers under her command. He stood well back from the window, in the shadow of the room, where he could still watch the balcony. There was no sign of movement there. He stepped to the window, then shouted once more.

"Cassandra! Show yourself!"

There was a long pause, then a head and shoulders appeared above the parapet. He recognized the princess. Her long hair was uncovered and stirred gently behind her in the breeze that was always present at these higher floors. She looked around, shading her eyes under her hand.

He called again. "Cassandra!"

She looked down and did a double take as she saw him. The movement was exaggerated and he knew she was acting.

"Why, Dimon, is that you?" she said, surprise evident in her voice.

"You know it's me!" he shouted angrily. Even at this distance, he saw her shake her head. He realized that she was using larger-than-normal movements so that he could recognize them, and his anger smoldered inside him.

"But I thought you'd be halfway to Sonderland by now," she said. "What happened? Did you forget something?"

"Yes!" he grated. "I forgot to kill you and your followers. But I'm going to set that right."

She seemed to consider this statement. "How do you

actually plan to do that?" she said eventually. "So far, it hasn't worked out too well for you."

"I've sent for extra men!" he told her. "This time, I'm going to winkle you out of that tower, no matter what it takes."

"You are?" she said calmly, and that calmness infuriated him even more.

"Yes, I am! I'm going to finish this, Cassandra, unless you surrender right away. This is your last chance!"

"I thought last time was my last chance?" she said. "Hadn't you better hurry? After all, you said Horace and Gilan were on their way from the north."

"I lied! They're still trapped in that blasted hill fort, if they aren't dead already! You're on your own—and this time I'm going to finish this business."

Dimon stormed away from the window and, a few minutes later, Cassandra watched him striding back across the bridge to the south tower.

She turned slightly to Ingrid and Merlon, who had been standing back from the parapet, out of sight. "Obviously," she said quietly, "he has no idea that Maddie and the Skandians are on their way to relieve Horace and Gilan. They may even be there already."

Ingrid nodded, but Merlon was frowning.

"I don't like what he said about sending for more men," he said.

Cassandra shrugged. "However many he's got, they can only come up that stairwell three or four at a time."

"Yes. But he's desperate now," Merlon said. "Really desperate. He's likely to try anything, no matter how many men it costs him."

Cassandra considered the statement. "That's true," she said. "We'd better be on our toes."

From the tower below them, the sound of hammering started once more. Cassandra leaned over the parapet, looking down. But of course, she could see nothing.

"Sounds like he's building again," she said. "He's a busy little fellow, isn't he?" She paused. "At least that'll give us some time until he's finished whatever it is."

23

THE SKANDIANS MOVED OUT FROM THEIR CAMP JUST AFTER
dawn, maintaining a slow jog along the path that Maddie had
blazed to the hill fort.

Maddie led the way, with Hal close behind her. Stig, Thorn
and Ingvar were in the rank behind them, and the others followed in two files. There was no talking. These were experienced
raiders and discipline was tight—and strictly enforced. All she
could hear was the rhythmic shuffle of their sealskin boots on
the leaf-mold floor of the forest.

Down among the trees, the light hadn't penetrated fully and
they moved in semi-darkness. But from time to time, when the
tree cover thinned, she could see the sky lightening in the east.
They were making good time and she estimated they would be
in position well before the time of the planned breakout.

Eventually, up ahead, she could see the open ground that led
up to the ridge above the Red Foxes' camp. She held up a hand
and the column came to a halt. Hal had warned the rest of the
men that if anyone disobeyed her signals or orders, they would
have to deal with him. As a result, they obeyed promptly. She
mimed to Hal what they had decided earlier: She would head up

the slope to reconnoiter, making sure there were no enemy patrols who might spot the Skandians moving into position.

Hal nodded and gestured for her to be on her way.

As she ghosted up the slope, the Skandians relaxed on the soft ground. Several of them uncorked water canteens and took long sips. There was no sleeping. Hal knew these men well, and he knew their tendency to snore like wounded walruses. He had gone to great lengths to impress on them that they were not to doze off while they waited for Maddie.

At the other side of the fort, Horace was preparing for the cavalry to sortie.

A five-meter-long ramp had been built from the walkway timbers. It lay ready by the north wall, where a gap had been cut in the palisade. The cut section was held in place by ropes. When the time came, these would be cast off and the section would fall outward, creating a gateway in the wall. Since the floor of the fort was a meter-and-a-half below the outside ground level, they had built an earthen step to provide footing for the horses as they left the fort.

Once the ramp was in place, the troopers would lead their horses down it, then mount and form up on the lower path. They would be seen by the enemy watchers below, of course, but as Gilan had pointed out, it would be too late for them to take any significant action. By the time they could report what the troopers were doing, Horace and his men would be halfway down the hill and in full sight of the enemy camp anyway.

A trooper came forward to report to him. "She's ready to lower, sir."

"Wait for the order," Horace said.

The man nodded. Already, the troopers were leading their mounts into position, ready to leave the fort. One of them was holding the bridle of Horace's battlehorse, Stamper. Horace would be the first man out of the fort when the time came.

He glanced at the sun. It was nearly time. He walked quickly now to the south wall and mounted the stairs to the ramparts. Gilan was leaning against the frame of the gate, studying the enemy camp below and the ridgeline farther out.

"Any sign of Maddie yet?" Horace asked.

The Ranger shook his head. "We should see her signal any time now," he told the tall warrior. "Maddie knows how important it is to stay ahead of the schedule."

Once they knew Maddie and her Skandians were in position on the southern ridge, they would begin the attack. She would signal to them with a flashing light—the sun reflected off a small polished-metal mirror. Their reply would be a horn blast. When she heard that, she'd know they were lowering the ramp into place. A few minutes after that, the south gate would open and Gilan would lead the archers out.

"There!" said Gilan, pointing suddenly to the ridge, where a light was flashing.

"Signal from the hill, sir!" called one of the sentries.

Gilan waved a hand in acknowledgment. "I've seen it. Well done." He grinned at Horace. "Time we heard how musical you can be."

"Hah!" snorted Horace. He took the horn from his belt, raised it to his lips and blew a mighty blast on it.

Gilan winced. "Not at all, apparently."

The light flashed one more time from the ridge.

"She heard it," Horace said.

Gilan frowned at him. "They probably heard it at Castle Araluen."

Horace ignored him and turned toward the stairs. "Let's get that ramp down," he said.

The archers were already assembling by the south gate. Six of them carried long ropes coiled over their shoulders—an idea Gilan had borrowed from the attackers several nights before. They would anchor them at the top of the hill and the men would use them to keep their footing on the slippery grass slope. He glanced around the ramparts now, catching the attention of the archers on duty there as sentries.

"Time to go, men," he called. "Get down to the gate."

There was a clatter of feet as the sentries hurried down the stairs from the walkway and formed up with the rest of their companions by the south gate. Gilan signaled to one of the men in the lead file, who stepped forward and raised the locking bar on the gate. The two halves moved apart a few inches. The archer looked at Gilan, a question on his face, but the Ranger shook his head, looking around to see the progress Horace's group was making at the north wall.

"Not yet," Gilan said.

As he watched, the cavalrymen released the ropes that held the cut section of the wall in place and shoved at it with long poles. It moved a few inches, stopped, then moved again as the troopers pushed harder. It swayed for several seconds, then fell outward with a resounding crash. Half a dozen men took hold of the ramp and ran it out through the gap in the wall, setting it down so the end overhung the edge of the path. They shoved it outward, until gravity took hold and the end tipped, falling to rest on the next terrace down.

Horace took hold of Stamper's bridle and led the horse as he scrambled up the earth step to ground level, then out through the newly made gap in the palisade wall.

"Come on, boy," he said.

Stamper's ears twitched nervously. He hesitated at the edge of the makeshift timber ramp, but Horace's firm hand on his bridle reassured him and he stepped onto the ramp, clip-clopping carefully down, head held low to watch where he was going. Horace felt the ramp vibrate as the next trooper followed him with his horse, then the next.

Stamper scrambled down the last meter or so, legs braced and moving clumsily until his hooves felt firm earth beneath them. He whinnied triumphantly, then followed Horace as he led the horse away from the ramp to a clear spot where the others could form up behind him.

Moving two at a time, the other troopers led their horses down the ramp. In five minutes, they were all assembled on the second tier of the path. At a signal from Horace, they swung up into their saddles, and he led the way down the spiraling track. Looking to the bottom of the hill, he saw two of the watchers who had been stationed there running to inform their commander at the main camp that the Araluen cavalry was coming out. He smiled grimly. They had a lot of ground to cover and he could see that he and his men would be in position on the southern face of the hill before the watchers reached the Red Foxes' camp.

Seeing the last of the cavalry leading their horses out through the gap, Gilan turned back to the archer at the unbarred gate.

"Open up," he ordered, and the man shoved against the two gates, pushing them wide-open. Gilan led the rest of the force out through the gate.

"Get those ropes fastened," he said.

Six men hammered pegs into the ground, then tied off the ends of the long coils of rope they were carrying. That done, they tossed the ropes downhill, watching them uncoil as they sailed through the air.

"Take hold," Gilan ordered.

The group of archers split into six files, moving to take a firm grip on the ropes, then beginning the descent. The long grass was slippery and the footing was treacherous, but the ropes kept them steady and stopped them falling. They half ran, half slid down the terrace to the second level of the path, then continued over the edge of that section and on downward.

Vikor Trask was resting in his pavilion. He had risen at dawn, as usual, to check on the hill fort and make sure the enemy were making no attempt to leave. Satisfied that the situation was unchanged, he had breakfasted, then returned to his pavilion to catch up on the sleep his early rising had cost him.

Now he was brought rudely back to wakefulness by the breathless arrival of one of his men, who shoved past the sentry outside the tent and hurled back the canvas door flap. The noise startled Trask, who sat up blearily on his camp bed.

"What is it?" he said angrily. He disliked being disturbed, and his men had strict orders not to enter his tent without permission. But the man's words soon dispelled his momentary annoyance, replacing it with a jolt of alarm and fear.

"General, they're coming out! It's an attack! The enemy are coming out of the fort!"

Trask threw his legs over the side of the bed and rose rapidly, fastening his shirt and looking around for his sword belt. Finding it, he buckled it around his waist, belatedly hauled on his boots, hopping awkwardly around the sleeping chamber as he did so. He grabbed the messenger by the arm to regain his balance.

"How many? Where are they?"

The man grabbed his arm in return and began dragging him toward the doorway. "Looks like all of them. The archers, anyway. They're coming out the main gate."

They blundered out into the open, Trask shielding his eyes from the mid-morning glare of the sun. He hurried to a vantage point close to his tent that commanded a view of the hill fort above them. He peered up the hill, and his heart began to race as he saw the group of armed men emerging from the gate, throwing ropes down the hill and beginning to descend to the next level of the track. He estimated there were about a score of them, which he knew to be the full complement of archers under Horace's command. But where were the cavalry? He looked urgently left and right and saw no sign of them.

Then a file of horsemen appeared, riding around the contour of the slope, already at the third level down from the fort. Twenty of them too, he estimated. He turned to the messenger who had woken him.

"Sound the alarm!" he shouted, and the man raced away to find a bugler. A few seconds later, the strident notes of the alarm call blared out and men began to spill from their tents, pulling on their armor and helmets, buckling swords around their waists. One of his subordinate commanders ran up to him.

"What are your orders, General?"

Trask hesitated, then indicated a line across the front of their camp, at the base of the slope. "Form a shield wall there," he said. "Two ranks. We'll let them come to us."

The commander saluted and ran off, shouting orders. Gradually, the milling mass of men began to form themselves into some sort of order, pushed and shoved into position by their sergeants and corporals. They moved into two ranks, shields locked together, spears set at an angle, facing the enemy uphill, with forty men in each rank. The remaining twenty or so men grouped themselves around Trask, as a mobile reserve. If part of the shield wall was threatened, they would provide support and reinforcement.

Still the archers swarmed down the terraces of the hill. On the right wing, the cavalrymen urged their horses, stiff legged against the slope, down to the final level, which was one terrace up from the base of the hill where the rapidly formed shield wall stood waiting. Ten troopers halted there, threatening the right wing. The others continued to move around the south face of the hill until they had joined the archers. They wheeled their horses around to face downhill. Only one gently sloping section of grass now separated them from the Red Fox force.

Trask glanced nervously from one group to the other. The ten mounted men, lances held vertically, remained threatening the right wing of his force. The combined group of archers and troopers faced the center of his shield wall. He heard one of his officers calling orders on the right and saw the right-hand end of the shield wall pivot back through ninety degrees, like a gate moving on a hinge, so that they stood square on to the troopers, facing them directly with shields and spears.

He heard a whisper of noise from the archers facing his center, then the scraping sound of arrows being released from their bows, and the first arrow storm was on its way.

"Shields up!" shouted the officer commanding the center of

the wall. The shields rattled and clashed together as the men raised them to deflect the arrows. Trask suddenly realized he was unarmored. He grabbed the nearest soldier by the arm and shoved him in the direction of his tent, stripping the man's shield from him as he did so.

"Get my armor!" he ordered, and the man ran off to do his bidding. Trask slipped the shield over his left arm and raised it to cover his head and upper body.

He was not a moment too soon. A second later, he staggered as an arrow slammed into the shield. It struck slightly off center and nearly tore the shield from his arm. He regained his balance and lowered the shield to look uphill. The archers were releasing another volley. Hastily, he raised the shield again, hearing cries of pain from his men in the shield wall as arrows found their way through the gaps and struck home. His mouth dried as he realized this would be the final confrontation. The enemy had committed all their men to this fight.

Then he calmed himself. He had them outnumbered by three to one. He'd lose some men, he knew. The enemy were skilled fighters. But sheer force of numbers would see him through. And with their entire force committed, the Araluens could do nothing to surprise him.

He smiled. Now all he had to do was make sure he stayed well clear of the fighting.

24

ON THE RIDGE ABOVE THE ENEMY CAMP, MADDIE LAY IN THE long grass and watched the opposing forces form up.

Her heart was racing. The Araluen force looked pitifully small against the Red Fox numbers. She could recognize her father at the head of the small group of troopers who stood ready at the right wing of the enemy's line. She saw a section of the shield wall angle back to face them. She licked her lips. They were dry with tension. Her father and ten men were facing probably forty enemy soldiers in a secure line, protected by shields and armed with spears. She scanned the enemy lines, seeing the smaller command group some distance behind the shield wall.

So far, she thought nervously, the enemy didn't seem to be making any mistakes—although the deployment of a shield wall was an absolutely basic tactic and involved no complex maneuvering.

As far as she could see, nobody in the enemy camp was looking back up the hill behind them. Everyone's attention was riveted on the archers and cavalrymen facing them.

She heard the whimper of arrows rushing through the air as the archers started shooting. Men in the Red Fox force began to fall. Now there was no way anyone was looking in her direction. She rose to a crouch, looked back at the waiting Skandians, and signaled them forward.

The sea wolves rose from where they were crouched in the long grass covering the hillside and moved forward. As they did, they moved into a wedge-shaped formation, with Thorn at its head and Hal and Stig close behind him. Then four more men followed, then six, and so on, with each successive line growing longer, so that the moving group, if it had been viewed from above, would have resembled a triangular wedge. Maddie waited until they had reached the crest of the ridge and motioned them to continue. She fell in close beside Hal. As they drew closer to the enemy, she would look for a good vantage point, from which she could cover Ingvar.

The Skandian formation moved down the hill at a fast walk, the rustle of long grass around their legs the only sound they made. Thorn ensured that all of them had secured their weapons and equipment so that they didn't rattle or clank or let out any other telltale noise.

Still, none of the Red Fox soldiers noticed the danger behind them.

But Gilan could clearly see them moving down the hill. He drew his sword and raised it above his head.

"Archers, rapid shooting!" he shouted, then, circling his sword in the air, he called, "Troopers! Forward!"

The cavalrymen had dismounted. Charging on horseback down the steep grassy slope would be too dangerous. The men would fight on foot. In each group of five, one trooper was assigned as a horse holder, keeping the horses ready for the time when the enemy broke and ran, and the cavalry could pursue them.

The men in the shield wall saw the small group of dismounted troopers advancing. They shouted a roar of defiance and brandished their weapons above their heads—swords, spears and axes, gleaming in the sun.

It was a mistake. As they raised their weapons, they inadvertently allowed their shields to drop. The archers were quick to seize the advantage offered and began to pour arrow after arrow into the gaps where the Red Fox warriors were exposed. Men screamed and fell as the cruel warheads slammed into them, penetrating mail coats and ripping into the bodies behind them. Half a dozen men in the front rank went down.

"Keep your shields up!" a sergeant yelled, and the gaps in the shield wall were quickly closed. At the same time, men from the second rank stepped forward to fill the place where their comrades had fallen. Once again, the shield wall was intact.

Now the troopers started to run, their shields up and their long lances held ready over their shoulders. As they came within range, they stabbed forward with the lances, staying out of the reach of most of the weapons of the men in the front row of the shield wall.

There was a series of resounding crashes as the lance points, with the impetus of the running troopers behind them, smashed into the shields, staggering the men in the front rank. The Foxes were ready for it, however, and the second rank leaned their weight into the backs of the men in front of them, straightening the line and holding them steady against the troopers' attack. Some of the lances penetrated, forcing their way between the shields, hitting bodies, legs and arms.

As the two struggling forces met, the archers, on a command, ran quickly to their right, so they could shoot without fear of hitting their own comrades. Once again, the deadly hail of arrows began to bring down men in the shield wall. As the angry Red Fox warriors turned to face this new threat, they exposed themselves to the darting, jabbing thrusts of the lances. Hastily, they swung back to face their original attackers.

On the Foxes' right flank, the section commander watched the small but dangerous group of motionless horsemen warily. So far, they had made no move. But he knew that as soon as he turned his men to aid their comrades in the center of the line, the enemy cavalry would charge into their exposed backs.

Back in his command position, well out of the fight, Vikor Trask watched anxiously. The crash of contact, the clash of steel on steel and the cries of wounded and dying men echoed across the field. He had no idea how to counter the implacable storm of arrows that was whittling down the numbers of his men. He had never faced a disciplined, concentrated force of archers on the battlefield before. He watched in horrified fascination as their flights of arrows darkened the sky, seeming to pour into the ranks of his men without cease. Many of them, of course, were stopped by the shields. But a lot were making it through the wall, or over it, as the archers raised their aiming point and directed a plunging barrage onto his men.

As the Red Foxes raised their shields to protect themselves from the plunging arrows, they exposed themselves to the lances and swords of the attacking troopers. The line took a pace backward. Then another.

"Hold position! Hold your line!" Trask yelled, his voice cracking with the strain. He didn't know what his men should do, what orders to issue. But he knew if they began to fall back, the order and cohesion of the shield wall would collapse, and they would be exposed to the vengeful lances of the troopers, and the murderous, plunging arrow storm.

He glanced fearfully at the threat of those ten cavalrymen on the right, still motionless, still waiting for the right moment to launch their attack.

Then, from behind him, he heard a mighty voice booming. "Let's get 'em!"

Trask wasn't to know it, but it was the celebrated battle cry of the Heron brotherband, and it issued from Thorn's powerful chest and lungs. It was a voice that was trained to bellow commands above the noise of the fiercest storm at sea. On this sunlit hillside, it carried clearly to Trask's ears—and those of the men around him.

As one, they turned to see a wedge-shaped formation of Skandians—recognizable by their sheepskin jackets, their huge round shields and their brass helmets, many adorned with ox horns—plunging down the hill toward them. At their head, barely thirty meters away, was a huge, white-haired figure, whose right arm seemed to end in a massive wooden club. Just behind him were two other warriors—one tall and broad shouldered and swinging a mighty ax around his head, the other slighter, slimmer and wielding a sword, with a kite-shaped shield on his left arm. Behind him was a terrifying figure, towering over the others, and with his eyes concealed behind two black tortoiseshell circles, which gave them the appearance of empty eye sockets. He carried a pole weapon, with a head that combined a spearpoint, ax and hook. He whirled it around his head, seeking a target.

The plunging mass of Skandians bypassed Trask's raised vantage point and smashed into the rear of his shield wall with a resounding crash of metal.

The white-haired warrior flailed back and forth with the mighty club that seemed to be part of his arm, scattering his enemies, sending them flying. The thud of his weapon striking home was sickening to the ear. It could be heard clearly above the bellowed battle cries and the screams of those who fell before his terrible onslaught.

Beside him, the tall warrior's ax dealt death at every blow. Like the white-haired club wielder, he scattered the men trying to face him, bludgeoning a trail through the line. And at the same time, the third member of the wedge point was fighting with studied control, his glittering sword point darting forward like a striking snake, sending his opponents sinking to their knees as they stared with horror at the flashing sword.

The black-eyed giant with the triple-headed weapon was wreaking havoc as well. Diverging from his comrades, he used the hook to jerk men off balance, then dispatched them with either a spear thrust or the ax head.

Trask saw that two of his men had worked their way behind the giant, their swords poised to strike him from behind. Suddenly, one of them reared up in agony, clutching vainly at an arrow that had magically appeared between his shoulder blades. The other, seeing his comrade's fate, turned to look up the hill, just as a second arrow smashed into his chest, punching through the mail shirt he wore and dropping him to the ground. The giant seemed not to notice, but Trask turned and looked behind him.

Forty meters back up the hill, a slim, cloaked figure stood on a large rock, a bow in his hand. As Trask watched, the bowman quickly nocked another arrow, raised the bow, drew and shot in one smooth, continuous movement. Turning to follow the arrow's flight, Trask saw yet another of his men go down.

As the discipline of his shield wall collapsed under the assaults from front and rear, Trask's men began to mill aimlessly, looking for an escape. Then a horn blasted out on the right, and the small body of cavalry that had been waiting there started to move. They trotted at first, then cantered, then went to a full gallop, slamming into the disorganized shield wall, scattering men left and right, rearing their horses to strike out at the men who faced them, discarding shattered lances in favor of sword and axes as they cut about them, leaning to either side out of their saddles.

It was the final straw for the Red Fox force. Their shield wall was broken, their cohesion and mutual support was gone. The ten cavalrymen who had stood in reserve now drove their horses into the disorganized ranks from the right wing, cutting, stabbing and smashing as they came. The Red Foxes began to withdraw to the left, but found themselves confronted by the screaming, merciless Skandians who had forced their way through to the middle of their line. The Red Foxes wavered, broke into small groups, threw down their weapons and ran, running to the eastern side, where there was no force in place to stop them, knowing there was no future in trying to surrender to the Skandians, now that the fury of battle had seized them.

As the broken force ran, Gilan's archers began to shoot again, cutting the enemy down as they tried to escape. Then, at a shouted order, the troopers who had attacked the center of the line raced back up the hill to where their horse holders waited. They mounted and set off after the running, demoralized army, gradually riding them down, their swords and axes rising and falling in a remorseless rhythm.

Trask looked around, his eyes wild and desperate. There was a saddled horse standing nearby, belonging to one of his men who had been detailed to carry messages. The man ran to his horse now, but Trask was too quick for him. Before the man could lay his hand on the bridle, Trask's sword took him from the back and he fell, clutching impotently at the deadly wound.

Trask swung up into the saddle, his sword still in his hand, and hauled the panicking horse's head around to the south. The way out was behind him—up the hill and over the ridge. He kicked his heels into the horse's ribs, sawing at the bridle, and forced the animal into a terrified run, heading up the shallow slope.

As the frightened horse gradually settled into a lumbering gallop, Trask noticed the slim figure in the cloak once more. Now, he realized dully, it wasn't a man. It was a young woman. And she had set her bow down while she took what looked like a length of cord from her belt. She stepped down from the rock outcrop where she had been standing and moved to intercept his path up the hill.

"So much the worse for you," he snarled, although she couldn't hear him. He set himself, raising the sword high over his head and standing in the stirrups, ready to cut her down. She made no move to evade him and he smiled cruelly. She was barely twenty meters away, standing side on, her right arm back behind her, her left leg advanced. He wondered what she was doing, then dismissed the thought. It didn't matter. Any second now, she'd be dead.

He heard someone yelling—an inarticulate, wordless sound of anger and fury—and realized that it was him. Then the girl's right arm snapped forward and she stepped onto her left foot, bringing something whipping up and over her head.

A fraction of a second later, he felt a thundering impact on his helmet, right in the center of his forehead. There was a loud *CLANG!*

Vaguely, he felt himself topple backward from the saddle and crash onto the soft grass. Then everything went black.

Maddie stepped forward and stirred the stunned figure with the toe of her boot, returning the sling to its place under her belt. "You're not worth wasting an arrow on," she said.

25

LATE IN THE AFTERNOON, TWO CROSSBOWMEN INCHED their way around the curve in the stairway just below the gap in the south tower stairs. Once in position, they began to shoot bolts from their crossbows at the narrow gap on the right-hand side of the barricade wall that Cassandra's men had erected on their side of the missing section of stairway. The bolts whipped through the gap, the first of them narrowly missing one of the defenders who were keeping watch. The others hastily drew back out of the line of sight, sheltered by the curve of the stairwell wall. One of Cassandra's archers stepped out onto the stairs and shot a few arrows in return. But his shots were rushed, and he was shooting blindly down the stairs through the narrow gap. As far as he could tell, his shafts had no effect.

"Save your arrows," the corporal in command of the sentries told him.

Reluctantly, the archer agreed and stepped back.

The corporal peered cautiously around the gap, then rapidly jerked back as another crossbow bolt flashed through, catching the edge of the gap and ricocheting wildly inside the eighth floor.

"Get back out of range," he said, gesturing to the men nearby.

Those bolts that did penetrate the gap tended to fly wildly, skidding and skittering off the walls and spinning end over end in all directions. Cassandra, summoned by a messenger, arrived to see what was going on. A soldier handed her a long shield and she slipped it over her arm before she approached the doorway to the stairs. The corporal, crouching behind a shield of his own, waved a hand warning her to come no farther.

"What's happening?" Cassandra asked, flinching as another bolt shrieked off the stonework and spun away into the stairwell. She raised her shield a few centimeters higher.

"A couple of crossbowmen," the corporal told her. "They're making a nuisance of themselves, shooting through the gap here, as you can see."

They both ducked as another bolt flashed through the gap. This one struck no obstruction and continued across the room, eventually thudding into the door of a weapons cabinet.

"Anyone hurt?" Cassandra asked.

The corporal shook his head. "Not so far. Jeremy got a nasty fright when the first shot came through the gap, but they're shooting at random and as long as we stay well back, we should be safe enough."

Cassandra was silent for several seconds, wondering what Dimon was up to. There seemed to be no point to the current attack, other than the vague chance that one of her men might be struck by a random shot. She shrugged. As the corporal said, the attack seemed to be of nuisance value only. Perhaps it was a measure of Dimon's frustration at his inability to winkle her out of her retreat, she thought. All the same, she felt an uneasy stirring in the pit of her stomach. Dimon usually didn't do anything without a good reason. But for the life of her, she couldn't see what that could be in this case.

Ten minutes passed and there were no more shots. She ventured a quick look around the edge of the barricade. The stairway below was empty. The crossbowmen had withdrawn, presumably frustrated that their shots had had no effect on the defenders.

"Put the sentries back in position," she told the corporal.

He nodded, then turned to call to two of his men. Their view through the narrow gap was restricted and they couldn't see the extreme outer side of the stairway. But they'd be able to see any major attack forming up.

Cassandra waited a few more minutes, her suspicions unresolved. Then she decided she was achieving nothing by remaining here. "Stay sharp," she cautioned. "Let me know if you see or hear anything unusual." Then she turned away and headed for the stairs to the eighth floor above them.

Neither she or the corporal was aware that, in addition to their seemingly wild shooting, the crossbowmen had shot eight bolts into the woodwork of the barricade, at varying heights and widths across the timber.

In the small hours of the morning, working in darkness, four of Dimon's men placed a narrow plank bridge across the gap in the stairway. The plank was on the outer edge of the stairwell, where the defenders' vision was limited. The two sentries on duty were taking it in turns to keep watch through the gap, but neither of them noticed the plank inching its way across nor did they see the four men who crossed it, moving almost silently. Any noise they might have made was drowned by the raucous singing of their comrades farther down the stairs. It had been going on for hours.

"They sound happy enough," one sentry said to the other, yawning prodigiously. He had been on duty for three-and-a-half hours now. His relief was due in half an hour. He was tired, cold and hungry. As a result, his concentration was lowered—which was why the attackers had chosen this time of the early morning.

Pressed hard against the rough timber of the barricade, with the yawning drop into the stairwell at their backs, the four men inched their way across the stairway, using the deeply embedded crossbow bolts as handholds. Each of them was burdened with two oil bladders, similar to the ones that the trebuchet had flung at the tower a few days before. The contents gurgled as the men moved across the barricade.

When they were in position, they hung the oil bladders from the crossbow bolts, setting them carefully in position, making sure the bolts were firmly embedded and wouldn't pull loose under the weight. Then, when all eight oil sacks were in position, hanging against the barricade, they made their way back to the plank bridge, crossed to the lower side and hauled the bridge back after them. One at a time, they withdrew back down the stairs to the lower levels. Shortly afterward, the singing died away.

On the eighth floor, the sentries yawned. "Where's our relief?" one of them asked.

"Late—as usual," his companion replied. He shrugged himself into a more comfortable position, then leaned forward to peer through the gap between the barricade and the stone wall.

"Nothing happening out there," he said morosely.

✦ ✦ ✦

Born out of desperation, and his mounting frustration at his inability to dislodge Cassandra from her tower retreat, this would be Dimon's most determined attack to date.

He had recruited an extra thirty-five men from members of the Red Fox Clan—fresh troops from the surrounding countryside who so far had not been involved in the attack on the castle. He called them together now in the vast hallway on the fourth floor.

"This time," he said, "we will drive Cassandra out of her tower. Or we'll kill her in the attempt. I'm not going to pretend that it'll be easy. She's a wily enemy and she has some good men with her. But I will pay a sum of five thousand royals to the men who win this battle for me."

He paused for effect, listening to the murmur that ran around the room. It was a huge amount, more money than most of them could dream of or even imagine. But it was worthwhile. It would keep them motivated, keep them forcing their way upward and forward as the men around them fell and died.

And while it was a massive amount, it didn't matter to him. If they succeeded, he would have the throne—and access to the vast riches that went with it.

"In a few minutes, we'll ignite the bladders hanging on the barricade wall. We'll set them alight with fire arrows. Once the wood is well alight, we'll put our new bridge in position and attack across it. Some of you won't survive this attack . . ." He saw his troops looking round at one another, wondering which of them would die in the next few hours. With the sublime confidence of fighting men, none of them expected to be among those who fell.

"But for those who do, it'll mean fewer to share those five thousand royals."

There were wolfish grins at those words. Every man there knew that he would be among the survivors. And every man there knew that he would be rich. Who cared how many of the others died? That simply meant more for those who lived.

"All right. Get yourselves ready. Full armor. Shields and helmets. They'll try to stop us before we get a foothold on the other side. Don't let them. Keep moving. Keep thrusting forward. Those behind, shove the man in front of you to keep him going. If he falls, take his place. Once the barricade has burned through, shove it out of the way. No quarter. No mercy. We need to get this done. Questions?"

One man raised his hand and Dimon pointed to him.

"Will you be leading us, lord?" the man asked, with a sardonic grin.

Dimon had been half expecting the question. He raised an eyebrow at the man. "I'd be entitled to a commander's share if I did. That'd be a quarter of the money. Do you really want to share with me?"

There was a rumble of laughter from the assembled men. "I thought not," Dimon said when it died down. "Anything else?"

Another man spoke without raising his hand. "Won't Lady Cassandra be able to flood the burning barricade from the upper-floor cisterns?"

Dimon shook his head. "The water from the cisterns would flow down the steps at floor level. There's no provision to divert it over the top of the barricade."

The man nodded, along with several of his companions. Dimon waited a few moments to see if there were more questions. There weren't. The men were already spending those five thousand royals in their minds.

"All right," he said, pointing to the door that led to the stairway. "Let's get moving."

On the eighth floor, the men on sentry duty heard the sound of heavy boots on the stone stairs below them—a lot of heavy boots.

"Stand to!" called Merlon, who happened to be taking his turn as commander of the sentries. "Jerrod! Go fetch Lady Cassandra."

The young lad he pointed to nodded and sprinted toward the stairs leading to the ninth floor. The others hastily gathered their weapons. The measured tramp of feet on the steps grew louder as the enemy approached.

"Ready, lads," said Merlon. "Spearmen to the front."

With the barricade in position, there was little for the archers to do. Merlon expected a straightforward attack across the gap in the stairs and, to counter that, spears were the better choice.

Then the crossbowmen were back, standing well down the stairs, concealed by the curving stone wall. They began shooting, sending their bolts slamming into the oil sacks, so that the sticky mixture of oil and pitch flooded out and saturated the timbers of the barricade. Once all eight bladders were split, the crossbowmen switched to bolts with oil-soaked rags wrapped around their heads. Men on either side of them leaned in with flaming torches and ignited the rags, and the crossbowmen shot into the glutinous oily mix on the barricade.

The flames flickered, then flared wildly as the oil and pitch took fire. Within seconds, the barricade was a wall of flames, and thick, choking black smoke boiled up over the top of the timber wall, filling the stairwell behind it.

The crossbowmen ceased shooting, standing ready to counter any move from the defenders above them. As they waited, men began to swarm up the stairs below them, carrying sections of a new bridge that would completely fill the gap in the stairs.

It was in three pieces. Under cover of the thick clouds of smoke, they placed them side by side across the gap, linking them together so that they formed one solid floor.

Merlon covered his face against the choking smoke. At that moment, Cassandra came running from the ninth floor. She took one look at the barricade, where flames were visible, licking hungrily through the gaps in the timber. She touched Merlon's arm.

"What's happening, Merlon?"

The grizzled old soldier met her gaze, then pulled away. "I'll take a look," he said, pushing through the narrow gap at the side. Cassandra reached out to grab him and pull him back.

"No!" she shouted. "Don't—"

At that moment, a freak eddy of wind cleared the smoke clouds from the barricade for a few seconds. One of the crossbowmen, standing ready down the stairs, saw the gray-headed sergeant leaning out through the gap between the barricade and the stone wall, raised his weapon and shot.

"They've got a bridge across the—"

Then the crossbow bolt hit him and he reared back, falling dead at Cassandra's feet.

26

Gradually, the cavalrymen returned to the site of the battle, their horses weary and streaked with sweat and foam, their swords and axes red with the blood of their fleeing enemies.

"A few of them got away into the woods," the lieutenant in charge reported to Horace. The commander had dismounted after sending his ten men to join their comrades in pursuit of the defeated enemy.

"How many?" Horace asked.

The lieutenant beckoned to an orderly nearby for a water canteen. He drank deeply, then shrugged. "Hard to tell," he said. "Maybe twenty. But they were broken up and disorganized. They ran in all directions once they made it to the trees."

"And the others?"

The cavalry officer grimaced. "They didn't make it to the trees."

Horace nodded, understanding. Infantry fleeing before mounted cavalry had little chance of survival, he knew. He made his way through the dead and wounded enemies who had fallen before the triple assault. He could see Thorn's massive form, standing with Hal and Stig. The old, one-armed sea wolf looked inordinately cheerful, he thought. But then, Thorn always loved a battle. He and Stig were talking eagerly, describing to each other the deeds they had performed during the fight.

Hal, by contrast, was somewhat pale and grim faced. No matter how many battles he fought, he could never become totally accustomed to the dreadful bloodshed that ensued. Horace dropped a hand on his shoulder, and the skirl turned, recognized him and smiled.

"Thanks," Horace said. "You arrived in the nick of time. I owe you. We all do," he added, indicating his men, standing in small groups talking or resting on the ground. Their small number of troops designated as healers were moving through the ranks of wounded Red Fox warriors, giving them what aid they could with their limited resources.

"There are no debts between friends," Hal said simply.

Stig and Thorn pounded Horace on the back enthusiastically. "Nice charge, your knightship," Thorn said. He delighted in mangling the correct titles of Araluen nobility. "You scattered them like ninepins."

"There weren't many left to scatter after you wild men got among them," Horace told him. He looked with interest at the massive club fastened to the stump of Thorn's right arm. He had heard of the weapon before, but had never seen it in action. "I wouldn't like to face that thing," he said.

Stig grinned. "Very few people do," he told the tall knight. Then Gilan joined them and they all called greetings to him. The Ranger Commandant had sailed with the Herons on several occasions in the past and they knew him well.

"Glad we could pull your irons out of the fire," Thorn told him cheerfully. "What do we do now?"

"Now," Gilan told him, "we head back to Castle Araluen and twist Dimon's tail for him."

Thorn smiled wolfishly. "I think I'd enjoy that," he said. He had met Dimon when they visited the castle some weeks prior, and he hadn't been impressed by the garrison commander then. Now that he had learned of his treachery, and his betrayal of Cassandra—a person Thorn held in high esteem—he thought even less of him.

Gilan was looking around the battlefield. "Did anyone see what became of their leader?" he asked. He wasn't concerned with the fact that twenty or so of the enemy had escaped into the forest. But if their leader was at large, there was always the chance he could rally them, and the idea of leaving twenty organized armed men behind them didn't appeal.

"He ran," said a voice from behind him. He turned and saw Maddie threading her way through the crowd, greeting the men from the two wolfship crews as she came. They seemed to be quite fond of her, Gilan thought. One of them, Ingvar, the giant warrior with black tortoiseshell circles over his eyes, stepped forward and, towering over her, engulfed her in a hug.

"I'm told you shot two of them who got behind me," he said.

Maddie smiled. "My pleasure to do so," she told him. "You seemed pretty busy tearing a great hole in the enemy line."

"Well, if I can't have Lydia here to watch my back, I'm delighted to have you to take her place."

She stepped forward and embraced her father. "Hullo, Dad. Are you all right?" She leaned back and looked with concern at the bloodstains on his chain mail and surcoat. "None of that is yours, is it?"

He smiled reassuringly. "No. I'm fine. Are you all right?" He still wasn't used to the idea that his daughter was a seasoned warrior and was quite at home risking her life on a battlefield like this.

She shrugged. "I wasn't in any danger. Hal kept me well back behind the main fighting."

Horace nodded his gratitude to the Skandian commander, who smiled in return.

"She wasn't that far back," Hal said. "And she saved Ingvar's life twice."

Maddie shrugged diffidently. "If I hadn't, someone else would have swatted them," she said. She realized her father was looking at her with a mixture of awe and nervousness and pride. She wished someone would change the subject. She was accustomed to looking up to her father, not the other way around.

"What about Trask, their leader?" Gilan repeated. He had questioned some of the surviving enemy soldiers to find the man's name.

Maddie switched her gaze to him. "As I said, he tried to run. He deserted his men and rode up the hill there." She indicated the slope where she had been stationed.

Gilan frowned. "So he got away?"

"Not quite. He thought it would be a good idea to ride me down." She paused. "It turned out it wasn't."

"You shot him?" her commandant asked.

She shook her head. "Hit him with my sling. Knocked him cold. He's tied up by that clump of rocks you can see. Thought you might like to take him prisoner," she added, looking back to her father.

"You thought right," Horace said grimly, and suddenly she thought it might have been kinder to the enemy general if she *had* shot him. As an invader, and leader of a rebellion against the crown, Trask would probably pay for his crimes with his life.

"We'll take him back to Castle Araluen for trial," Horace said, as if reading her thoughts. She decided to say no more about the subject. Trask deserved everything he got, she thought. But she didn't have to dwell on his eventual fate. She indicated the enemy soldiers, most of them wounded, who sat or lay on the grass around them.

"What'll we do with this lot?" she asked.

Horace hesitated. That question had been troubling him. "We can't take them with us," he said. "Some of them can't walk and those that can would slow us down."

"And we can't leave our healers to look after them," Gilan put in. "There are too many of them and we need the healers for our own men."

Thankfully, they had suffered relatively few casualties. They had lost two troopers and an archer killed in the battle, and another eight men had been wounded. But even that number would keep their healers busy on the trip back to Castle Araluen. The wounded could travel in the cart, which was still perched at the top of the path, outside the main gate.

"Strip 'em and leave 'em," Thorn said curtly. "They don't deserve anything more." He had no sympathy for mercenaries, and even less for the rebels who put his friends at risk—and Thorn counted Cassandra and her family as his friends.

"How many of them are there?" Horace asked.

Gilan, who had made a count, replied. "About thirty of them here, wounded to one degree or another. And twenty-odd who ran off into the forest. The others we don't have to worry about."

The others were those who had died in the battle or in the ill-fated retreat to the woods. Horace sighed. It wasn't an easy decision that faced him, but then, he thought, he hadn't asked these men to invade his country. Or to rebel against his wife. Finally, he made up his mind.

"Collect their weapons," he said. "All of them—even knives. We'll throw them in the river. I'm not leaving armed men here to cause trouble through the countryside, wounded or not. Then strip them. Leave them with their shirts and trousers. No boots. No coats. They can take shelter in the fort. We'll leave the tents there for them so they won't die of exposure. But they won't be able to travel very far with no boots or weapons or proper clothing. We'll leave them what medical supplies and bandages we can spare and they can take care of one another. That's the best I can do for now."

Maddie looked at him, her head tilted in a question. "For now?"

He nodded. "Once we've finished this business with Dimon, I'll come back and collect them. They can stand trial if they're locals. If they're Sonderlanders, we'll put them ashore on the Iberian coast."

Thorn grunted. "I'd throw them in the river with their weapons."

Gilan grinned at him. "You say you would, you old warhorse," he remarked. "But you're all talk."

"Either way," Hal said, "let's get busy collecting their weapons while they're still in shock. If they recover a little, they might not like the idea."

The troopers, archers and Skandians went to work collecting the weapons from their defeated foes. Horace sent half a dozen troopers out to find weapons discarded during the

headlong retreat to the forest. Once the Red Foxes were disarmed, they were stripped of their armor, outer garments and
boots. They stood or sat shivering in their underclothes, thoroughly dejected. One or two tried to resist, but their former
opponents were fully armed and vengeful and they soon saw that
their protests would be to no avail.

Finally, Horace addressed them. "We're leaving you here.
You're unarmed and some of you are badly injured. We'll leave
you some medical supplies—whatever we can spare. Those who
are not so badly hurt can look after the others. Winter is coming
on and if you try to run you won't get far without warm clothes.
There are tents in the hill fort and we'll leave them there for you.
I suggest you make use of them, and repair the fort walls. The
locals might not take too kindly to having a bunch of would-be
rebels wandering loose. I'll spread the word around the local villages so they'll know you're here—and they'll be on the lookout
for you. It might not be a good idea to try any tricks on them."

One of the lightly wounded men raised a hand. "What will
we eat?"

Horace jerked a hand at the fort once more. "We'll leave
some food for you," he said. "But we need most of it ourselves.
You'll have to forage for whatever else you can find."

"But we could starve," the man complained.

Horace turned a steely gaze on him. "Perhaps you should
have thought of that before you chose this course," he said. "I
really don't have too much sympathy for you. Once we've put
down the rebellion at Castle Araluen, we'll come back and collect you."

He cast his gaze around them. Few raised their eyes to meet
his. They were cowed and miserable, and that was the way he

wanted it. He waited a few more seconds, then concluded. "I suggest you start making your way up to the fort. We'll help the worst cases get up the hill. After that, you're on your own."

Slowly, the defeated men began to straggle up the hillside to the fort. Horace detailed half a dozen troopers to help them. Within an hour, the remnants of the Red Fox army were ensconced inside the fort, squabbling among themselves over the tents that were still pitched there.

Horace and Gilan listened to the arguing. It was obvious that the survivors had divided into two factions—the Sonderland mercenaries and the Araluen rebels. The two friends looked at each other and shrugged.

"There'll be little cooperation among those two groups," Gilan said.

Horace shrugged his broad shoulders. "Not our problem," he replied. "Let's get on the road to Castle Araluen."

27

MADDIE ELECTED TO TRAVEL OVERLAND TO CASTLE ARALUEN with her father and Gilan and their men, while the Skandians returned by ship. The two groups set out the following morning, agreeing to rendezvous at the pier northeast of the castle, where Maddie had first met the crew of the *Heron*. The Skandians headed for the point on the river where they had beached the *Heron*. From there, they would sail back to the coast, turn south and take the River Semath inland once more.

The Araluens struck to the west, looking for a shallow spot where they could ford the river. They found a convenient place seven kilometers away, where the river widened and shallowed. The little force crossed to the south bank once more.

The village of Harnel was located on the north bank close to this spot and Horace sent a messenger, alerting the villagers that the remnants of the defeated Red Fox force were sheltering in the hill fort, and directing the village headman to raise the local militia and take them into custody.

"It'll take at least a week for them to get the militia together," he said to Gilan and Maddie. "But I don't think the Foxes will go anywhere in that time."

"Pity you couldn't have got them to lend a hand sooner," Maddie remarked.

He glanced at her. "We didn't have time. The Foxes were pressing hard on our heels. On top of that, they're not really a trained fighting force and they would have been badly outnumbered by the rebels."

Maddie nodded as she thought of the local militia—mainly farmhands and laborers, unskilled and poorly armed with hoes, pitchforks and axes—facing the mercenaries. In times of war, when the militia was assembled, they were usually equipped and then trained for several weeks by the regular army.

"Will they be able to handle them now?" she asked.

Horace smiled. "The Foxes are injured and they're unarmed. They'll be hungry and cold as well. I imagine they'll be quite glad to be arrested. Particularly if it means they're fed."

They rode on, heading south through the forest, then emerging onto cleared farmland on the second day. Maddie enjoyed the companionship of her father and Gilan. For his part, Horace continued to look at her with some wonder and a certain amount of pride, shaking his head from time to time. He hadn't seen a lot of his daughter over the previous three years and he was impressed by her quiet self-confidence and her skills. Will had taught her well, he thought. But then, who better to teach her?

Gilan did most of the talking. He was eager to hear details of how Maddie had infiltrated the Red Fox Clan's meeting and discovered that Dimon was their leader. She related the details with a Ranger's typical self-deprecation and understatement.

Rangers didn't boast, Horace realized.

Gilan quizzed her about the secret tunnels and stairways inside the castle as well. "I'd always heard there were secret passages in the castle," he said. "But I never met anyone who had seen them. I actually thought they were just a myth."

"They're real enough," Maddie told him. "And just as well they are."

"How did you find them?" he asked.

"I went through the old blueprints and plans of the castle. It was Uldred's idea, actually."

"Uldred?" her father interrupted. "The head librarian?"

"Yes," Maddie replied. "He told me to look for discrepancies in the dimensions of places like the lower dungeon rooms. When I did, I saw that the lower cellar was several meters shorter than the one above it. I hunted around and found a hidden doorway in the end wall. It opened into the room where the tunnel entrances are located."

"Simple when you think of it," Gilan said, shaking his head. "I should have done that myself."

"And how many of these tunnels are there?" Horace asked, his mind going ahead to consider the problems that would face them when they attacked the castle.

"I found three. One is the way in and out of the castle. It goes under the moat and emerges in a clump of trees halfway down the hill to the forest. The second leads to the concealed stairway that goes up the south tower. The stairway is a series of ladders hidden behind a false wall. That was how I managed to reach Mum and make sure she was all right.

"The third one is the most useful for us now. It leads up to the gatehouse, where the mechanisms to raise and lower the drawbridge and the portcullis are located."

Horace nodded thoughtfully. "As you say, that's going to be very useful. But the gatehouse will be well guarded, that's for sure."

"Sure to be," Maddie agreed. "But nothing I can't handle—particularly if I've got a dozen or so wild Skandians backing me up."

Horace rubbed his chin. "Yes, I imagine a dozen wild Skandians might cause absolute havoc in there." He smiled grimly as he pictured the scene. "Don't think I'd care to be part of the garrison if that happened. It'll be decidedly unhealthy for them."

"And serve them right," Gilan said, a note of savage satisfaction in his voice.

"Handy people, Skandians," Maddie said. "They were amazing the way they smashed into the Red Foxes. They went through them like a battering ram."

"They're incredible warriors, sure enough," Horace said. "Man for man, they'd beat any soldier I've ever seen." He looked around. There was a small stream running through the fields to their left, its bank lined with trees. He pointed to it.

"We'll make camp there for the night," he said. "Tomorrow, we'll rendezvous with Hal and his men."

The Skandians were waiting for them when they reached the little dock early the following afternoon. The land party had forded the Semath river at a convenient point two kilometers to the east. Hal and Stig strode along the riverbank to meet them as they rode up.

"Been waiting long?" Horace asked, after they had exchanged greetings.

Hal cocked his head to one side. "We got here after sunset last night," he said.

Horace smiled ruefully, rising in his stirrups to ease his

backside, aching after hours in the saddle. "Looks like that's the quicker way to travel," he said, nodding in the direction of the neat little wolfship tied up at the dock, its heron figurehead rising and falling with the wavelets and giving the ship the appearance of a living creature. "More comfortable too."

Hal nodded. "We made good time. But then, we had plenty of rowers," he said. "So what's the plan now?"

Horace cocked one leg over the saddlebow and slouched comfortably. "We'll take a look at the castle," he said, "and see if anything dramatic is happening. All going well, we'll get into position to attack tomorrow morning."

"And the attack plan?" Hal asked.

"Maddie knows a secret tunnel into the cellars of the castle. From there, a hidden stairway leads to the gatehouse. She's suggested that she leads you and the other Herons through there and you take the gatehouse. Then you can let the drawbridge down, and we'll come in and start whacking Dimon and his men."

"Sounds like a good idea," Hal said. "Nice and simple. Not too much to go wrong."

"Just as long as you and your men can clear out the gatehouse," Gilan said.

Stig turned a wolfish smile on him. "Oh, we'll clear them out, never fear," he said. "You just make sure you're ready to come riding in and take all the glory."

"What about *Wolfbiter*'s crew?" Hal asked. "Do you have anything special in mind for them?"

"Nothing special. They'll come with us and knock heads together once they're inside the walls."

"They're good at that," Hal said.

Horace nodded. "So I'd noticed. Now let's go and take a look at the castle. We've got spare horses if you'd like them."

Hal hesitated. "They'd be cavalry mounts, wouldn't they?"

Horace replied, straight-faced, knowing the Skandians' aversion to riding. "Well, we didn't bring any gentle old ladies' palfreys with us," he said mildly.

Hal considered the offer, then shook his head. "We'll walk," he said firmly. "Give me a minute and I'll fetch Thorn."

The six of them set out a few minutes later, Hal, Thorn and Stig on foot and Maddie, Gilan and Horace walking their horses to let the Skandians keep up. They made their way up the slope and stopped as they reached the crest, where they had a clear view of the castle.

Smoke was pouring from the south tower, close to the top, billowing out of windows and arrow slits.

"I don't like the look of that," Horace said, the worry evident in his voice.

"Mum's flag is still flying," Maddie pointed out, but her father continued to look concerned.

"It's upside down," he said. "That's a distress signal."

"She did that days ago," Maddie told him. "To warn me they were under attack. And look, the smoke is coming from the eighth floor. The ninth floor is still undamaged by the look of things."

But her words did little to lessen Horace's anxiety. "All the same," he said, "I don't think we'll wait till tomorrow. How long will it take you and Hal's men to get in position?"

Maddie estimated distances for a few seconds, then replied. "We'll circle down through the trees. I don't want Dimon to see us. Maybe two hours?"

"Do it then. Stig, can you run down to the ship and get the rest of your crew up here please? And tell Jern to bring *Wolfbiter*'s crew up to join us." Stig set off back down the hill at a fast jog. Horace continued: "Gilan, fetch our men up here as well."

Gilan nodded. "What do you have in mind?"

Horace answered, his eyes never leaving the south tower, with the long banner of dark smoke trailing from it. "I think I'll let Dimon and his men know we're back," he said. "That might distract them from whatever they're doing in the south tower. And it'll give Maddie and the Herons time to get through the tunnel to the gatehouse."

Gilan wheeled Blaze and cantered down the slope, following in Stig's footsteps. Unconsciously, Horace eased his sword in the scabbard a few inches, making sure it was clear and ready to draw.

"How will we let you know we're in the gatehouse?" Maddie asked. "We'll need some kind of signal, won't we?"

Horace finally looked away from the burning tower and regarded her calmly.

"We'll see the drawbridge coming down," he said. "That'll be enough."

28

Stricken with grief, Cassandra dropped to her knees beside the loyal old sergeant. She touched his face gently, fighting back the tears that sprang to her eyes. But Merlon was dead.

She felt a rough hand on her shoulder. "Move back, my lady!" a voice cried. She looked up. One of the archers was urging her away from the danger zone by the gap. Reluctantly, she allowed herself to be led to relative safety. Then she disengaged herself from the man's grasp and pointed to the still figure of the sergeant.

"Get him out of there," she said, her voice breaking up with emotion.

The archer shrugged. There was no point to it, he thought. Merlon was dead already. Then he saw the look in Cassandra's eyes and hurried to obey her.

"All right, all right. Whatever you say," he muttered, dragging the still form into the room. Then he hurried back closer to the doorway onto the stairs, bow ready. But he could see nothing through the clouds of smoke, even though he knew the enemy must be crossing the new bridge across the gap.

"That barricade won't last much longer," he said. It was well alight and burning fiercely. As he spoke, a section on the far side collapsed, the burned timbers giving way to a heavy blow from a battleax. Cassandra looked and nodded agreement. They had only minutes left before the barricade timbers burned through and were hacked or shoved aside by the men attacking across the bridge. She waved three men out onto the stairs.

"Stop them coming through," she said.

Coughing in the thick smoke, their eyes weeping, the men shuffled out onto the small landing by the door, spears in hand, and stood ready. A gust of wind sent a tongue of fire curling through the barrier and they hastily moved backward, up the stairs. Then, as the flames subsided, they moved down again, standing ready for the attack that must come at any minute.

Cassandra felt a cold hand of fear clutch her heart. Once the barricade was down, the way would be clear to the ninth floor as well. She turned and saw Ingrid standing nearby, a pike in her hands. She beckoned the girl over.

"Take three or four men up to the ninth floor and barricade the doorway onto the stairs," she said. "Nail timber beams across it, then pile tables, chairs, beds and cupboards against it. We've got to stop them coming through there once the barrier down here burns through."

Already, she was preparing herself for the fact that she would have to retreat with her men to the ninth floor. The internal timber stairs that led upward from the eighth floor could be quickly dismantled when they did.

There was a loud crash as another section of the barricade gave way in an enormous shower of sparks. An armored man stepped through the gap, a massive war hammer in his hands.

He had used the heavy weapon to smash through the burned-out section. Now he moved toward one of the spearmen who barred his way, swinging the hammer in a horizontal arc. The spearman gave ground desperately, crabbing across the stairs back toward the doorway. The armored man followed, but failed to see another defender on his left side. The second defender was one of the archers, but he had armed himself with a long spear. Now he drove the heavy head into the attacker's side, which was exposed as he followed through on the hammer strike. The spearpoint hit stout chain-mail armor and was deflected. But, even though it didn't penetrate, the force was enough to crack two of the attacker's ribs and send him staggering, the hammer falling from his hands. As the archer readied his spear for another thrust, a second attacker stepped through the gap in the barrier, his sword swinging in a diagonal sweep. With a startled cry of pain, the archer fell back on the steps, his spear clattering on the stonework as he dropped it.

Cassandra came to a sudden decision. She was losing men, and more and more of Dimon's troops were forcing their way into the gaps that were appearing in the barrier. Her men were outnumbered and there could be only one outcome to this battle. They might kill a lot of Dimon's men but, in the end, superior numbers would tell in a simple face-to-face battle like this. There was only one course open to her: retreat to the ninth floor and pull up the stairs.

"Get back! Get back!" she yelled to the defenders on the stairs. "Shut the door and barricade it! Fall back!"

There was only one man remaining from the three she had waved out onto the stairs a few minutes previously. He stumbled back through the smoke and embers. Ready hands dragged him through the door, then the door itself was slammed shut and the heavy locking bar dropped into place.

"Barricade it!" Cassandra yelled. "Tables, chairs, anything you can find! Pile it up against the door and then get up to the ninth floor."

Her men went to work with a will, hurling furniture against the door. After a few minutes, she decided they'd done enough to delay the enemy sufficiently, and she led the way to the internal flight of stairs that led to the ninth floor, yelling at the top of her voice.

"Grab as many spare weapons as you can! Then get up the stairs to the ninth floor."

They gathered up spears, pikes, swords and bundles of arrows from the weapon racks, then staggering under their burdens, made their way up to the next floor. Cassandra, standing by the bottom of the stairs, urged them on, looking back fearfully at the door. She could hear heavy blows being rained on it. Some of the lighter items piled against it toppled and fell to the floor. They had only minutes before the door gave way.

"Keep moving!" she yelled. "Get up the stairs!"

The last man shuffled awkwardly up the steps, burdened by an armful of pikes and spears. She looked at the door once more, saw it shudder inward under another series of heavy blows. There was a gap now between the door and the doorway on the right side. As she watched, it widened a little more.

She turned and ran up after the last of her men. As she came level with him, he dropped four of the pikes he had been carrying and stopped, trying to retrieve them.

"Leave them!" she shouted, shoving him upward. She stooped and picked up two of the pikes and followed him, emerging breathlessly onto the ninth floor. She looked around, saw Ingrid, who nodded to her and pointed to the door, where a pile of heavy items blocked the way. Cassandra knelt and peered down into the floor below. The door moved again, and the furniture piled against it shuddered and moved back a few more centimeters. The room was already thick with smoke, but now more began swirling through the narrow gap around the edge of the door. She gestured to the wooden steps she had just ascended. They were held in place by two curved brackets that fitted flush to the floor. The rails were secured by metal spikes.

"Pull these spikes out!" she shouted, and her men leapt to obey. One of the spikes jammed and she looked around, saw a man standing with a battleax in his hands and pointed at the wooden bracket.

"Smash it!" she said. "I want these stairs down!"

The axman stepped forward, steadied himself and swung at the rail. The ax bit deeply into the wood but failed to break it.

"Again!" she screamed. She could hear the sound of the piled furniture at the eighth-floor door toppling and moving, could hear more heavy blows against the door and the shouts of the men on the stairs as they sensed they were close to winning this battle. The axman swung again and this time the rail splintered, leaving the wooden stairway unsecured.

"Push it loose!" she ordered. She shoved the head of one of the pikes she had been carrying under the top stair and began to lever it up and out. Others joined her and suddenly the entire staircase—really nothing more than a giant wooden ladder— slid back over the empty space and fell to the floor below with a resounding crash. One of the side supports cracked under the impact. It didn't matter, she thought. Dimon's men couldn't put the stairs back in place while she held the upper floor. Their only access now was via the main spiral staircase.

She flattened herself on the floor, leaning down through the square hole where the steps had been until she could see the doorway. As she watched, the piled furniture collapsed and the door swung inward, stopping when the gap was thirty centimeters wide. A renewed shove from the other side pushed it completely open, and the attackers flooded into the eighth floor, the first of them staggering as the door suddenly gave way.

They stopped, puzzled for a few seconds as they found nobody barring their way. Then one of them looked across to where Cassandra's head and shoulders were visible, peering down at them.

"There they are!" he yelled, and led the rush forward.

"Clear the way, my lady," said a voice behind her.

She turned. It was Thomas, the senior archer. He stood ready with his bow, an arrow nocked to the string. Understanding what he intended, she rolled hastily to one side. Thomas stepped forward, drew back the arrow, then aimed through the square hole in the floor at the massed attackers below and released. Before the arrow found its mark, he nocked and shot another. Two shrill screams came from below and he shot again. There was another cry of pain. Then a rush of feet below told her that the enemy troops were seeking cover from the deadly arrows. She smiled her thanks.

"Good shooting, Thomas."

He nodded to her, eyes still intent on the hole in the floor as he searched for another target. Cassandra looked around, saw a large wardrobe standing against the wall.

"Bring that here," she said, and four men took hold of it,

dragging it closer to the hole where the stairs had been.

"Topple it over and slide it across the hole," she said. The thought had occurred to her that if Thomas could shoot down through the stairway aperture, those below could hurl weapons up through it—possibly more of the oil bladders that had destroyed the barricade on the stairs.

Grunting with the effort, two of the men shoved the wardrobe over so that it crashed on the floor. Then all four took hold, and they slid it across the hole, blocking it. The volume of shouting and threats from below was reduced dramatically.

Cassandra rose to her feet, dusting herself off. Then an idea struck her.

"Let's take a look at that doorway," she said, hurrying across the room to the door that led into the main stairwell.

Ingrid and her men had done a good job. Several heavy beams were nailed across the door, and a selection of beds, tables, bookshelves and chairs were piled against it to reinforce it. Cassandra nodded approval, then looked up at the ceiling. As she had recalled, the pipes from the cisterns above, designed to stop the tower from burning, led across the ceiling at this point to several outlets at the top of the wall. She pointed to one of them. It was a lead pipe and could be cut and bent easily.

"Move that pipe so it can flood the door," she said. "Make a hole in the top of the door to accommodate it. If they try to set fire to the door, I want to be able to put it out."

Her men set to work, cutting the pipe, then making an aperture in the top of the doorway so they could direct water out and down the door itself. They were none too soon. They had barely finished when she heard footsteps outside the door, then the sound of flint and steel as the men there struck a flame. Through the narrow gaps in the door, she saw an orange light spring up outside, smelled the thick stench of oil and pitch.

"Now!" she called to one of her men, who was standing by the drain cock from the cistern to the pipe. He spun the valve and water gushed out of the pipe, flooding down the outside of the door. She heard men cursing in surprise, then saw the flames go out. She let the water run for a few minutes, soaking the door, then turned it off.

"Keep an eye on them," she said. "If they try lighting it again, open the valve once more."

She moved wearily away from the door, found a chair that hadn't been used in the barricade, and slumped onto it, wondering what she hadn't thought of. Thomas, who was her senior man now that Merlon was dead, approached her diffidently. He was loath to disturb her, particularly with bad news. She noticed him hesitating and smiled wearily.

"What is it, Thomas?"

He cleared his throat nervously, then spoke. "You'll need to ration the food, my lady," he said. "We left most of our supplies downstairs. We've barely enough to last us for three or four days up here."

She shrugged fatalistically. "Don't worry about it. We may not last more than three days." A few days ago, when they had held control of the stairs, her archers could shoot down into any attackers and hold them off with little fear of retaliation. They had no tactical advantage here. All they could do now was stave off Dimon's attempts to force his way into their retreat.

It was a simple arm wrestle, and Dimon seemed to have found men who would keep fighting on, no matter how many casualties they took in the process. Probably, she thought bitterly, he had promised them riches. He could certainly afford to.

Eventually, they would break down the door into the stairwell. They'd plug or divert the water and burn their way in. She looked around desperately. They needed a fallback position. She pointed to the wall opposite the door.

"Build another barricade near the wall," she told Thomas. "We'll fall back there if they break in." *When* they break in, she thought to herself. But before Thomas could move, a deep voice countermanded her order.

"No, Cass. Defend the door. It's your best chance."

She looked around, startled, to see her father, dressed in his shirt and trousers, and carrying his long sword, moving toward her. With a stab of guilt, she realized she had forgotten all about him.

"Dad!" she said in alarm. "You shouldn't be out of bed."

He smiled grimly at her. "I'm fine, Cassandra." And in truth, when she looked at him, he *did* look better. There was color in his cheeks now, and the lost, shadowed look in his eyes was gone. Perhaps the challenge of fighting against the invaders had stirred his spirit and given him new vigor. His leg was bandaged and he was still limping, but he pointed the long sword back toward the door.

"Stop them there. It's your best chance. They can only come at you two at a time through the doorway and they'll be in each other's way on the stairs. If you try to fight them back there"— he indicated the spot where she had ordered Thomas to build a second redoubt—"they'll be able to come at you from all sides. Hold the door and trust that Horace is on his way."

She realized he was right. She looked at Thomas, who was regarding her inquisitively. She nodded. "Do as the King says, Thomas. Get the men ready. We'll stop them at the door." She smiled sadly at her father and rose from the chair. "And for goodness' sake, will you sit down? You may think you feel better but you're still not healed."

Her father returned the smile and sank gratefully onto the chair she had vacated, his injured leg held stiffly out before him.

Thomas shouted his orders, and her men began to form up at the door, weapons ready. They'd keep the attackers out for a while, Cassandra thought. But she didn't have enough men to hold them back indefinitely. Sooner or later, superior numbers would tell. The attackers would sweep them aside and take control of the ninth floor—as they done with the floor below.

On the floor below, Dimon was exultant. They had finally driven Cassandra back into her last possible refuge. Now that she was fighting at close quarters, and was fighting blind behind the blocked doorway, her archers held little threat for his men. Now, he told himself, it was only a matter of time before he had her at his mercy.

He smiled at the thought, then turned as there was a small commotion at the door. A soldier was looking wildly around for him, his chest heaving with the effort of having run up from the fourth floor. From his lack of armor, Dimon recognized him. He hadn't been part of the current attack, but was one of the men from his original group. As he watched, the man caught sight of him and hurried across.

"My . . . lord!" he said, still panting heavily. "There . . . are . . ." He stopped, breathless, and Dimon gestured angrily at him.

"Calm down. Get your breath. There are what?"

"Men, my lord. Soldiers. Sir Horace and his men. They're at the gate."

29

DIMON WENT DOWN THE STAIRS AT A RUN.

He reached the fourth floor, then made his way out through the ironbound door onto the battlements overlooking the massive castle gate. His heart sank as he saw the body of mounted men drawn up on the parkland facing the drawbridge. Behind them, two ranks of archers stood ready, although they were currently out of bowshot. Another group of about twenty men were formed up loosely beside the archers. He saw the huge, multicolored round shields and horned helmets and cursed quietly. Skandians, he thought, wondering vaguely where Horace had found them.

"They must be the *Heron*'s crew," he muttered to himself, although there seemed to be more of them than he had seen when they had arrived at the castle several weeks before.

The soldier who had alerted him to the newcomers' presence looked at him curiously. "What's that, my lord?"

Dimon angrily dismissed his question. He was counting the enemy. There seemed to be about sixty of them—a few more than he had in his own force, counting the losses they had sustained during the engagements with Cassandra. But at least the enemy were outside the immense walls of the castle, and he was safe inside.

Sitting on his battlehorse a little ahead of the troopers was an unmistakable figure. Tall, broad shouldered and with his distinctive round buckler slung over his left shoulder, Horace was easy to recognize, even if he hadn't been accompanied by a rider bearing his standard—the green oakleaf.

Dimon looked to his left. One of his men was leaning on the battlements, a crossbow propped against the wall beside him.

"Can you reach him with a shot?" he asked.

But the man shook his head. "He's no fool, my lord. He's out of range. Besides, if I try to shoot, I'll draw twenty or so arrows from those archers of his. They outrange me—and they rarely miss."

And that, thought Dimon, was probably the real reason for his reluctance to shoot at Horace. Coward, he thought, scowling at the man, who steadfastly ignored his contemptuous look.

As Dimon turned his attention back to the force outside the gate, he saw Horace bring the buckler round to his front and urge his horse closer to the walls. There would be no chance of shooting him now, Dimon thought. Horace had the reflexes of a cat, and he'd stop any crossbow bolt before it could hit him.

The tall knight stood in his stirrups and held his cupped right hand to his mouth.

"Dimon!" he shouted, his voice carrying clearly to the battlements. "Show yourself, you treacherous snake!"

Dimon started in surprise as he heard his name called. How did Horace know that he was in command of the rebels? He hesitated to answer.

"Dimon! Show yourself!" Horace called again, his voice echoing off the granite castle walls.

Dimon shrugged mentally. There was no point in pretending that he wasn't here. Horace obviously knew what had happened. There was a stone step beside the battlements, and he stepped up onto it and shouted back.

"Horace! Here I am!"

He saw Horace's head move slightly as he scanned the walls, then stop as he recognized the figure high above him.

"Open the gates and lay down your weapons," Horace called.

Dimon laughed. "Do you think I'm mad? There's no way on earth that I'm letting you and your men inside these walls."

"I'll give you one chance to surrender. And then—"

Dimon shook his head and cut him off. "And then what? You'll storm these walls with sixty men? I'll be delighted to see you try. Now I'll give you one chance: Ride away and give us free passage to the coast."

"Or what?" Horace demanded.

"Or I'll burn out your wife and her men in the south tower. Her life is in your hands, Horace. Don't put it at risk."

Horace laughed, but there was a hollow sound to it. He pointed to the tower. "You'll burn her out, will you? Looks as if she's put your fire out."

Dimon craned around to look at the south tower. The thick clouds of black smoke pouring from the windows on the eighth floor had lessened and had turned white as Cassandra allowed water from the cisterns to flood down, turning the smoke to steam. As he watched, even the white steam diminished to a series of small wisps. He cursed to himself.

"Now I'm warning you and your men," Horace continued. "If

you harm one hair on Cassandra's head, there will be no mercy. I will kill every one of you."

Even at a distance, the grim sincerity in his voice was obvious. Dimon felt a momentary frisson of fear. Horace was not an enemy to take lightly. He was a highly skilled and dangerous warrior—the champion knight of Araluen. Dimon began to wonder whether he could somehow use Cassandra's life as a bargaining chip to allow his escape. Horace's next words cut across the thought.

"And here's something else. Any of your men who surrender now will be given free passage. They'll get a head start of eight hours to go in any direction they choose. I give my word that they won't be pursued in that time."

"Can they keep their weapons?" Dimon asked. Another thought was forming. He might somehow be able to disguise himself and leave with those of his men who chose to surrender.

"Are you joking?" Horace replied. "They will be disarmed and we'll take a close look at every one of them—just in case you had the idea of sneaking out with them."

Dimon's heart sank further at the words. He was not going to trick his way out of the castle, he thought.

But then, Horace and his men were going to have a hard time getting in. Maybe some kind of compromise would be possible in the coming days as he continued to hold them off. The longer the stalemate went on, with Horace unable to force his way in, the more likely Horace would be to see reason.

"That sounds like a worthwhile offer," said a voice close behind Dimon. The words were spoken in a conversational tone, not shouted to Horace. Dimon turned angrily and saw eight or nine men who had followed him down from the tower—the mercenaries he had contracted to force Cassandra to surrender.

He rounded on them in fury. "What are you doing here?" he demanded. Suddenly, he understood why the fire on the upper floors had gone out. These men had abandoned their attack when he had rushed down the stairs to the battlements.

The man who had spoken was uncowed by his anger. "We wanted to see what we were up against," he said. "We didn't sign up to fight Sir Horace and his men. You said we just had to capture a woman and a few of her soldiers. Now we're looking at troopers and archers. And there are Skandians there as well. We're not fighting them."

The men around him nodded and muttered agreement.

"So you're afraid to face Horace, are you?" Dimon sneered.

Again, the man showed no reaction to his manner. "Any sane man would be. As I said, we didn't agree to fight him."

"Have you noticed that he's outside the walls—and you're inside?" Dimon continued sarcastically. "There's no way he can get in."

"And there's no way we can get out while he's there. I don't plan to be caught like a rat in a trap. He's offering us a way out and I'm thinking of taking it."

Dimon drew his sword and took a step toward the surly group. But the sound of half a dozen swords being drawn echoed around the battlements as the men closed up around their spokesman. Dimon stopped and lowered his own sword. He tried not to let his desperation show. This willingness to surrender might spread to the rest of his force if he continued to argue with this group.

"Pay us our five thousand royals and we'll be on our way," said another of the turncoats.

Dimon laughed bitterly. "Pay you? For what? I hired you to bring Cassandra down from that tower. So far, you haven't managed to do it. I'm not paying you a lead penny!"

The man shrugged. He hadn't really expected Dimon to hand over any payment, but it had been worth a try. "Then we'll leave anyway," he said, and his companions mumbled agreement.

Dimon capitulated. It would be better to be rid of them quickly, before the rot could spread. He slammed his sword back into its scabbard.

"All right. Tuck your tails between your legs and run," he said. "And good riddance. But take another look: There's a Ranger out there. Wherever you run to, he'll track you down. All Horace is promising is an eight-hour start."

"That sounds good enough to us," said the original spokesman. He stepped up to the battlements and shouted to the figure below.

"Sir Horace! Ten of us are coming out!" Then, gesturing to his companions to follow, he led the way to the stairs leading down into the courtyard. Dimon followed them for a few paces and called to the men below.

"Let those traitors go!" he said.

The guard in the courtyard reluctantly opened a small wicket gate beside the main gate, and shoved a narrow plank bridge across the moat. The ten deserters made their way across it, tossing their weapons to the grass as they reached the far side. Then the plank bridge was withdrawn and the wicket gate was slammed shut and barred.

Dimon watched as the small group were searched and closely inspected by the Ranger. Then they were stripped of their armor and boots and shoved on their way, heading for the coast.

In the tower, Cassandra was puzzled by the sudden cessation of the attack on the door. She stepped closer to the barricade and tilted her head, trying to hear what was going on. There was a concerted rush of feet on the stairs, then silence fell. She frowned at her father.

"What do you think is going on?" she asked.

Then Ingrid called to her from the door leading out onto the balcony. "My lady! Come and see! It's Sir Horace! He's back!"

Cassandra dashed out the door to the balcony. She hurried to the wall and leaned out so she could see the parkland beyond the main gates. Sure enough, there was a body of men gathered there, in neat ranks. Archers and troopers, she saw. She smiled as she recognized a third group—Skandians.

And several paces ahead of them, accompanied by his standard bearer, was Horace, sitting astride his battlehorse, his armor gleaming in the sunlight. She laughed out loud. She had never seen a more welcome sight in her life. Sensing someone moving beside her, she turned to see her father.

"It's Horace," she said, pointing. "Now Dimon will have something to think about."

Her father shrugged. "Horace still has to get inside the walls," he said. "And nobody's managed that in the last hundred years."

"He'll manage it," she replied confidently. "He's got Maddie to help him get in."

Quickly, she told him of the plan she had discussed with

Maddie, for the girl Ranger to lead a party through the secret passages to the gatehouse and let the drawbridge down.

He smiled as she told him. "So she found the secret tunnels, did she? Good for her."

Involuntarily, they both leaned out to peer down the hill to the small clump of trees and bushes that concealed the tunnel entrance. There was no sign of movement there. A thought struck her—a way to let Horace and Maddie know that all was well in the south tower. She called to Ingrid, who hurried to her side.

"Go and bring down my flag," she said. "Then send it up again, right side up."

"Yes, my lady," Ingrid said, a broad smile on her face. She hurried away to do Cassandra's bidding.

"Now we'll just sit tight until Maddie lets down the bridge," Cassandra said to her father. "Then we'll go down and join the party. I've got a few things to say to Dimon."

30

MADDIE LED THE HERONS SOUTHWARD IN A LONG ARC, remaining inside the trees and out of sight until they reached the small clearing where she had kept Bumper. From time to time, she would halt the sea wolves and creep to the edge of the tree line, concealed by her cloak, to spy out events at the castle.

She nodded to herself, satisfied that her father was keeping the Red Foxes' attention away from the cleared ground below the castle, and the small copse where the entrance to the tunnel was concealed. She and her group would have to cross that open ground to reach the tunnel and she didn't want anyone in the castle to see them when they did.

Eventually, they reached a point in the trees below the castle, and she paused, surveying the terrain once more. She sensed something was different in the south tower. She looked closely at it. The dark smoke had ceased billowing from the windows and arrow slits. Now, only a few wisps of steam remained.

"Well done, Mum," she said quietly. She realized that her mother must have flooded the fire set by Dimon and his men with water from the roof cisterns. She could see heads moving above the balcony wall on the ninth floor, but it was too far to recognize individuals. Then her heart leapt as she noticed the flag, now flying upright. It was obviously a signal to her and to Horace that all was well on the ninth floor of the tower.

She moved back inside the cover of the trees and approached Hal. "Are you all set?" she asked.

He nodded, then indicated the waiting members of his brotherband. He and Stefan were carrying torches they had pre-pared on board the *Heron*—rags tied round lengths of wood and soaked with pitch to keep them burning for at least half an hour.

"Should we light these now?"

She shook her head. "Wait till we're at the tunnel mouth. If we start up the hill with burning torches, we could be noticed. In fact," she said, glancing around and studying the clear ground, "we might move a little farther west and angle up the hill to the tunnel. That'll put the south tower between us and the men on the walls."

"Good idea," said Hal. Then he turned to his men. "Right, let's get moving."

Maddie led them a hundred meters to the west, until she judged that the bulk of the south tower would provide them with adequate cover from observers on the wall. As they crouched ready inside the tree line, she spoke to them softly.

"Stay low and move slowly. Rapid movement attracts the eye. Make sure you have nothing on you that might catch the sun's rays and send a reflection up the hill."

She waited while the men checked one another's clothing and equipment, ensuring that no metal was left bared. They had elected not to bring their shields with them, reasoning that they would be too bulky in the narrow confines of the tunnel. She was glad to see that they didn't wear the traditional Skandian horned helmets. Instead, they all wore knitted watch caps, with a small heron symbol on the front. Their clothing was dull-colored—leather and sheepskin for the most part—and that would help them move up the hill without being seen. She nodded to the first group. Stig, Thorn, Jesper and Edvin were ready to move out.

"Remember," she said once more, "low and slow. Use the long grass as much as you can, and don't bunch up. Go."

Thorn led the group out. Stig waited until the one-armed sea wolf had gone ten meters, then followed. Edvin and Jesper left similar gaps. She watched them move furtively up the hill, crouching to use the cover of the long grass as much as possible, and angling across the slope to reach the small copse of trees. As Edvin crept in among the small bunch of trees, she signaled for the next group to move out.

Ulf and Wulf, the identical twins, went next, with Ulf leading Ingvar, holding him firmly by the wrist. The big sailor's eyesight was poor in the late-afternoon light, and Ulf was able to warn him whenever they reached rough patches in the ground. The head of Ingvar's long weapon was wrapped in a piece of canvas, so that it wouldn't catch the light and cause reflections. She saw Ingvar stumble once on a rough piece of ground, but Ulf's secure grip saved him from falling. The two brothers waited until Ingvar had regained his balance and composure, then set off again, with Wulf dropping back to trail behind them.

They moved more slowly than the first group, but they eventually reached the sanctuary of the trees with no sign that they had been spotted from the castle walls. Not that that was conclusive, Maddie thought. They might have been seen without the defenders raising the alarm or shouting. Then she shrugged.

If they were seen, there was little Dimon could do about them. He had no idea about the concealed tunnel entrance, or about the tunnel itself. As far as he would know, they were hidden in the small clump of trees and bushes and well away from the castle walls.

"Are we going?" Hal asked beside her.

She realized she had been delaying while she considered the situation. She roused herself with a jerk and nodded. "Let's go," she said. "Follow me."

She glided out into the open ground, with Hal and Stefan behind her, trying to mimic her movements and rhythm as closely as they could. She kept her cowl up so that she was able to keep an eye on the castle as she went, without exposing the pale oval of her face to potential watchers. Once again, there was no indication that they had been seen. A few minutes later, she guided her companions into the shelter of the small clump of trees. It was now quite crowded in the little clearing, with ten of them crammed together.

Hal looked around curiously. "Where's this tunnel?"

She moved to pull the screening bushes to one side, exposing the dark hole of the entrance. The men with torches began to reach for their flints and steels but she stopped them.

"Wait till you're inside the entrance before you light the torches," she said. "Even in daylight, they might see the flash of flint and steel from the castle."

Hal and Stefan nodded their understanding. A struck flint created a brief but brilliant flash of light, and it could well be seen if someone was looking in the right direction.

She moved into the tunnel entrance and found the lantern she had left there when she had come this way, days before.

There was still plenty of oil in its reservoir, and she raised the glass, exposing the wick. She nodded to Hal, beckoning him forward into the dark recess.

"Give me a light for this, please," she said.

Hal quickly struck sparks from his flint into a small pile of tinder, then blew on it to raise a tiny flame. Maddie found a small dry stick and put it into the flame to get it burning. Then she transferred it to the oil-soaked wick of her lantern. The light sprang up immediately, intensifying as she closed the glass. She held it up while Hal set his torch aflame, then Stefan's.

The yellow light flared, but it only seemed to accentuate the darkness of the tunnel, stretching away from them toward the castle.

"I'll lead," she told Hal. "You bring up the rear."

Hal nodded and moved aside to let the others past. Stig came first, then Thorn, looking nervously about him.

"We're going in here?" he said doubtfully.

Stig looked at him in surprise. Thorn was fearless in battle. It had never occurred to Stig that he might be nervous in confined spaces. The tall first mate found the tunnel's confines unpleasant, but nothing that he couldn't handle.

"Are you all right, Thorn?" he asked.

Thorn made a nervous gesture with the hook on his right arm. "I'm fine," he said. "I'm fine." But his voice belied the words. It was pitched a little higher than normal.

More Herons tried to enter the tunnel behind Thorn, but he wasn't moving. They all looked at him.

"I can hardly see my hand in front of my face," Thorn said nervously, peering around in the darkness.

Ingvar, behind him, grinned easily. "Welcome to my world,"

he said. "That's normal for me." He realized that his spectacles—tortoiseshell lenses pierced by tiny holes to help him focus—would be virtually useless in the darkness. He took them off and put them away in a pocket. Peering around owlishly, he realized that, even though his vision was blurry, he could see the light of the torches and the dark shapes of his companions. "Let's go," he said.

But still Thorn hesitated.

"It's just a little tunnel, Thorn," Jesper said, the amusement obvious in his voice. "Nothing to be frightened of. No booger-men in here."

"Shut up, Jesper," Thorn said, his voice tight.

Jesper opened his mouth for another sally. It was rare that he felt superior to Thorn in any way, and the opportunity to crow about it was almost irresistible.

"Yes. Shut up, Jesper," Hal said. His voice wasn't tight. It was firm and grim. Jesper heard the underlying threat and closed his mouth.

"Just let's get going," Thorn said.

Maddie caught his gaze and nodded reassuringly. "It'll only be a few minutes, Thorn," she said. "And we've got plenty of light."

"Okay. Okay. It's going to be fine," Thorn said, speaking rapidly. "Let's get going, shall we?"

Maddie decided there was no point in trying to reassure him any further. Best to get the ordeal over with, she thought. She knew that some people had an inordinate, unreasoning fear of dark, confined spaces, and the tunnel definitely fit that description. She held her lantern high and set off, walking slowly so that the men behind her could keep their footing on the uneven ground.

The lantern and the torches threw an irregular, flickering light over the rough clay walls and roof of the tunnel as it embraced them. Behind her, she could hear the shuffle of sealskin boots on the ground as the Herons followed in her footsteps. Occasionally, one of them would grunt as he brushed against the cold, clammy walls. They were all bigger than her, and there was less room for them. Something to be said for being small, she thought, grinning to herself.

She became aware of another sound, a constant, harsh, sighing noise. She realized it was Thorn's heavy breathing as he strove to keep his panic in check.

"Are we nearly there?" he asked, his voice a hoarse whisper.

She turned to look back at him, smiling encouragement. "Not far now. We'll be under the moat in a minute or so."

"Under the moat," he groaned. "Did you have to tell me that?"

"Hope the roof doesn't collapse while we're there." That was Jesper again, Maddie realized. She wondered if he ever knew when to keep his mouth shut.

Thorn's heavy breathing came faster and faster at the thought of the tons of wet clay and water that would be above them. Then, as they started forward once more, moving down toward the moat, he let out a startled cry.

Maddie stopped and turned to him again. "What's up?"

His eyes were wide in the yellow light of her lantern. He had his hand up above his head, feeling the empty air above it.

"Something touched me," he said, his voice shaking. "Something touched my hair."

"It was probably a root," she told him. "They hang down through the top of the tunnel. They scared the devil out of me first time I came through here. But you get used to them."

"I don't plan on getting used to them," Thorn replied. "I plan on getting out of here as soon as possible."

She led on and they followed. She sensed that they were under the moat and called back softly. "We may get a little water dripping down here and there. But it's quite normal and nothing to worry about."

"So you say. I just . . . Nyaaaah!" Thorn's statement was cut off by his cry of alarm. Once again, he was feeling the empty air above his head, brushing his hand back and forward as if to ward something off.

"That was you, Jesper." Stig's warning voice came out of the dim recesses behind them. "If you do it again, I'll break your arm."

Jesper sniggered. It was as well that, in the darkness, he couldn't see Thorn's malevolent glare.

Hal's voice came from the rear of the party. "Cut it out, Jesper," he said. "Or you'll be baling out the ship all the way back to Hallasholm."

Jesper could tell when his skirl was serious. And he was serious now. He mumbled to himself about people not being able to take a joke. But he didn't bother Thorn again as they continued.

A few minutes later, they emerged into the concealed room at the end of the tunnel. The room was small and they were crowded together, but already Maddie could see color returning to Thorn's pale face.

He returned her gaze apologetically. "Sorry about that."

She shrugged. "No matter," she told him.

But Stig was puzzled. "I don't get it, Thorn. You've never

been worried about small spaces before. You go belowdecks on the ship without any problem."

"That's different. That's not underground. I don't like the feeling of being underground."

Jesper opened his mouth to comment, then wisely changed his mind and closed it. Maddie heard sounds coming from the cellar beside the small secret room where they waited. She held up a hand for silence and pressed her ear against the door. Voices, she realized. Listening carefully, she could just make out their words.

". . . stay down here while Horace attacks. We'll be caught like rats."

"Would you rather go up and tell Sir Dimon we've decided not to stay here? Someone's got to guard these prisoners, after all."

"Why? They're locked in their cells and not going anywhere. We're not really needed here."

Thorn had pushed forward to stand beside Maddie, his ear close to the door as well. He frowned in concentration, then looked up at her. *Two of them?* He mouthed the words, making no sound.

Maddie nodded.

Thorn beckoned Stig forward and pointed to the wall, again mouthing his words, reinforcing the meaning with hand signals. *Two men. You take the one on the left. Me the right.*

Stig nodded his understanding, loosening his battleax from the iron loop on his belt that held it in place and removing the canvas that covered the metal blade. Thorn was already unstrapping the hinged hook that took the place of his right hand and forearm, and taking his club hand from a sack strapped to his back. Quickly, he slipped the stump of his arm into the leather socket, then pulled the straps tight with his left hand and his teeth. He moved his arm back and forth, testing that the club was securely in place, then gestured to Maddie, pointing to the door.

She moved to the spring-loaded door lock, but he held up his left hand to stop her, then turned to the other Herons, again mouthing and miming his words. *Just two of us. The rest stay here.*

The Herons nodded. Thorn and Stig would be more than capable of dealing with the two guards. And if they all barged into the cellar at once, they'd get in one another's way. Satisfied that they had got the message, Thorn nodded to Maddie once more. As she reached for the door release, she took a moment to marvel over the rapid change in Thorn's manner. He had been nervous and uncertain in the tunnel. Now he was confident and back in control. She had a feeling that the guards on the other side of the door would pay dearly for Thorn's former nervousness.

She pushed on the door lock, and the door into the cellar sprang open.

31

"SIR HORACE," SAID THE LEADER OF THE CAVALRY TROOP, "there's someone waving from the south tower balcony."

Horace looked up to the tower. Sure enough, someone was waving a towel or a pillowslip from the balcony that ran around it. He thought it might be Cassandra but couldn't be sure. He stood in his stirrups, drew his sword and held it over his head. Then he twisted the blade back and forth to catch the sun, creating a series of flashes to acknowledge that he had seen the signal.

"I imagine they'll move down the stairs once we start through the gate," he said. Then, satisfied that the signaler on the balcony had seen his reply, he re-sheathed his sword and settled back in the saddle.

Gilan moved Blaze up beside Horace's battlehorse. The Ranger had been off to the left, watching the hill below them.

"I thought I saw men moving up the hill toward that grove of trees Maddie pointed out," he said quietly.

Horace nodded. "So she's in position. How long did she say it would take them to get through the tunnel?"

He knew the answer but he was reviewing the timing for the coming events in his mind.

"Ten to fifteen minutes," Gilan told him.

Horace chewed his lip thoughtfully and glanced at the sun, sinking lower in the western sky. Already the shadows of the trees on that side were stretching across the grassy hillside toward them. He estimated that there were two hours of daylight left. More than enough time to get the job done, he thought. He gestured to the cavalry leader.

"We'll start to move forward. Archers," he added, turning in his saddle to address the men on foot, "keep an eye on the battlements. They've got crossbows up there. Anyone looks like shooting at us, pick them off immediately."

There was a low growl of assent from the bowmen.

Horace glanced left and right, making sure his men were ready, raised his right hand, then lowered it forward. The mixed force moved together with a jingle of harness and equipment. On his right, the Skandians from *Wolfbiter* stepped out as well. They were in no fixed formation. They strode toward the castle with their weapons in their hands and their shields ready.

They had gone fifteen meters when a crossbow bolt whizzed past Horace, missing him by several meters. Instantly, he heard the rapid slapping sound of several bows releasing, and the whimper of arrows fleeting toward the walls. A moment later, there was a cry of pain, and he saw a man fall back from the battlements, his crossbow dropping from his hands and falling to the moat far below. Another bow released and a second crossbowman dropped back into cover just in time. Inadvertently, as he jerked back, he hit the release trigger on his crossbow and his shot arced high and wide of the approaching men. Horace saw Gilan riding with an arrow nocked to his massive longbow, his eyes narrowed as he scanned the battlements. Horace looked to see if Dimon were visible, but the Red Fox leader was staying out of sight. With an archer of Gilan's expertise seeking him out, it was a wise decision, Horace thought.

"Far enough," he said, raising his hand in the signal to halt. They were close enough now to waste no time when the drawbridge came down. "Shields up," he added and heard the clatter as the troopers brought their shields around to their front to protect them from further crossbow bolts. The archers had no shields, but they moved quickly to take up position behind the halted cavalry, where the armored men and horses would protect them from shooters on the walls, while still enabling them to shoot in return.

"Don't forget your own shield," Gilan said quietly beside him.

Horace belatedly let his buckler slip around to the front. He glanced at his companion. "What about you?"

Gilan shrugged. "I'll stay behind you and that massive beast you're sitting on."

Horace gave him a pained look. "That's no way to talk about a thoroughbred battlehorse."

Gilan sniffed disdainfully. "Thoroughbred ox, more like it," he said. Stamper and Blaze didn't seem to share their riders' sniping. The two horses whinnied at each other in a companionable way. Behind them, two archers released another pair of arrows at figures on the battlements. There was a further cry of pain.

"Your men are doing well," Horace remarked.

Gilan glanced back at them before replying. "They were the pick of the bunch," he said. "They're all expert shots."

He was still speaking when he suddenly raised his bow, drew

and released. The arrow hissed away, and five seconds later there was another yell of pain from the defenders on the wall.

Horace grinned at him. "You're not so bad yourself."

"Just keeping them up to the mark," Gilan said. He fidgeted with his reins for a few seconds, then glanced down the hill to the copse of trees. "Wonder what's keeping Maddie?" he said. "She should be through the tunnel by now."

"Be patient," Horace told him. "Nothing ever goes to time in a battle."

"Be nice if it did, just this once," Gilan grumbled in reply.

In the south tower, Cassandra's men had opened the door to the stairs and moved down to the eighth level. Seeing none of Dimon's men present, they replaced the section of stairs that they had removed when they first sought shelter in the tower. Now, fully armed, they stood ready to make their way down to the lower levels.

On the ninth floor, Cassandra called to Ingrid, who was keeping watch from the terrace. "Any sign, Ingrid?"

"No, my lady," the girl replied. "Sir Horace and his men have moved closer to the gate, but there's no sign of Maddie and her Skandians yet."

"Don't get edgy," Duncan told Cassandra. "Nothing ever goes to time in a battle." Unknowingly, he repeated Horace's phrase to Gilan.

Cassandra looked at him, noting the long sword in his hand. "Where do you think you're going?"

"I'm coming with you," he said. The tone in his voice brooked no argument, so she decided not to waste any time with it but to accept the inevitable.

"All right," she said. "But stay back behind the men. You're not fully fit yet."

Duncan nodded agreement. He wanted to be in at the end of this battle, but he realized he couldn't play an active part. He was realist enough to know that, if he did, he could well be putting his own men at risk as they protected him. He'd have to be content to observe, and to advise Cassandra if necessary.

They started down the winding stairs. Cassandra placed three of her troopers in the lead, armed with long spears. Three archers followed them, then Ingrid with four troopers ranged around them. The remainder of her men followed, also in threes, with Duncan in the center, screened by a wall of bodies and armor.

"Take it slowly," she cautioned the men in the lead. "We don't want any unpleasant surprises." She glanced quickly at Thomas, who was in the lead rank of archers. "We'll stop at the sixth floor, unless we run into any resistance. I can check the main gate from there."

Thomas nodded. They had to tread a fine line. They needed to be ready to join in the fight as soon as the drawbridge was down, leaving the stairway at the fourth level and moving across to the keep. But if they moved too early, they could be isolated by Dimon's men.

A few floors later, Thomas called a quiet command to the leading three troopers. They stopped in place, their shields up and their spears ready. There was no sign of any opposition. He turned to Cassandra and jerked his thumb at the door beside them. "We're at the sixth floor, my lady," he said.

Cassandra licked her lips nervously and moved toward the door, turning the iron loop that activated the latch. The door was unbarred and the latch lifted easily. She pushed the door open a meter or so and peered around. There was nobody visible. A corridor led away to left and right, with doors visible on either side. This floor was used for accommodation, she knew. Those doors would lead to bedrooms, and they would have windows overlooking the courtyard and the main gate.

Quietly, she drew her *katana* with a muted *shring* of steel on wood and leather. She opened the door farther and stepped into the corridor.

"Wait, my lady," Thomas said. He gestured for a trooper to go with her, and followed her himself. The three of them crossed quietly to the nearest door. Holding her sword ready, Cassandra reached for the door handle and turned it.

This door was unlocked as well. The well-oiled latch lifted and the door swung into the room. Cassandra stepped quickly through the doorway, sword pointing left and right, ready for danger. There was nobody present, and she moved farther in, making room for her two guards to join her.

Assuring herself that there was nobody lurking in ambush in the corners or behind the floor-length drapes, she walked quickly to the window and heaved the heavy curtains open.

From this lower level, Horace and his men were hidden from her sight by the walls, but she could see through the courtyard gateway that the drawbridge was still up and no attack had begun so far. Dimon's men lined the battlements, all peering outward at the attacking force. But there was no outcry, no sound of weapons clashing against one another.

She turned to Thomas. "We'll wait on this floor until the fighting starts," she said. "Then we'll go down those stairs and join in. Tell the men that Dimon is mine. Nobody else is to touch him."

Thomas regarded her curiously for a several seconds. She was small and slim, although he knew she was well muscled and skilled in the use of the *katana*. He decided that he wouldn't like to be in Dimon's shoes when she caught up with him.

"I'll spread the word," he said.

32

Thorn and Stig erupted into the cellar as the door sprang open. The two guards who were stationed there looked up and cried out in alarm. They had no idea where the two Skandians had come from. The door was carefully disguised and blended into the stone walls of the cellar. Now, without warning, a gap had opened and two yelling sea wolves burst into the cellar, their weapons drawn.

Thorn's man was closer and he struggled to draw his sword. But in his haste, he caught the crosspiece in the loose loop of his belt and only managed to have it halfway out of its scabbard before Thorn was upon him.

The Skandian battlemaster swung his massive club in a backhanded swipe, catching the guard in the left ribs and cracking three of them. The force of the blow hurled the guard backward, and he crashed into the unyielding stone wall behind him. His eyes glazed briefly, then he slid down the wall and lay crumpled on the floor at its foot, unconscious.

The second man had a little more time to gather his wits. He was armed with a spear and he lunged now at the terrifying one-armed man who had just dispatched his companion. But Thorn had the reflexes of a cat and was carrying his saxe in his left hand. He deftly trapped the spearpoint with the big knife's blade and twisted it downward so the iron head rang against the stone floor, striking sparks. The result was that the second sentry was effectively disarmed. Stig, reluctant to use his battleax against an unprotected man, changed his tactics and leapt high in the air, right leg bent at the knee and drawn back for a flying kick.

It caught the guard in the solar plexus, and the air was smashed out of his lungs with an explosive *WHOOF!* He, too, was catapulted across the room to slam against the stone wall behind him. Any breath he might have had remaining was driven out of his lungs by the impact. Like his companion, he slid unconscious to the cold stone floor of the cellar.

Thorn regarded the two inert bodies with a satisfied smile. "All clear," he called to the waiting group in the secret room.

Hal and Maddie emerged into the cellar, looking around curiously, then seeing the two figures slumped against the far wall. The rest of the crew followed them, fanning out through the cellar. Hal stirred one of the guards with the toe of his boot. There was no reaction.

"Nice work," he said quietly.

A querulous voice sounded from one of the cells close to the door. "Who's that? Is someone there?"

Maddie recognized the voice of Timothy, one of her mother's senior retainers. Timothy was no warrior. He was in charge of the castle dining room whenever Cassandra had important guests. She stepped to the door of the cell, pulled the bolt free of its hasp and shoved the door open. Timothy, white-haired and thin, emerged, blinking in the extra light.

"Princess Madelyn!" he exclaimed in surprise, puzzled by

her appearance. She was dressed in a camouflaged Ranger cloak, woolen breeches and a leather jerkin and was carrying a recurve bow that was nearly as tall as she was. "What are you doing? What's going on?"

Maddie smiled reassuringly at him. "We're taking back the castle, Timothy," she told him. Then, looking around the cellar, she asked: "How many of you are down here?"

"Seven or eight of us. It's hard to be sure. They brought some in after I was locked up."

Maddie gestured to Stefan and Edvin, who were peering around the cellar. "Can you let the others out of their cells, please?"

The two Skandians began to unlock the doors and push them open. Gradually, the imprisoned castle staff—five men and three women—emerged into the cellar, looking around fearfully as they saw the armed and ferocious-looking Skandian warriors gathered there, then staring in surprise at the crumpled bodies of the two guards.

"It's all right," Maddie said quickly. "These are my friends. You're quite safe."

The prisoners huddled together, matching Timothy's puzzled expression as they recognized Maddie. None of them had ever seen her dressed this way. They were used to seeing her in fine gowns and dresses. This leather- and wool-clad young woman, armed with a bow and two knives at her belt, was something outside their experience.

"She looks like a Ranger," one of them whispered to his neighbor.

Maddie heard the exchange and smiled. "That's what I am," she said, and there was a buzz of surprise from the group. They were all house servants, she saw, stewards and maids and wait-ers. They definitely weren't warriors.

"Perhaps you'd better wait here until we've got rid of Dimon," she told them.

But Timothy scowled at the name. "I'd like to help," he said, and several others voiced their agreement.

Maddie shook her head. "You're not armed and you're not trained for battle," she told them. "With the best will in the world, you'd get in our way. These men"—she indicated the Herons—"won't have time to look after you. They could be hurt trying to protect you."

Timothy looked about to protest, but Hal stepped forward and laid a hand on his forearm.

"I appreciate the offer, Timothy, but we're trained to fight as a team, and it could be dangerous for all of us if you come with us."

Reluctantly, Timothy accepted the good sense of it. He looked around and caught sight of Thorn, and the massive club on his arm. He took a pace toward the white-haired Skandian, recognizing a champion warrior when he saw one.

"You," he said. "What's your name?"

Thorn appraised the elderly servant. He admired the man's courage. He knew Timothy would be willing to fight against Dimon's men, given the chance. He also knew that he would probably die if he did.

"I'm called Thorn," he said quietly.

Timothy stepped closer, leaning forward to place his face only a meter or so from Thorn's. "Well, Thorn, when you catch up with that traitor Dimon, I'd like you to give him a wallop from me with that big club of yours."

Thorn's face split in a wolf-like grin. "I'll be happy to oblige,

Timothy. And I might give him an extra one from me," he assured the elderly servant.

But Maddie interjected, smiling. "I think my mum might have other ideas about that," she said. "She wants Dimon for herself."

Hal nodded several times. He'd heard stories about Cassandra's fighting prowess. "I wouldn't care to be Dimon if she cuts loose with that sling of hers," he said.

Maddie shook her head. "She won't be using a sling. She's been training with the Nihon-Jan *katana*. She plans to slice him up into little pieces."

"And I'll wager she'll do it too," Hal said. Then he looked around at his men, relaxing in the cellar. "It's time we got that drawbridge down," he said.

The Herons gathered themselves, checking weapons and equipment.

Thorn held up his hand. "Just a moment, Hal. There's something I need to take care of first."

Hal nodded, sensing what Thorn had in mind. He saw his old friend looking keenly around the crowded cellar, seeking someone out. "All right, Thorn. But don't be too long about it."

"I'll only be a minute or so," Thorn said, his eyes still roving across the group of people. Then they stopped as he saw whom he was looking for and stepped toward him.

"Ah, Jesper, my old friend. Don't skulk back there among the others. Come and join me."

In truth, Jesper was stooping slightly to remain hidden among his comrades and the released prisoners, and trying to avoid Thorn's gaze. He had thought it was funny to tease Thorn when they were in the tunnel and the old warrior was oppressed by the confined space, the shifting, uncertain light and the sense of being far below ground. Now, he realized, it hadn't been so funny after all. He backed away as Thorn pushed through the surrounding people. But he didn't move quickly enough, and the old sea wolf's hand shot out and gripped a handful of his jerkin at the shoulder, pulling him forward, holding him up on tiptoes, off balance.

"Would you like to touch my hair now, Jesper?" Thorn asked, his voice sinking to a fierce whisper. "Maybe make some remarks about the moat caving in on us?"

Jesper struggled to free himself. But Thorn's grip was unbreakable.

"It was a joke, Thorn. That was all. Just a joke."

"A joke, my friend? No, I don't think so. A joke is when everyone can have a good laugh together. But when you do something that's spiteful and hurtful and causes misery to someone else, that's *not* a joke. That's cruelty."

"No. I didn't mean it that way. I—"

Thorn suddenly shoved Jesper violently backward. Jesper slammed into the stone wall behind him, the impact driving the breath from his body. Gasping for air, he slumped to the ground.

"Now get up," Thorn told him. "And next time you make a joke, be sure it's really funny."

Thorn hauled him to his feet, where he stood swaying uncertainly, trying to fill his lungs with air.

Hal waited a few more seconds until he could see that Jesper had recovered. Then he exchanged glances with Maddie.

"All right," he said. "Lead the way to the gatehouse."

33

MADDIE LED THE WAY BACK TO THE SECRET ROOM. SHE stopped at the threshold, looking back at the two slumped figures of the guards. "Should we tie them up?" she asked.

Hal considered the idea, then shook his head. "I think they'll stay quiet for a while yet."

Timothy heard the exchange and stepped toward her. "There are plenty of manacles down here . . . ," he began.

Maddie smiled. "It is a dungeon, after all."

Timothy nodded. "We'll make sure they're not going anywhere," he said grimly. There was an angry growl of assent from the other former prisoners, and Maddie decided that, if the guards were smart, they wouldn't be seen to wake up anytime soon.

"We'll leave them to your tender mercies then," she said, and beckoned to the Herons to follow as she stepped back into the concealed room. She caught Thorn's eye. "No tunnels this time, Thorn. We're not going underground. There's a secret passage that leads to a spot under the gatehouse, then a series of ladders that will take us up. My lantern and one of the torches should give us plenty of light."

At her words, Hal re-lit the torch he had carried through the tunnel under the moat. Maddie's lantern was still burning.

"I'll bring up the rear," he said, then added, "Jesper, you stay with me."

"As you say, Hal," said Jesper. Maddie moved to the door on the extreme left of the room and pressed the latch. The door sprang open, revealing the passage behind. Unlike the tunnel under the moat, this was well-formed from rock and stone and had evenly shaped walls and plenty of headroom. It was nothing like the cramped, dark, damp-smelling tunnel through the clay that had brought them into the cellar. The lantern light illuminated the first five or six meters of the passage, then the darkness closed in again. Thorn looked at the well-formed walls and ceiling and heaved a small sigh of relief. It was cramped and confined and he didn't particularly like it. But it didn't cause that gut-loosening fear that he had felt in the tunnel when the damp clay and earth seemed to be pressing in on him. Maddie glanced at him, her eyebrows asking a question, and he nodded gruffly.

"I'm fine," he said. "Let's go."

She led the way into the passage, holding her lantern high to cast its light as far as possible. From behind them, Hal's torch added its flickering glow, giving them plenty of light.

The floor of the passage was smooth and even—again unlike the rough, uncertain footing that they had found in the moat tunnel. Their sealskin boots whispered on the stone as they followed the small cloaked shape in the lead. Maddie looked back at Thorn, and he saw her teeth gleam in a smile.

"Not far to go," she told him. "It'll start to angle upward in a minute or so."

She had only gone through this passage once before, but it

was perfectly straightforward with no awkward turns or dangerous spots. A few seconds after she had spoken, she felt the floor beneath her feet begin to slope upward and she knew they were close to the ladders that led up into the gatehouse. Behind her, she could hear the regular shuffle of feet on the stone floor. There was no other sound.

She was pleased that, this time, she couldn't hear Thorn's loud, nervous breathing. The one-armed man seemed to have his claustrophobia well in check. She looked back at him again. His face was half concealed in shadow, but he was pressing on without any sign of hesitation. She found herself admiring his control. True courage, she believed, consisted of facing up to one's fears and defeating them. That was what Thorn was doing now. For herself, she had no fear of small, dark places so there was no courage involved in her making her way through this passage. But for Thorn it was a different matter, and she realized that for him to walk quietly behind her through this small space, lit only by the yellow flame of her lantern, was an extraordinarily brave action.

The light from her lantern shone on a new sight in front of them. It was the first of the series of ladders that would lead up to a concealed door that led into the main floor of the gatehouse. She called back over her shoulder.

"Nearly there. Now it's time to climb."

They bunched up at the base of the first ladder, peering upward, trying to pierce the darkness above them. There were two ladders per floor, she knew, and the gallery they were heading for was on the same level as the battlements—the fourth floor. That meant eight ladders in total. She looked around the faces that surrounded her, making sure everybody was ready. She was about to turn back to the ladders when Hal held up a hand to stop her.

"Just a moment," he said. "Where do we come out?"

"We'll come out onto the main floor of the gatehouse. It's about halfway up the building, on the same level as the battlements. The controls for the drawbridge are located there."

Hal considered her answer, then came to a decision. "In that case, I'm moving up to come with you. Thorn and Stig will go out first—after Maddie has checked the situation. I'll follow them. The rest of you"—he looked round at the attentive faces of his crew—"follow on in the normal battle order. Clear?"

There was a rumble of assent from the crew. Hal handed his torch to Edvin, who would now be bringing up the rear, and pushed his way through so that he stood behind Thorn and Stig. Jesper followed him, elbowing to be in front of Ingvar, who had re-donned his tortoiseshell spectacles.

The big warrior looked at Jesper with some amusement. "Hoping to win back a little favor?"

Jesper scowled and ignored him. That was precisely what he had in mind, but he wasn't about to admit it.

"Everyone ready?" Maddie asked. Then, without waiting for an answer, she turned to the ladder. "Then let's go." She had a sudden thought and turned back to them again. "These ladders are quite old. Place your weight carefully and keep your feet as close to the sides of the rungs as you can. No more than two people on a ladder at the same time, all right?" When they nodded their understanding, she added: "We'll form up on the landing when we reach the top."

She started up the first ladder. It was near vertical and she felt a familiar twinge in her hip as she set her weight on her right foot for the first time. Then it eased and she began to climb, moving quickly. She felt the ladder vibrate beneath her feet as Thorn began to climb after her.

She reached the first platform and stepped around to the second ladder. Below, she heard Stig begin to climb. Then Thorn joined her on the platform and she gestured upward.

"One down. Seven to go," she said, and began to climb once more. Thorn let her mount half a dozen rungs, then started up after her. As she'd advised the others, she placed her weight carefully. She reached the top and stepped onto the small platform, waiting for Thorn. When he arrived, she started up the next ladder.

They were past ground level now and daylight was visible through narrow, carefully concealed arrow slits in the outer wall. Up they went, stepping around at each of the small platforms that separated the ladder flights. They had climbed six ladders so far, which meant they were on the third floor. Two flights to go. The gatehouse control room, the bridges that joined the keep to the four towers and the battlements themselves were all on the fourth level.

Maddie's thighs were feeling the strain, the muscles aching as she kept pushing herself up and up.

Below her, she could hear the soft patter of feet on the ladders, and the occasional grunt of effort from the Skandians. She noticed there was no sound from Thorn. He moved up and up in a steady, effortless rhythm. Years of training and actual combat had hardened his muscles and honed his fitness.

She reached the final platform, before the last flight up to the fourth floor, and paused, regaining her breath. Thorn stepped up beside her. Behind him, Stig saw them stop and he paused halfway up the ladder he was climbing.

"Everything all right?" Thorn asked her quietly.

She nodded. "Just getting myself set," she said. She was casting her mind ahead to the point where she opened the door into the gatehouse control room. She had no idea what she would find there. The place might be deserted. Or it could be packed with Dimon's soldiers.

The most probable scenario would be somewhere between those two: maybe a dozen men stationed there. After all, it was a key point in the castle's impregnable defenses—the one potential weak point. Dimon would hardly leave it unguarded, she knew. But he didn't have a large number of men, and the walls were under threat from Horace's force outside. She shrugged. No point wondering, she thought. Best thing she could do was get on with it and see what the situation was—and then turn these Skandians loose on whoever was in the gatehouse. She smiled grimly. She quite enjoyed leading a force like this. There was a definite sense of invincibility about these wild northmen.

She looked at Thorn again. He was waiting patiently, sensing what was going through her mind. She grinned. "All right. Let's get going."

She moved quickly up the last ladder, then stood to the side on the platform, waiting for the others to join her. Thorn and Stig crowded onto the platform with her, then Hal. She saw Jesper's face level with the platform floor. He was standing on the upper part of the last ladder. There was no room on the platform for any more people. She called softly down the shaft.

"That's all for now. Hold your positions, then get up here fast when you hear the door open."

Not an ideal situation, she thought, to have her force strung out down the ladders. But at least their three premier warriors would be ready to charge into the gatehouse. That would give the rest of the crew time to get up the ladders and join them.

She pushed past Stig and Thorn. They were both bulky men and took up a lot of the available space on the small platform. She studied the door leading into the gatehouse. It was fitted with a spring-loaded latch, similar to the one in the cellar. She looked around to make sure the others were ready, received a nod of confirmation from Thorn and pressed the lock.

The click as the door sprang open a few centimeters seemed deafening. But there was no reaction from the gatehouse. She eased the door open a crack farther and peered through.

The gatehouse was a vast stone room, lit by high windows set in the stone walls. The outer wall was formed by the huge draw-bridge, now closed and standing upright. The floor space was relatively free, with only the control area for the bridge and the massive chains and cogs that raised and lowered it. The main machinery was in the level below. To her left, a short ladder led to a timber platform set against the wall, overlooking the room. Probably a supervisor's position, she thought.

She counted ten men in the big room. Some were relaxing at a large table and chairs set in the middle of the room; others were peering out the arrow slit windows either side of the bridge itself, presumably keeping an eye on the force threatening them from outside. One man was close by the door where she watched, but he was preoccupied with the task of painting heavy, protective grease onto one of the support chains for the bridge. He had a leather pail of grease in one hand and a large brush in the other. A wooden gantry stood beside him, allowing him access to the higher parts of the chain, and a long-handled battleax was leaning against it. Two other soldiers stood a few meters away, both in armor and both wearing swords.

She withdrew into the small chamber at the top of the ladder and beckoned the three Skandians closer to her.

"Ten men in all," she said softly. "One close by." She pointed to where the man stood greasing the chain. "Maybe four meters away. Two more men a few meters farther on." Again, she pointed in their direction. "Both armed but their swords are in their scabbards. The rest of them are across the room, either sitting at a table or looking out the arrow slits."

"All armed?" Thorn asked, his face only a few centimeters from her ear.

She nodded. "Swords. Spears. Chain mail. But none have their weapons drawn."

Thorn looked at his two companions. "I'll take the one closest," he said. "You two look after the other two. Then we'll sort out the others. Our boys should be up here by then," he added.

Stig and Hal nodded. They had done this sort of thing many times before.

Thorn looked at Maddie. "Where will you be?"

"There's a small platform off to the left, about two meters up," she said. "Probably an overseer's position. I'll get up there and cover you all." Unconsciously, she touched the tip of her bow where it stood out above her shoulder. It would be easier to leave it slung while she climbed the ladder to the platform she had seen, and once there it would take her no more than a few seconds to have it ready for action.

Thorn nodded, then flexed his right arm, moving the massive club in a small circle. "Ready, boys?" he asked.

Hal and Stig answered in unison. "Ready."

"Then let's get 'em!"

34

The door flew open with a crash as Maddie hurled her weight against it. She went through first, angling off to the left to clear the way for the three Skandians.

Quickly, she mounted the timber stairs to the small platform, unslung her bow, selected an arrow and nocked it.

The men in the room reacted with shock and surprise at the unexpected intrusion. Fear struck their hearts as they recognized the newcomers as Skandians. It was that fear and sense of panic that initially saved the man Thorn had targeted. He was crouched by the massive chain, paintbrush in one hand and a leather bucket full of thick, lubricating grease in the other. He jerked upright in alarm and the paintbrush went flying one way, the bucket another. He turned to reach for the ax leaning close by, but he was too slow. Thorn was almost upon him, the massive club hand ready to strike.

Then it all went wrong.

Thorn's boot came down on the discarded paintbrush, thick with grease. His leg shot out from under him and he crashed over onto the floor, the breath coming out of his body in an explosive gasp. Stig and Hal were already heading for the two spearmen close by, who were moving to intercept them, and had no time to turn back to Thorn's aid. As the old sea wolf scrambled to regain his feet, he saw the painter seize the ax and swing it diagonally down at him. He threw up his right arm, with the massive club on its end, to parry the blow.

The blade was deflected from its downward trajectory, but it bit deep into the wooden head of the club, driving it to one side. The head of the club lodged in the framework of the timber gantry, and with Thorn's elbow on the floor also trapping it at its base, the shaft of the club shattered in the middle.

The former painter withdrew the ax and readied it for another blow at the old sea wolf, who was now rolling desperately away to escape the ax. Maddie drew back an arrow, but the timbers of the gantry were obstructing her shot and she hesitated.

Then a figure bounded from the doorway and into the control room, sword drawn and a snarl of fury on his face. The axman saw him and turned to face him. But Jesper's sword shot forward and took him in the center of the chest. With a startled cry of pain, the axman dropped his weapon, straightened up, then crashed over backward to the floor. As he fell, Jesper withdrew his weapon, then turned to face one of the soldiers who had been at the table and was now charging across the room to finish the helpless Thorn.

Jesper parried two desperate sword strokes, then swept the other man's blade to one side with his own. The man was left wide-open to the saxe that Jesper held in his left hand. Jesper struck swiftly, then stepped back as his opponent went down.

At the same time, Stig and Hal were engaging the two spearmen. Stig swayed to one side, avoiding a low thrust, then arced his battleax up and over. The spearman withdrew his weapon and held it in both hands above his head to parry the stroke. To his horror, the ax sheared through the stout ash shaft of the spear, then continued down, almost without pause. His last sound was a strangled cry of terror.

Hal was more clinical. Where Stig relied on brute force and the smashing impact of his ax to break through his opponent's defenses, Hal used speed and precision. He trapped the spear-head that came at him, deflecting it to one side, then stepped inside the long weapon and lunged with lightning speed at the spearman's unprotected body. His sword bit through the chain-mail shirt his opponent was wearing, almost as if it weren't there. Another of Dimon's men fell, with the same surprised and hor-rified look on his face.

Now more of the Herons were pouring through the door and into the gatehouse control room, yelling as they echoed Thorn's war cry of "Let's get 'em!"

Led by the massive, terrifying figure of Ingvar, they stormed across the room as the soldiers at the table desperately tried to draw their weapons and defend themselves. Ingvar stabbed at one man with the spearpoint of his voulge and, almost in the same motion, caught the back of another's mail collar with its hook and jerked him forward. As the man stumbled, off balance, Ingvar smashed him in the chest with a flat-footed kick and sent him flying.

Ulf and Wulf were close behind him, identical in appear-ance, and both spreading terror and confusion as the startled defenders thought they were seeing double. The gatehouse gar-rison began to throw down their weapons and hold up their hands in surrender. First one man, then two more. Then the swords and axes fell to the floor in a clattering shower as the men begged for mercy.

Stefan and Edvin, last to arrive on the floor, regarded the scene with mild disgust.

"They might have left some for us," Edvin said in an aggrieved tone.

Stefan shrugged. "They never do."

Maddie slowly replaced her arrow in its quiver, then came down the stairs from the platform. She grinned at Hal.

"Looks like you didn't need me," she said. He nodded, then they both looked to where Jesper was helping Thorn to his feet. The white-haired old warrior regarded his shipmate for a few seconds in silence, then he threw his left arm around him and drew him forward in a crushing bear hug.

"Thanks, Jes," Thorn said simply.

Jesper nodded once or twice, then replied, "I think I owed you, Thorn."

But Thorn shook his head. "We're brotherband; you don't owe me anything."

For a minute or so, nobody said anything. Then Hal took control of the scene. He gestured to the disarmed garrison members. There were five of them still standing, their hands held high in surrender.

"Ulf and Wulf, secure those prisoners."

"Aye-aye, Hal," Wulf replied, and he and his brother began shoving the defeated group, herding them into a corner of the gatehouse, their orders reinforced by the menacing figure of Ingvar looming in the background.

Hal strode across to the arrangement of levers and cogs that raised and lowered the drawbridge. "Now, let's see how we can get this bridge down," he said, studying the controls with a keen eye.

He had never seen the workings of a drawbridge before, but he was a skilled engineer and designer and it took him only a few moments to figure it out. The huge bridge was raised and lowered by heavy chains, which ran through the floor they were standing on into the lower recesses of the gatehouse. They were controlled by a large windlass, with room for half a dozen men to turn it. In addition, to make the work easier, the bridge was fitted with a counterweight, so that only a relatively small effort was needed to raise it. The counterweight in this case was the heavy portcullis—the grilled barrier that came down across the entrance to the castle when the bridge was raised. As the bridge went down, the portcullis went up, and vice versa.

While it took some effort to raise the huge bridge, lowering it was a relatively simple matter. There was a brake on the windlass that could be thrown off as the bridge started to move. Once the brake was off, gravity took over and the bridge would simply fall down, bringing the portcullis up and opening the way into the castle.

Hal gestured to his men. "Ingvar, get that windlass turning. Stefan and Edvin, give him a hand."

As they moved to the windlass, Edvin grinned ruefully at Stefan. "We never get to do the fighting," he complained. "We only get the donkey work that comes after it."

Which was patently untrue. Over the years, the two of them had done more than their share of fighting. Stefan merely grunted and together they grasped the spokes of the windlass. Ingvar towered over them and began to heave. The wheel didn't move. Hal walked quickly to them.

"You have to release the brake," he said. "Then stand clear once it's moving."

He grasped the brake lever that inserted a massive iron stop into the cogwheel at the side of the windlass, and hauled it back. The three Herons heaved once more, and the windlass began to turn easily. The bridge started to go down, and Hal called to them.

"Let go and stand clear!"

They stepped back from the windlass, which began to turn faster and faster as the bridge gathered momentum. The massive chains either side clattered over the pulleys, shedding flakes of rust as they went. There was a mighty rumble from the depths of the gatehouse as the bridge dropped and the portcullis rose. Then the foot of the bridge crashed down on the far side of the moat, rebounding a half a meter in the air, then coming to rest in a cloud of dust.

"Hope we didn't break it," Edvin muttered.

Hal shrugged. "It's not our bridge."

Light flooded into the gatehouse through the gap that had been closed by the bridge. Below them, the Herons saw Horace spurring his horse forward, leading a charge across the bridge and into the castle yard.

"Time to give them a hand," Thorn said, and led the crew toward the heavy timber door that opened onto the battlements.

Dimon turned in horror as he heard the massive rumbling sound from the gatehouse. He went pale as he saw the bridge starting to descend, moving faster and faster with each meter. Below him, outside the walls, the attacking force had heard the telltale sound as well and they cheered loudly, then started forward toward the castle.

"Get down to the yard and stop them!" Dimon yelled to the men on the battlements.

There was no further purpose in remaining on the battlements. His men, about thirty in number, started to clatter down the stairs leading to the courtyard below. But once he had seen them start down, Dimon held back. He could hear the clatter of hooves on the wooden bridge, and he knew that Horace's cavalry would sweep his own men aside in a matter of minutes. The courtyard was no place for him, he decided.

Dimon hesitated, wondering which way to go, then the door to the gatehouse swung open and he saw Thorn, Hal and Stig coming at a run, the rest of their crew behind them.

A few of his men, who hadn't yet made it to the stairs, turned to face them. Since Thorn's massive club had been destroyed, he and Stig had changed positions, so that the *Heron*'s first mate led the way onto the battlements' walkway. He smashed into the four men who had stopped to bar their way. His ax swung in a shining arc in the late afternoon sun, and his first opponent went down. As the second slid under the deadly arc of the battleax and drew back his sword to lunge at the tall figure, Thorn crouched and leapt forward, stabbing at the man with the saxe that he held in his left hand.

The man gave a startled grunt and dropped the sword. He staggered away to lean against the castle battlements, sliding slowly down to the walkway as he did.

That left two. Hal engaged the first, parrying the man's wild swings with his own sword, then immediately cutting back in a lightning series of short, sharp strokes. The man gave way before the deadly onslaught, parrying desperately, only just managing to deflect the whirling sword at the very last minute each time. He felt a chill of fear clutch his heart as he realized he was seriously outmatched. He would have thrown down his sword and yielded, but he had no time. If he dropped it, the Skandian's sword would be on him before its owner could stop.

In total panic, he turned to run, but Hal leapt forward and, reversing his sword, brought the heavy hilt down on the back of the man's head, sending him sprawling unconscious on the boards of the walkway.

The fourth man had made the mistake of trying to engage Hal as the skirl was preoccupied with his unfortunate comrade. He was armed with a spear, and he lunged underarm at the Skandian. But, fixated on his target, he hadn't noticed the massive form of Ingvar looming. The huge warrior reached over Hal's shoulder and batted the spear aside with his voulge, sending it flying out of the man's grasp with the force of the impact. The would-be attacker drew back a pace and fumbled for the sword at his waist. But Ingvar was too quick. He snagged the hook of his voulge into the chain mail bundled at the man's shoulder and jerked him forward, off balance. It was Ingvar's favorite fighting technique with his unique weapon, and one that few opponents were ever ready to counter.

The man stumbled as he was jerked forward. In a flash, Ingvar disengaged the hook and reversed his weapon, swinging the heavy ash-wood shaft in a horizontal arc to smash against his opponent's head. It would have been a telling blow no matter who delivered it. But with Ingvar's mighty strength behind it, it lifted the defender off his feet and hurled him several meters through the air. As he hit the planks, he slid another half meter, then lay still.

Dimon watched, horrified, as his men were brushed aside with apparent ease. He glanced quickly around, looking for sanctuary. The Skandians were between him and the gatehouse. There was a flight of stairs leading to the courtyard below just a few meters beyond him. But he knew the scene down there would be one of further disaster for his men.

That left the east tower, behind him. From there, a hump-backed stone bridge led across the gap to the fourth level of the keep tower. There was no way he could escape from the keep, with Horace's men in the courtyard. But it offered temporary safety from the wild Skandians. He turned and ran.

35

STAMPER'S HOOVES THUNDERED ON THE ROUGH PLANKS OF the drawbridge as Horace urged him across and into the castle courtyard. Two of Dimon's men stood at the open gateway ahead of him in a vain attempt to stop him. The one on his left thrust upward with a spear, but Horace caught it on his buckler and flicked it away. The next instant, Stamper's huge shoulder slammed into the man and hurled him back onto the flagstones.

The second man looked at the armored figure and the massive battlehorse bearing down on him. He was armed only with a sword, and he knew that was an entirely inadequate weapon for this situation. He turned and ran, dropping his sword as he did so, seeking the shelter of the lower levels of the gatehouse. Maybe they'd find him later and take him prisoner, he thought, but at least he'd be alive.

Stamper careered across the courtyard like a four-legged battering ram. A group of five stood before him, huddled together for mutual protection, their spears and swords held out like the quills of a hedgehog. Feeling the pressure of Horace's knees in a well-known signal, Stamper reared, lashing out with his huge front hooves, smashing and scattering the spears that had been held up to stop him. The men before him fell back in terror as Horace wheeled the horse on his hind legs and reached to cut backhanded at them with his sword. Two of them fell. The others turned and ran, only to be pursued by a trio of cavalrymen who had followed Horace across the bridge.

One of the running men managed to surrender in time, falling facedown on the stone paving, his hands above his head in a desperate gesture of self-preservation. The others weren't so lucky.

The courtyard was a scene of confusion and terror and noise as the cavalry hunted down the outflanked defenders. Horses thundered this way and that as the troopers spotted and chased after new targets. The ironshod hooves struck sparks from the flagstones that paved the courtyard.

Gilan rode calmly into this scene of devastation. It was not his role to take part in the wild cavalry charge that Horace had led—although, had he felt he was needed, he would have joined in. But he was confident that Horace and his highly trained troopers could take care of the ragtag Red Fox soldiers. He rode with his massive longbow across his saddle bow, an arrow nocked and his eyes searching the faces of the enemy. He had set himself another task.

A soldier leapt forward from behind a stone buttress, a long pike in his hand. Seeing the rider moving at a steady walk, with no sword or shield, he took him for easy prey and ran at him, the pike drawn back for a massive killing stroke.

But this was no easy prey. This was a fully trained Ranger, armed with the Corps's most deadly weapon. As the yelling man charged, eyes wild, Gilan drew and shot him, almost as an afterthought. The heavy arrow, with the full force of Gilan's eighty-five-pound longbow behind it, spun the running man around, sending him staggering back, so that he lost his footing. He crashed to the ground and lay still. But Gilan, knowing his shot was good from the moment it had left his bow, wasn't looking at him anymore. His eyes roved the courtyard and the battlements above.

He was searching for Dimon, but there was no sign of the treacherous guard commander.

On the sixth floor, Cassandra felt the vibrations running through the building and heard the loud rumble of the descending drawbridge.

"Come on!" she shouted to her men and led the way down the stairs.

They had reached the fifth level when they heard the sound of running footsteps on the stairs below them. Moments later, a small group of escaping Red Foxes, who had retreated into the ground level of the south tower to save themselves from the deadly swords and lances of the cavalry, pounded into view.

As before, Cassandra had placed three of her troopers in the lead. They stepped forward now and engaged the panicked former defenders. She drew her *katana*, in case one of the men made it past her troopers, and called back to her father.

"Stay well back, Dad."

But her caution was unnecessary. In less than a minute, after a short, bitter engagement, the three Red Fox soldiers were lying wounded and bleeding on the stairs.

"Pick up their weapons," she ordered. "We'll take them prisoner later."

She gestured for the troopers to continue down the stairs.

They moved slowly, ready for any further interruptions. But there were none and they reached the fourth level without incident. Her men stood back to let her through to the front. Cassandra shoved the door open and peered out onto the bridge that led to the keep—where Maikeru had given his life for her. She felt a quick stab of sadness as she thought of the faithful Nihon-Jan swordmaster, then led the way out onto the bridge.

"I'll avenge you, Maikeru, never fear," she muttered to herself. With her *katana* in hand, she moved across the arched bridge. Her men followed, weapons ready, senses tingling with anticipation.

They reached the door that led into the fourth-floor level of the keep. Only a few old bloodstains remained to show the spot where Maikeru had fallen to Dimon's cowardly attack, when the rebel leader had ordered two crossbowmen to shoot Maikeru down as the swordmaster defied them.

Cassandra felt a hand on her shoulder as she moved toward the door. She looked back and saw Thomas close behind her.

"Let someone else go first, my lady," he said.

She nodded, seeing the sense of his suggestion. She had no shield, no armor, just her sword. It would be all too easy for an attacker waiting in ambush to kill her.

She stepped aside and beckoned the same three troopers forward. One of them, taller and broader than the others, took the lead. He had his shield up ready and he set his lance to one side, handing it to one of his companions. Then he drew his sword. Cassandra nodded approval. The shorter weapon would be more effective in the confines of the doorway.

The trooper paused at the closed door, leaning forward and turning his head slightly to listen. Hearing nothing, he gestured to one of his companions to come forward, nodding at the iron loop that formed the door handle. His comrade reached down and carefully turned the handle, raising the latch on the inside of the door. He looked at the swordsman, who nodded again. Then he flung the door open and leapt aside as his companion went through, sword ready, shield raised, turning in a quick half circle to make sure the way was clear.

He relaxed, rising from the crouch he had fallen into as he went through the door, lowering the point of his sword to the floor.

"All clear, my lady," he said, then stepped back out onto the bridge in order to let Cassandra lead the way.

36

Maddie shoved her way through the Skandians who were bunched in the gatehouse doorway and emerged onto the battlements' walkway.

Hal and Ingvar were dealing with their opponents as she stepped clear of the gatehouse. She had her bow ready now and an arrow on the string. She leaned to see past the struggling knot of men in front of her and saw a familiar figure at the far end of the wall.

Dimon was heading for the door into the east tower.

"There he goes!" she yelled, and stepped past the fighting men for a clear shot at him. But she was a fraction of a second too late, and her arrow thudded into the timber door as Dimon slammed it behind him. She started running along the walkway toward the tower, nocking another arrow as she went. Behind her, she heard Hal calling for her to wait but she ignored him. She saw Dimon's head and shoulders appear above the parapet of the humpbacked stone bridge and loosed another shot. But she rushed her aim, and the arrow skittered off the parapet half a meter behind him. She cursed herself. Will would have berated her for such a hasty, clumsy attempt. She ran faster. If she could reach the east tower before Dimon made it to the keep, she'd have a clear, unimpeded shot at him.

She threw herself at the door handle and turned it, shoving the heavy door. But it refused to budge. For some years, it had been warped by time and weather, and the castle staff had grown accustomed to leaving it ajar. But Dimon had slammed it with all his strength and the twisted timbers now jammed tight. She threw her shoulder at the door, feeling a sudden, jarring pain as she struck it. But she also felt it give a few centimeters, so she redoubled her efforts. At the fifth assault, the door flew open, sending her staggering into the tower anteroom. The second door, leading to the bridge, had been kept in better condition and it opened easily as she turned the handle and pulled it inward, wincing as her bruised shoulder took the strain.

She darted out onto the bridge, in time to see Dimon disappearing over the raised section in the center of the span. She brought up her bow but she was too late. A few seconds later, she heard the door into the keep slam open and shut as he went through it.

She ran, knowing that if she didn't keep him in sight once he reached the keep she might lose him altogether. There were too many options open to him: the stairs leading up and down, or the three other doors onto the bridges leading to the south, north and west towers. Once he reached any one of the towers, he could go up or down. It was vital that she didn't lose him.

She pounded across the bridge, her quiver slapping her thigh as it jolted up and down with her movements.

She reached the door and was about to plunge through it when her tactical training cut in. It would be all too easy for Dimon to simply wait beside the closed door for her to blunder through, and then cut her down from behind. She stopped a few meters short of the door, letting her breathing settle. She still felt the same urgency to regain sight of the Red Fox leader, but she knew she had to go carefully and the frustration built in her. She waited a few seconds, listening at the door for any slight sound on the other side. Then, she twisted the door handle and kicked at the door so that it slammed back on its hinges. Anyone waiting there would have been smashed by the heavy timbers.

But there was nobody behind it. The door rebounded violently from the stone walls and would have slammed shut again if she hadn't raised her foot and placed it against the door, stopping its violent movement. She nocked an arrow and moved forward.

Dimon charged into the big open hall that formed the fourth floor of the keep and paused, unsure of which way to go. He had a vague idea of heading for the south tower and going down the stairs. Reason told him that if Cassandra descended from the upper floors, she would cross the bridge to the keep. If he could reach the south tower before she appeared, he could go down to a lower level and elude her. From there, he could make his way through the maze of corridors and rooms and stairways and possibly find a way out of the castle. There were drains and waste pipes leading to the moat, he knew. If he could find one, he could possibly get away.

Of course, he had just as good a chance of finding a way out in the north or west towers. But the idea of getting behind Cassandra appealed to him. She would be unlikely to look back the way she had come, and that might give him extra time to make his escape. So he started for the south bridge, his sword in his hand and his triangular shield on his left arm.

Horace dragged back on Stamper's reins, bringing the big horse to a stiff-kneed, sliding stop on the cobbles. He was outside the ground-floor door to the keep. Two Red Fox soldiers had just entered and were hurrying to bar the door against him. He went up the steps at a run and slammed a flat-footed kick into the door. He heard cries of alarm and the crash of falling bodies as he did so. The door flew open and he saw the two soldiers rolling on the floor, desperately seeking to regain their feet.

One of them came up and then immediately went down again as Horace's sword flickered forward like a serpent striking. The other wisely remained on the floor, rolling away from the terrifying sight of the Kingdom's champion knight, his sword blade red with blood. He clasped his hands over his head in a useless protective gesture, shoulder blades twitching expectantly as he waited for the sword to strike him. But Horace was already past him and running for the wide stairway that led to the upper floors, taking the risers two at a time without slackening his pace.

Dimon was up there somewhere, he knew. Horace had seen the traitor crossing the bridge as he had fought his way through the defenders in the courtyard. And he had seen Maddie racing after him. He felt a cold fear as he thought of his daughter facing the treacherous Red Fox leader. Dimon was an expert fighter, he knew, and he had no real idea of Maddie's skill level. She was a Ranger, and that should be enough. But she was also his daughter and that fact put fear in his heart as he thought of her facing Dimon in single combat.

He went up one flight, then two, barely breaking stride. He knew Dimon would have reached the fourth floor when he crossed the bridge, and he continued up the third flight of stairs without pause. At the fourth, he slowed a little. Like Maddie, he knew that too much haste now could well leave him open to ambush as he reached the top of the fourth flight. He slowed his pace, his sword ready in front of him, his buckler high and covering his left side.

Dimon was halfway to the south doorway when it opened, and Cassandra stepped into the hall, her *katana* gleaming in her hand. At almost the same moment, he heard the eastern door slam open and turned to see Maddie advancing through it, a bow in her hand, arrow nocked on the string.

"Stop right there, Dimon," Maddie called. He was surprised to hear that her young voice was surprisingly confident and firm.

Maddie was an excellent shot with a bow, but an even better one with her sling. However, she had elected to use the bow as it was a more threatening weapon. Most people looked at a sling and saw only a relatively harmless-looking loop of leather thongs. The fact that it could hurl a lead shot so that it smashed through armor and bone wasn't obviously apparent.

A bow, with a barbed warhead set on the arrow, was a different matter.

Except in this case. Dimon had a totally mistaken opinion of Maddie's skill with a bow, born of her keeping that ability a secret when she'd returned to Castle Araluen. He laughed scornfully.

"Playing with grown-up weapons, Maddie?" he said. "You forget, I've seen you shoot."

"Stay out of this, Maddie!" her mother called. "He's mine."

"You can have him, Mum. I just want to even things up," she said. Then she spoke to Dimon again. "Your shield. Left and right upper corners."

He frowned, not understanding. "What about—" he began, but suddenly felt two slamming impacts against his left side as Maddie shot twice. His mouth dried with fear. She had moved so quickly that he had barely seen her release the first arrow, then draw a second, nock it and shoot again. Now he looked down and saw two arrows embedded through the left and right upper corners of his triangular shield, just as she had predicted. On the left-hand side, the armor-piercing bodkin point had punched through the leather and wood of the shield and protruded ten centimeters on the other side.

He appraised her with a new level of understanding, taking in the cowled, camouflaged cloak and the wool-and-leather leggings and jerkin. She was dressed and equipped as a Ranger, he realized. And she had just shown a Ranger's skill with a bow, hitting his shield twice in such quick succession. He had underestimated the princess from the start, he realized. And now he knew instinctively that she had been the major cause of his failure.

"Let's make this a more even match," she said. "Get rid of that shield."

He hesitated. From behind him, he heard Cassandra's angry voice.

"Stay out of this, Maddie. I can manage him with his shield."

"I'm sure you can, Mum. But you'll manage him much more easily without it." Her eyes came back to Dimon and they were cold and hard. "Now get rid of that shield," she said once more, the arrow making a commanding gesture.

Seeing his hesitation, she called again. "If you don't, I'll put the next arrow through your knee. That should cramp your fighting style."

He flinched at the thought of one of those heavy, armor-piercing arrows tearing through his knee, cutting tendons, smashing bone and ligaments. From their many practice bouts, he knew only too well that Cassandra was an agile and fast opponent. The thought of fighting her with one leg disabled sent a shudder up his back. He'd be lucky to last thirty seconds in such a bout. He released the hand grip on the shield and shrugged his arm out of the retaining straps, letting it fall to the floor with a loud clatter.

"Do you swear you'll let me go free if I win?" he asked Maddie.

She gave him a totally humorless smile. "No. I swear I'll shoot you down."

Before he could answer, Cassandra chipped in. "But at least you'll have the satisfaction of killing me first," she said.

He turned back to her, meeting her steady gaze. That was true, he thought. And with everything lost in his attempt to seize the throne, he might as well have that one final satisfaction. He turned to face her, whirling the sword in a series of fast circles to get the feel of its balance and loosen his wrist.

A new voice stopped him in his tracks.

"Hold it right there, Dimon!"

Horace was emerging from the staircase, fully armored in chain mail and helmet, his round buckler, emblazoned with his oakleaf symbol, on his left arm. Horace's hair might be showing streaks of gray, but he still moved with an athlete's grace and agility. That, combined with his size and obvious power, made him a truly daunting figure. He reached the top of the stairs and moved toward the Red Fox leader. Dimon had frozen in place, faced by three very real threats.

"That's far enough, Horace!" Cassandra called to him, the authority clear in her voice. "This is my fight. Stay out of it."

"I'm your champion," Horace pointed out. He had been appointed Cassandra's official champion when they married. As such, he could fight in her stead if she were ever challenged to combat.

"Not this time," Cassandra said, her voice tight.

"She's right, Dad," Maddie told him. "This is her fight." Then, in a lower voice, she added, "But if he even looks like hurting her, I'll kill him."

He hesitated, unhappy with the situation. Seeing him weaken, Cassandra spoke again. "I mean it, Horace. Stay out of this."

"Yes. You can fight me after I kill your wife," Dimon said sarcastically.

Horace started forward, but a gesture from Cassandra stopped him. She was a born princess and she was used to commanding—and being obeyed. The door behind her opened and three of her men moved into the room, followed by her father, limping and leaning on his sword. He had heard the exchange from outside on the bridge.

"Cassandra's right, Horace," Duncan said. "If she's going to rule this Kingdom, she should be the one who ends this rebellion—and this rebel."

"You're assuming, of course, that I won't kill her," Dimon sneered.

Duncan eyed him impassively. "She shouldn't have any

trouble with scum like you," he said calmly. He leaned back against the door with a sigh as he took some of the weight off his injured leg. He was confident in his daughter's ability to deal with the traitor—and equally confident that, if she looked like she was losing, his granddaughter would settle the matter for her. She was a protégée of Will and Halt, after all, and he knew they were pragmatists who held no false ideas about giving an enemy a fair chance—particularly one as evil as this.

Dimon looked back at Cassandra, standing in her ready position, the *katana* held forward in her two-handed grip. Her face was pale and set in a determined expression. She looked ready to meet him. Again he swung the sword in a few preparatory circles.

"You're going to die," Dimon said softly, beginning to shuffle forward.

Cassandra stood her ground.

"Yes," she replied. "But not today."

37

Cassandra and Dimon moved in slow circles around each other, swords ready. From time to time, one or the other would feint an attack to try to draw some reaction, and a possible mistake, from the other. But so far, neither one of them had committed to a real assault. The sword tips moved in small circles as the two fighters kept their wrists and arms fluid and loose. Tight muscles meant slow reactions—and slow reactions could mean death.

Then, without warning, Dimon launched himself forward in an attack, his left leg leading in a long stride, the foot stamping down as he completed the move. His sword swung down twice. Either blow would have split Cassandra from shoulder to waist, but she avoided them easily, swaying first left, then right, to let his blade slam down onto the floor of the keep. Then Dimon launched his third blow. Where an opponent might have expected him to withdraw after the second vertical slash, he brought the sword up and across in a backhanded slash.

Maddie felt her father tense beside her as the wicked blow flashed toward Cassandra. It was an excellent move, the sign of an expert swordsman in complete control of his weapon. But

Cassandra was ready for it. This time, she intercepted Dimon's blade with her own, and the room echoed to the ringing shriek of steel scraping on steel. The point of her sword spun in a small circle that deflected Dimon's blade, causing him to stumble slightly as his sword met no real resistance. For a fraction of a second, his left side was exposed and Cassandra cut at it, hitting him high on the left arm and slicing through the chain-mail sleeve of his hauberk as if it were wool. A bright red line of blood sprang up across his arm and he danced away clear of her, cursing softly as he surveyed the wound.

No serious damage had been done. It was a shallow cut only, as the chain mail absorbed most of the force of the cut. And it was his left arm, which would not affect his ability to fight—at least, not in the short term. If the combat continued long enough, the loss of blood might sway things in Cassandra's favor. But neither combatant was planning on a long fight.

They resumed their slow circling, the hall silent except for the shuffle of their boots on the floor as they moved around each other, keeping both feet in contact with the floor to maintain their balance.

Blood dripped slowly from Dimon's left arm, but not in sufficient quantities to weaken him. Cassandra's strike hadn't caused serious injury, but it gained her a psychological edge. The sudden burning impact of her sword blade on his arm had reminded Dimon of how quickly she could react and strike. If the cut had been twenty centimeters higher, it could well have sliced into his neck.

He eyed her with new caution as they circled. Then he feinted an attack and she darted back out of range before replying with her own. He dodged as well and for a few seconds they feinted and retreated, feinted and retreated, both of them aware that one of these mock attacks could suddenly become real and they would be fighting for their lives again.

Cassandra was on her toes now as she darted in and out, feinting, searching for an opening, looking for a reaction from Dimon that was a fraction of a second too late. She was breathing steadily, drawing oxygen into her lungs through her nose in long, deep breaths. The *katana* maintained its defensive circling movement in front of her. *Your shield*, Maikeru had called it.

Then Dimon attacked again in earnest. He swung a controlled series of strokes at her, backhand, forehand and overhead, never overextending himself or leaving himself open to an instant riposte from her. She danced backward lightly, staying away from him. If their blades locked, his superior weight and strength would give him the advantage, and she was all too aware of the heavy dagger in his belt. If her *katana* was trapped by his sword, it would take only a second for him to draw the dagger with his left hand and drive it into her ribs.

Back they went, down the length of the big, empty room, the swords ringing together, scraping, sliding off each other. Notches appeared in Dimon's blade as it impacted against the super-hardened steel of the *katana*. But they weren't enough to reduce his sword's capacity to wound and kill. He pursued her down the hall as she backed away, cutting and striking at her.

Then he overextended himself once, and instantly she went on the attack, slashing at his head and shoulders, then sweeping down to cut at his legs. Now it was Dimon's turn to retreat, his boots slithering and sliding on the floor in a rapid rhythm. He parried desperately. Cassandra's slashing attack was giving him no time to counterattack in his turn. All he could do was defend.

Sweat began to streak his forehead as he worked to keep that glittering blade away from his body, arms and head. The ring of steel on steel filled his ears. Then Cassandra missed a beat in the remorseless rhythm of her attack, and he sprang back, opening space between them as her attack ran out of impetus.

Again they faced each other. Again, they circled. Their breath was coming faster now, due to their exertions and the adrenaline rush that was filling both their bodies.

Dimon feinted. Cassandra stepped back smartly, then feinted herself, making him give ground. A worm of worry was forming in her mind. They were very evenly matched. The outcome of this contest rested on a knife blade—or, more correctly, a sword blade. Dimon's power and strength was balanced by Cassandra's speed and agility. But, as Maikeru had told her weeks before, the longer the contest continued, the more her advantages would be eroded.

As she tired, she would slow down, perhaps only fractionally, but enough to give Dimon the edge he needed. His advantage in stamina and strength would be less affected, she knew.

They engaged in another series of strokes and counterstrokes and she realized that Dimon's thoughts were running along similar lines to her own. He was committing her to violent movement and action, planning to tire her and slow her down. He knew their relative advantages and disadvantages as well as she did. He knew that the more he could engage her and force her into violent exchanges like this, the more quickly she would tire.

She leapt back, disengaging. He started to come after her, hoping she might be off balance, but realized that she was ready for him, her sword poised over her right shoulder, preparing to strike. He stopped and smiled mirthlessly at her.

"Feeling the heat?" he sneered.

She remained steady, her eyes locked on his, looking for a hint that he was about to attack again.

"How's that arm?" she asked. "Looks painful."

He forced a laugh. "It's just a scratch. Hardly cut the skin."

Then he leapt back a long step as she came at him while he was still speaking. He hadn't expected that. He'd have to stay on his toes, he told himself. She was a very dangerous adversary, and he would have to take his time tiring her out. If he tried to rush it, he could well lose this fight.

Cassandra resumed her defensive stance, the *katana* held in both hands, centered across her body, her left foot slightly advanced, knees bent, ready to react to any move he might make.

She shuffled forward, forgoing the circling motion. Dimon retreated, moving back away from her. Then he darted his sword at her and she stopped. They reversed the movement, with him sliding forward, her shuffling back. There was no sound in the room except the slither of their boots on the floor and the occasional shriek of steel sliding across steel.

The impasse continued for several more minutes. Then Dimon launched a savage attack at her, bludgeoning her sword with his own, beating down at her without finesse or subterfuge. She gave ground, parrying desperately, feeling the power of his strokes—power that she couldn't hope to match. He wasn't trying to find a weakness in her defense. He was simply battering at her, making her use up her reserves of energy and sap her stamina. She backed away down the hall, eventually coming up short against the western wall, where weapons were stacked in racks—spears, pikes and long-handled axes. She stood with her back to them, twisting her sword desperately from side to side, deflecting some of his strokes but forced to simply block others—to stop them in midair with the strength of her arms and wrists.

Dimon's breath came in a series of savage grunts as he struck at her, time after time. He could feel his own muscles tiring, but he knew the effect on her would be even worse. She had backed away from him as far as she could. Now there was nothing for her to do but to match him, blow for blow, strength for strength.

Her muscles ached. Her wrists felt weak and vulnerable as she reacted to his attacks—for that was all she could do, react. She had no time or energy to counterattack. She was trapped against the wall, trying to foresee each stroke of his blade, trying to interpose her own. She was fighting purely on the defensive and the nonstop effort was beginning to tell. She knew she was going to have to end this fight in the next few minutes. If she didn't, Dimon would end it for her.

Watching from his position by the stairwell, Horace's expert eyes followed the course of the combat. Worry and fear gnawed at his innards. Maddie had moved around the stairwell to join him.

"She's tiring," he said quietly to Maddie. "She's slowing down."

Maddie nodded grimly. She had seen the same thing. She had been present when Maikeru had dissected the relative skills and weaknesses of Cassandra and Dimon. She knew that the longer the fight continued, the less her mother's advantage would be.

Cassandra, watching like a hawk, saw Dimon's rhythm change slightly. The next blow was slightly slower than the previous ones, not as well aligned. While his constant offensive was causing her to tire, it was also sapping his own energy. As the blow began to descend from high above his head, she threw herself sideways, out of the way. She hit the floor with her shoulder and rolled desperately to move out of his reach. He cursed as she evaded his stroke, but recovered almost instantly, leaping after her and striking down at her as she was on the ground.

Almost instantly. The fractional delay was enough for her to roll away and bound to her feet, then dart clear of him. Once more they faced each other, both breathing heavily. Dimon noted with fierce satisfaction that the point of her *katana*, extended toward him in its defensive posture, was held slightly lower than it had been some minutes prior.

He smiled savagely at her. "Not so easy when it's for real, is it?" he taunted.

Then he saw her head jerk back in the familiar giveaway sign. Almost immediately, she took a long step forward, released her left hand from the *katana* and lunged overhand at him in a single-handed stroke. Without the warning signal from her head, she would have caught him napping and the blade would have driven deep into his chest.

Forewarned, he slipped her blade to the side and delivered a lightning-fast counter-lunge. It missed a vital spot by centimeters as she twisted desperately to her right. The blade scored across her ribs, opening a long, shallow slash in her side. Blood welled out instantly, staining her jerkin.

Horace and Maddie gasped in horror. Maddie began to raise her bow, fearing that her mother was nearing the end of her tether.

"She'd stopped doing that," she muttered to herself. Obviously, in her fatigue, Cassandra had allowed the potentially deadly mistake to creep back in.

Then, unbelievably, as Dimon closed in on her, Cassandra repeated the same dangerous thrust—but this time without the giveaway head movement. Caught totally unawares, Dimon watched in horror as her sword slid past his, moving on a slightly downward path. It sliced easily through the chain mail covering his torso and buried its point deep in the left side of his chest.

He looked at her in surprise. "You didn't . . ."

But he got no further. His words choked and he felt his knees buckling. The wound she had delivered was a mortal one and he knew it. He tried to strike at her one last time, but suddenly his sword was too heavy for his wrist and it fell away with a ringing clang as he released his grip. He dropped to his knees, staring up at Cassandra.

What he didn't know, and what Maddie didn't realize, was that Cassandra's first giveaway head movement had been intentional, designed to lull him into a false sense of superiority, so that he never saw the second overhand lunge coming at him until it was too late.

She was fading from his sight as blood welled down his body inside the chain mail. Suddenly it was hard to retain his balance as he knelt before her and, slowly, he fell forward, hitting the boards facedown.

But he never felt the impact. He was beyond all feeling.

Cassandra had remained facing him, sword ready for an instant response if he was faking. Now, she finally relaxed. She stepped back from him and wearily lowered her sword point to the ground.

It was as well that she did, as she was almost instantly engulfed by Horace as he swept her into his arms. For a long moment, they embraced each other, with Maddie hovering around them, trying to find a way to hug her mother.

Finally, Cassandra spoke. "Let me go, you great black bear. My ribs are hurting."

Chastened as he remembered the cut that had scored across her ribs, Horace released her and held her at arm's length instead. Maddie managed to find a way into the family huddle when he did and tenderly put her arms around her mother's neck.

"I was so terrified for you!" she blurted. "I thought you'd forgotten what Maikeru had taught you."

Cassandra smiled grimly and looked at the still body on the floor of the hall. "So did he."

Then she drew back and turned to the stairs as she heard the thudding of multiple feet coming up from below. Maddie stepped clear and raised the bow that she still held in her left hand, an arrow ready on the string. Horace's hand dropped to the hilt of his sword and he turned as well.

The Heron brotherband, led by Hal, stormed up the stairs and into the vast hall. For once, Edvin and Stefan had shoved their way to the front, jostling Stig and Thorn aside as they fanned out on either side of Hal, their weapons drawn and ready for action.

"It's all over," Maddie told them, jerking a thumb at the still body of Dimon, facedown on the floor.

Edvin and Stefan exchanged an exasperated glance. "Isn't it always the way?" Edvin said angrily.

Stefan nodded. Words failed him.

Then Edvin's training came to the fore as he saw the blood seeping slowly down Cassandra's side. He was the healer aboard the *Heron*, trained in treating wounds and injuries.

"Better let me look at that, my lady," he said, sheathing his sword and stepping toward her. Gently, he pulled her shirt away from the wound and unstrapped his medical kit from his belt.

Hal relaxed, sheathing his sword and regarding the three Araluens.

"Nice to see a family that gets on together," he said. Then, eyeing the assortment of weapons they all carried, he added, "And it's just as well you do."

EPILOGUE

Maddie unpacked the last of her traveling clothes and stowed them away in the small hanging space in her bedroom. She looked around the cozy little cottage and smiled. It was nice to be home, she thought. Castle Araluen was beautiful and imposing. But the cabin in the trees that she shared with Will held a special place in her heart.

Her mentor was due to arrive home later in the day, she had learned from Lady Pauline when she called at Castle Redmont to pick up Sable, Will's border shepherd. The dog now lay watching her, her muzzle on her front paws and her eyes wide-open following Maddie around the room as she unpacked.

Word of events at Castle Araluen had yet to reach Castle Redmont. Gilan and Horace had ordered that the news should be suppressed for the time being. That way, they hoped that any remaining Red Fox rebels would be unaware of Dimon's defeat and so would be easier to round up and arrest. The prisoners they had taken at Castle Araluen and at the hill fort had provided them with a long list of names of co-conspirators.

Of course, Gilan had written a detailed report for Halt and Will, and the rest of the Ranger Corps. These documents were being distributed throughout the Kingdom now by fast courier. The Rangers, in turn, would inform their respective barons of what had taken place. Maddie herself had brought copies for Will and Halt. Halt's she had left at Castle Redmont. Will's lay on the battered pine table in the main room of the cabin.

She saw Sable's head rise from her paws and turn quickly toward the door. A few minutes later, Maddie heard the soft clopping of hooves coming down the dirt trail from the castle. She shook her head at the dog.

"How do you always know?" she said, marveling at the animal's acute hearing. Or maybe it was Sable's sense of smell that told her that her master was returning. She followed the black-and-white dog as Sable rose and padded out of the bedroom toward the front door of the cabin. Sable was too well trained to bark at Will's approach, but her heavy tail began to fan back and forth as she moved out onto the small verandah, eyes glued on the trail where it exited from the trees.

Minutes later, a cloaked figure mounted on a shaggy gray horse appeared out of the shadows under the trees. From the stable behind the cabin, Bumper whinnied a greeting. Tug's head rose in reply. Will rode slowly out into the sunlit clearing in front of the cabin and raised his hand in greeting.

"Welcome home," Maddie called, and he smiled in reply. "Any luck in the west?"

He made a face, then shook his head. He and Halt had been sent to investigate further activity from the Red Fox Clan in the northwest of the Kingdom.

"Wild-goose chase," he said, as he reined Tug in beside the verandah. "A couple of fanatics shouting slogans and trying to stir up the countryside. Not that they had much luck with that.

Halt threw them in a duckpond and that seemed to cool them down. Baron Hexel locked them up in jail for good measure."

She nodded to herself. The rumors of activity in the north-west had obviously been a distraction, intended to keep Halt and Will away from the main action in the east. Dimon had planned his rebellion thoroughly.

Will dismounted and Maddie stepped down from the veran-dah to take Tug's rein. The little gray gave her a friendly nod.

"I'll take care of Tug for you," she said.

Will smiled his thanks. "That's kind of you. Any coffee ready?"

"There's a pot on the stove. I made it five minutes ago," she told him and saw the anticipatory gleam in his eyes.

"That's even kinder," he said. "How was your holiday?"

"Oh, you know how it is," she said. "It was lovely to see Mum and Dad and catch up with things at Araluen. But after a week I was bored and wanted to be back here."

"I'm sure a few weeks of peace and quiet did you good," Will said. He lifted his saddlebags and bedroll from Tug's back and slung them over his shoulder. "Is Evanlyn well?" he asked.

When Will had met Cassandra for the first time, she was traveling under the assumed name of Evanlyn. In all the years that had passed since, he had never become accustomed to call-ing her Cassandra.

"She's fine," Maddie told him. "Dad too. They send their love."

"How did Horace and Gilan make out with that Red Fox nonsense north of Araluen?" he asked.

Maddie shrugged. "They sorted it out. No big drama."

She turned away to lead Tug to the stable, hiding her grin as she did so. After a few paces, she casually called back over her shoulder.

"There's a dispatch from Gilan on the table."

"I'll read it while I have coffee."

Tug followed her to the stable, where she unsaddled him, brushed him down and rubbed him with an old horse blanket. Then she put him in his stall next to Bumper. The two horses nuzzled each other over the rail that divided their stalls. She filled Tug's drinking trough and ladled some grain into his feed bin. Bumper looked at her accusingly, and she gave him some extra grain as well. Then she gave each horse an apple from the cask outside the stable door and returned to the cabin.

Will looked up as she entered. He was sitting, sprawled in his chair, the dispatch open in one hand and his coffee cup in the other. He raised an eyebrow at her and brandished the report.

"Bored after a week? No big drama?"

She shrugged diffidently. "Well, I didn't want to make too big a thing out of it all," she said, not meeting his eyes.

He looked back at the dispatch again. "Gilan says you did very well," he said. "Very well indeed."

"Really?" she asked, unable to hide her pleasure. "What does he say, exactly?" She was young enough to like the idea of someone praising her—particularly when that someone was the Commandant of the Ranger Corps.

"He says you've learned not to yell out when someone steps on your hand. That's good to hear," he said, glancing earnestly at the dispatch.

"Is that all?" she asked, her voice rising with her disappointment. "He must say more than that!"

"I don't think we want you getting a swollen head," he said.

He folded the dispatch and put it away inside his jerkin. She dropped her gaze, shuffling her feet in embarrassment.

"No. I suppose not," she said awkwardly.

Will decided he'd teased her long enough. "He also says I should be very proud of you."

She looked up at him. His face was a mask, and for a long moment, the silence stretched between them. Finally, she could stand it no longer.

"And are you?" she asked tentatively.

Will smiled at her. "Oh, very proud indeed."